DIRTPICKERS

Edie May Hand is a writer from County Meath, Ireland. She graduated from University College Dublin in 2019 with a joint honours in History of Art and English Literature. She has been writing for over a decade. Edie began *Dirtpickers* as part of Maynooth University's Creative Writing Masters Programme, for which she received a first-class honours degree in 2024. *Dirtpickers* is her debut novel and she is currently working on her second.

DIRT PICKERS

EDIE MAY HAND

MANILLA
PRESS

First published in the UK in 2026 by
MANILLA PRESS
An imprint of Bonnier Books UK
5th Floor, HYLO, 105 Bunhill Row,
London, EC1Y 8LZ

A CIP catalogue record for this book is
available from the British Library.

Hardback ISBN: 978-1-78658-625-4
Trade paperback ISBN: 978-1-78658-663-6

Also available as an ebook and an audiobook

Jane Hirshfield, 'Late Prayer' from *The Asking: New & Selected Poems*
(Bloodaxe Books, 2024), reproduced with permission of Bloodaxe Books.
www.bloodaxebooks.com @bloodaxebooks (Twitter/Facebook) #bloodaxebooks

The author received financial support from the
Arts Council in the creation of this work.

1 3 5 7 9 10 8 6 4 2

Typeset by IDSUK (Data Connection) Ltd
Printed and bound in Great Britain by CPI (UK) Ltd, Croydon CR0 4YY

The authorised representative in the EEA is Bonnier Books
UK (Ireland) Limited.
Registered office address: Block B, The Crescent Building
Northwood, Santry
Dublin 9, D09 C6X8, Ireland
compliance@bonnierbooks.ie
www.bonnierbooks.co.uk

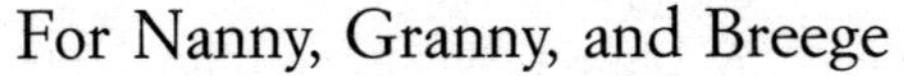

For Nanny, Granny, and Breege

Tenderness does not choose its own uses.
It goes out to everything equally,
circling rabbit and hawk.
Look: in the iron bucket,
a single nail, a single ruby –
all the heavens and hells.
They rattle in the heart and make one sound.

Jane Hirshfield, 'Late Prayer' from
The Lives of the Heart

August 1981

LITTLE MAUDE ROWE SITS in the crick, her pockets heavy with gold, the blood on her face turned to powdered rust. Her feathers drowned, tarred in crimson. Beside her, the setting sun makes a shadow of Denny, whose new clothes are fit for a man far smaller. He is perched on a rock, hands folded in his lap, eyes like pearls in the dusk. At his feet, the baby sinks its fingers into the dirt. The woman – Opal – talks to Denny, her shaking hands scrubbing at his face with wet rags, as if that will wash all the blood off. She asks Maude to watch the boy and the baby and Maude does watch, but she also imagines a pack of coyotes sniffing their way toward the bank to eat the children. She imagines looking on and wondering if she would feel anything at all.

*

The brief plains are flooded, sodden leaves rotting around their ankles. Denny takes Maude's hand in his own, tacky with the blood that could not be washed away, and drags her through the forest's packed pines. The boy, he carries; small fingers squeezing at Denny's discoloured neck, his face tucked and hidden from the dark, heavy night.

They reach the truck, its bed containing all manner of things that Denny's mind struggles to catalogue. It was Opal's doing – she worked as if drawing from a list she has spent years writing. Plenty of food, a sack of something soft; what little she could carry in arms that struggled to keep hold of the baby. Opal knows to pack only what will keep, which is not enough. She grabs a tarp from a neat stack of logs and throws it over the top. She bundles herself and the baby into the front, slides along the seat. The baby has stopped its howling. It has stopped making any noise at all.

Denny does as Opal does, because it is all he can bear to do. He climbs into the driver's seat, the boy in his lap, shaking. Maude turns, despite it all, and leans on Denny's shoulder a moment, the shotgun cradled in her arms once more. He twists the key and the headlamps flicker to life; the cassette plays a jilted tune that his father must have stopped, halfway through a song. The light is a terrible thing.

*

Over the white din of the road, cars shooting past like bullets, the buzzing of neon signs a cluster of wasps whipping its way through the air and burrowing into the tunnel of your ear. You'll call me Ma, the woman tells the children. You'll call him Da, she says of Denny, who is not Maude's father, but something else entirely.

Never before has Maude spent so long on the road. Her legs hurt, her tailbone has turned numb. The boy can't climb the stairs to the room that Ma got for them from the man behind the counter – doesn't seem to know how – and instead bends forward to take them at a crawl. His felted trousers have holes in them where his white kneecaps peep through like two tiny moons. There are cuts there, and on his hands too; scritch-scratch crosshatch, crescents curling between. Maude holds the railing and lets her palm catch on the peeling paint. The walkway stretches long and narrow, with identical green doors, brass numbers and locks. Further down, a group of men are talking with a spit bucket between them. She looks over the railing, across the lot they have parked the truck in; lights reach into the night sky, spaced evenly along the street. Cold, grey, painted in yellow and white lines; so precise, yet so ugly under the garish electric glare. When they pass the men who cluster around the bucket, Da grabs her and the boy by their shoulders and squeezes hard. He lets go once they arrive at door number fifty-four.

Behind it, a sticky carpet worn thin to a rough, greying weave. It is varying shades of green and brown, lifting at the corners where the skirting has grown damp. Pebbled wallpaper the colour of rust, tacky to the touch. There are pictures on the wall, smudged landscape paintings of sunny places, and brass lights on either side of the dresser – like what they use for their oil lamps – only one of them working. Two beds, wide and covered entirely by yellow quilts; the silk shredded and frayed in large patches. On one nightstand, a small book with a navy covering sits. The pages are as thin as rolling paper, with tiny letters and a gold ribbon down the middle. Maude knows it's the Holy Bible – like the one Pa's friend Sarge kept at his breast, kissed before bed each night. Next to it lies a box of tissues. She yanks two, almost a third, to wipe at her hands; then the shotgun, where her fingerprints are surely plenty.

Opal gives her a damp towel to make a proper attempt. She passes another to the boy, who wraps it around himself like a blanket, then she takes a drawer from the dresser and pads it with pillowcases, nestling the baby inside, the poor thing; with her pink knit cardigan, socks slipping from her feet; auburn hair in misshapen tufts, curled around her ears, squeezed tight between reddening fists. The baby baulks, her round face scrunched into something impossibly ugly, and raises her arms in a demand to be held once more. Denny should do it, because he is the one who took her in the first place; passed her off to Opal when it seemed the weight of her was far too similar to what had been taken from him in his exile, all those years before. But it is cruel – their collective grief and grievances toward one another are not the fault of anyone here. This baby ought not to suffer for the awkwardness – the way Denny cannot meet Maude's eye, the way he regards the boy with the kind of recognition one would never spare a stranger. With hair so blond, there's no mistaking him.

'That's Gideon's son,' Opal says to Denny.

'Yeah.'

Together, they watch carefully as the boy pulls himself to a stand in front of the long mirror nailed to the wall by the bathroom, and inspects his reflection so closely that his breath has begun to mist the glass.

'I couldn't just leave him behind.' This is the truth. Little fingers that hooked over the windowsill, curious gaze peering across the lip so he could find the source of all the noise.

'What's his name?' Denny asks. He should know. By right, he should have been there when the name was given, when the dirt was smeared and the water from the golden creek was scattered in droplets across the boy's forehead and he was pronounced a citizen of the Silver Valley. Godfather, maybe, a guardian in some capacity that foresaw the bizarre and twisted fate they all, five years later, have found themselves tangled in.

'You don't remember? I think it's—'

'It's Billy,' Maude says, hardly sparing them a glance from the window.

Denny hums with vague discontent and removes the baby from the drawer, as if the act of pleasing her will quiet his thoughts. It's muscle memory, supporting her at the neck when she is likely too old now to be in need of it. But in other ways, he gets it right: the calming hums and gentle bouncing, wiping the spit from her mouth with the clean sleeve of his borrowed shirt. He so clearly knows what he's doing. Opal does too – it was her job, once, loath as she is to admit it – but it's easier when they can walk and talk, communicate with her; or at least begin to.

Billy was easy. She took him by the hand and led him down the porch steps without any fuss. Told him they were going somewhere safe, somewhere better, and *no*, his Gid would not be joining them. The boy had taken it in stride, like that man never made up the entirety of his world, and Opal thought she could cope with things if it was just him; but then it was Maude, then Denny and a baby in his arms. It was five of them in a flatbed truck, packed like sardines and praying that they wouldn't get pulled over.

In Denny's lap, the baby fusses, kicking her bare, fat legs out and loosening the pins on her makeshift diaper.

'Quit,' he says none too gently, voice rough from the swelling of his throat. But it goes unnoticed by the baby, who grabs and paws insistently at his clothing as if she must dig to the very centre of him.

'And what's her name?' Opal asks.

Denny raises a shoulder.

'Well, she must have one.'

'And you think I'd know it?'

The baby looks nothing like anybody she knows. Though, for all her years in the valley, Opal knew so few. She was never good at such things; not in the way that James used to be, and once he was gone, she became even worse. Each evening spent on the crumbling back porch of her trailer, a glass of tepid water and a stubby, unsmoked square, watching the absolute *nothing* of people and basking in the peace it brought her. But now, there is only this to focus on: their shared sorrow or lack thereof; the blood painted thick and crusting in their nail beds. The baby gurgles, spit bubbling along the seam of her mouth.

She's pretty, with a single dark brown beauty mark above her left brow. Babies are not pretty, they are large, rounded foreheads and fat, hidden chins. This baby looks like a person, even though she is a year old, at most.

'You're the one who brought her.'

Opal can't say she wouldn't have done the same for an infant, but being here, in these conditions, is no mercy. She couldn't leave Billy. Even when she knew what it meant to care for him – for any of them: the factors involved in making sure they are fed and rested and kept clothed and clean. She took him and she took Maude, but a baby makes all the difference. It makes everything that bit harder.

'Is there any more of the—' she starts. Denny looks at her, his bruised, bloodshot eye bulging. Maude's gaze lands on her too, accusing. Why bring it at all if not to pay their way? Just as she had done before: with her grandmother's trinkets, her father's medals. They have nothing else. 'The gold?'

'Just sell it,' says Denny. Maude's grip on the window ledge slackens. Her sharp chin drops, black eyes fixed on her lap like any objections are simply lying there, ready to grab. She had been so eager for them to take it: Baron's coat heavy on her slight shoulders, pockets stuffed with clinking treasure; cheeks splattered with red flecks like freckles, something bone-white stuck in her hair. She's cleaner now – from their stop at the creek, from the towel – but still, her eyes are clouded by what she saw.

'Are you sure?' Opal asks. She hates being the one to do it, but Denny's not fit to leave the room. For all his seeming confidence, she has no idea where the bounds of his social abilities lie. He's not accustomed to this world in the way that she is and comes across as odd at the best of times – though prior to her move to the valley, Opal had been a city girl through and through, and this is decidedly not *that*. To send him off with jewellery to sell and provisions to buy would be akin to throwing him to the wolves. Perhaps, if it were another time, or some other pieces of jewellery, she might be more willing. But it's not right to do that to him, not after the night they've had. He nods, brief and gruff and refusing to meet anyone's eye with his only good one.

Taking the boy's hand, she pulls his shirt over his fuzzy head, strips him of his trousers, and drags the top sheet halfway down the bed. She will bathe him in the morning, when her back no longer aches so much from packing the truck. Of them all, Billy is the cleanest – despite the muck, despite the sticky, scentless sweat that has coated his neck with gritty lines caked in dust. He smells of smoke, though, and his clothes are musty beyond salvation; she tosses them into a pile by the bathroom door, knowing that she will have to give their soaking a fair attempt before she gives up entirely. Her clothes – and Maude's, Denny's, even the baby's – cannot be salvaged; painted with blood that has dried and bled again, framing the edges with a yellow tint.

The blinds billow in the midnight breeze and make grey the shadows. They cast strips of pink neon light across the floor that bend on collision with the bed, the wall, the ceiling. Maude sits in it, still and waiting, the shape of her in a jagged outline that stains the carpet. She watches for something that Opal cannot yet fathom because they never gave her the full picture: Maude, a warning in the dark, hair stringy and tear-soaked, blood-soaked. Denny came soon after, a silent spectre whose face was swollen and scarlet, a baby under his shirt to protect it from the mess. And she *knows* them – in ways that she perhaps wishes she didn't – how they move and speak and stick their limbs tight together as if the space of being is far too much for them to take up. She knows the sadness has sunken its teeth in.

There is a TV on the right-hand corner of the dresser. It's a model that appears to have come out around the time she and James moved from the city. Such a long while, and yet she feels in her feet as if she could step back into that life and have everything be so perfectly as it was. The exhaustion must be getting to her. She turns the TV on, and it flickers into static. That should be enough to mask the silence while they sleep, but still there is the urge to see something, anything, of the world as it is now: wrap her head around what has changed, while Opal has lived on in a strange and stagnated life.

'This?' Billy shoots up in the bed and points at the TV, entirely unsettled by its fuzzy white light.

''S a television,' Denny says, perched on the other bed. From the window, Maude cuts him with a look of both betrayal and confusion. 'For watchin' the pictures.'

'Snow,' says Billy.

'Looks more like a rainstorm to me,' says Denny.

She will go when it's light: cross the road to the strip and hope there is a pawn shop, an antiques mall, anything to get rid of the awful weight in Maude's jacket. Then there will be the convenience store, a gas station, maybe. She will buy diapers and formula, bread, gallons of water to load into the bed of the truck. Other things, too. She only has clothes for herself, some of James's old things; these will do for a while, but eventually people are going to become suspicious of them and their three bedraggled children. Their girl, almost a teenager and their baby, only one. Their boy, about to turn five, looking nothing like either of them, with his translucent skin and cherubic cheeks, his corkscrew curls near white in the dim lights.

'Rest,' she tells Billy. He is fit to do so without direction: half-lidded eyes, downturned and flickering, he watches the static television from his shredded silken pillow; arms flat at his sides, hands bunched against the covers. 'Where's your toy?'

He makes a noise, smudged and incoherent. *Muh*, it sounds like. *Muh*. He points again to the lamp by the mirror, around which he's wrapped the stuffed animal; long limbs a tangle, looping the base several times over. Opal retrieves it, tucks it – coarse, worn fabric made of old upholstery with buttons for eyes – under his neck.

'Will you sleep?' she asks.

He does not say yes, or any variation of the word. He does not nod or hum. He simply sleeps. She slips under the cover too, close enough for Billy to reach if needs be, resting her head in the crease between his pillow and her own. Her back to Denny, to Maude and the baby, she tries to sleep. She tries not to think.

Nothing more is said. Nothing is decided. Denny won't let the baby sleep in the drawer, he won't let Maude sleep on the floor. But Denny's never had much say in what that girl does. So, Opal holds the boy and Denny holds the baby, and Maude lies between them, a tired little island, floating all on her own.

*

Last night, Denny rifled roughly through Maude's coat pockets, shaking her down like a criminal in the motel reception. The clerk gaped, slack-jawed, hand twitching toward the phone before snapping it back at Opal's warning glare. This small violence was solely for the sake of a chain so weighty and golden that it bought the five of them two days' board and silence. Denny tossed it down on the counter like it burned to the touch, regarded it with such wariness Opal wondered if perhaps he could feel the spirit of Baron Rowe lingering between its links.

Beside the boy as he slept, still as a stone, she dreamt of the children and their wet, red faces, blind with wanting. The black woods and how they stretched on forever as they ran. Leaves and branches curling around her ankles like warped fingers. Of catching a bus – returning to Chicago like nothing ever happened, like she and James had never left. Taking up a job with the Sanders, the

Weixlers, old Mr March, and riding the L home every day to her cramped and lonely apartment. The windows were all wide open, and the noise of Chicago crawled through the cracks like the stray cats her mother always fed, even though they could never afford to. Opal dreamt all of this and let her mind pretend – that tragedy never struck, that the valley was simply an ill-thought money racket, not a death trap that would do its best to swallow them. Which it did, slowly, savouring each slice.

Her wish for a real, true dream instead of a memory woke her. Her eyes, dry and spent, tried to make shapes in the overwhelming dark, but the most she could grasp was the dawn through the blinds. In the shadows it cast, she gathered her things. Quiet, so as to not wake the children, she had no chance to give herself anything but a whore's bath over the crusted sink. Disturbing the baby was the least of her problems, with Denny awake and pretending not to be. Billy slept like the dead, but Maude was an unknown variable, limbs curled around each other, tense even in repose. Opal has done this before – cared for children that are not her own, but who seek in her everything their own mothers ought to give them freely – and she can do it again.

This town sits in a valley too; a different one – flat and low, hemmed by lush green and mountains that climb to whitened peaks despite the heat of summer. All her life, she's never been so far north. Five years ago, head out the passenger window of James's Buick – the cool spring breeze on her skin from the ice that had yet to thaw, every one of their earthly belongings in the trunk and backseat – she had thought that would be the end of it. She had thought, foolishly, that the valley would become her home.

Hand drifting to her hair, she smooths it down and busies herself in a way that seems comfortable, natural. In that other valley, somebody was always watching. Squinting through windows. Trailers and cabins tucked too close together for any kind of privacy – noise at night always remarked upon at the following day's breakfast. But here the people move about as if she is but an insignificant blip in their day. It's less of a town and more a slice of road, sandwiched by a selection of stores that seem to all sell the same things. Somewhere to pass by, this close to the border. Which is freeing in a way that this situation she has found herself in is absolutely not – it's nothing like the city she left behind, but it's far better than the lows of the valley she longs to bury deep.

Heady with it, she takes the pavement readily and finds herself running through every conceivable surname she could grant them all in their new life. Aster is not an option: Aster is James's name and was never truly hers; it belongs to family he still has in Edison Park, who know nothing about what became of him, only that he would rather hedge his bets on a poor girl and the promise of work up north than spend another second in the family business. At the antiques mall, she hands over three chains and an eighteen-carat signet ring in exchange for a thick stack of bills, and when asked for a name, she gives one belonging to a dancer from her old company; one she doesn't like enough to keep forever, but that serves its purpose in the moment. Then there is Rowe – Maude's name – certainly not. Knowing next to nothing of the family's origins makes it too high a risk. As for the other names from the valley, had any feelings of fondness remained, she might have considered them. But they never did a thing for her when it mattered.

The truck will have to go too, she's decided, and not just because she wishes to shake herself of the associations – the smell in the seats, fingerprints on the window – but because it will get them caught, with the pink slips in the jockey box registered to Baron Rowe, no doubt. But a place like this will care little for the details, and she can sell it for parts if she has to. Her old neighbours worked in a shop just off the Dan Ryan in Canaryville that dealt exclusively in scrappage, and she had heard enough to know that the truck holds some stock by virtue of its size alone. She can swap it for a neater model, then, something less obvious; cart Denny and the kids across the border no matter how hard her head tries to drag her in the other direction. Her heart is another matter best left alone. It's not in Chicago, nor the valley. Perhaps it is simply in her hand and she can put it wherever she wants.

Her shoulders ache with all she's bought – for the baby, mostly, and Denny's swollen face. She avoided the small grocery store, seemingly run by a husband and wife with wide eyes and endearing smiles, instead choosing a gas station right at the edge of town where men gathered in their low jeans and overalls to swap small talk before work; the kind of place she wouldn't be remembered. Paper bag brushing her chin, hair falling from its delicate hold, Opal breathes for a second if only for herself. Takes advantage of this moment of relative peace for all it's worth, because once she sets foot back in that motel room, she will have to be what they need. Give herself over to the children, to this drifting, hollowed-out man. She will have to be someone else for them, it seems. A mother she is not and likely never will be, but if she looks and feels the part it might become true.

On the way back to the motel, there is a barbershop, walls panelled in thin strips of pine a garish orange through the grubby window. Perfect, she thinks, knowing she would have had to do the job herself over the browning bathroom sink if not for the spare change stuffed in her pockets. Food bought and plans made for the truck, she can take this time before her life must begin again, no clear end in sight. Her free hand presses flat against the glass door, the bell ringing above her head. Opal can be what they need, but she has to mould it around the shapes that are already there. She never thought herself to be part of the life that had been cultivated for them in the valley. She is not Denny, who was made and remade by the hand of his father. She is not James, who is long dead in an empty grave. She is herself, whether she lives in that dark hole or not.

*

The door clicks open a sliver, slicing a line across the thick shag carpet. Opal's shoulder cuts through, bare and red from the heat outside. She's been gone all morning – rolled from bed without disturbing the boy, slipped into her boots, tied her long hair into a knot at the nape of her neck. Denny watched her silhouette, the dark shape of her against thin curtains, the steel of her spine straightening, hands low on her hips. The little sigh she released, quickly hidden by her palm. Now, as he coaxes the baby into sipping some water, Opal props a large paper bag against the legs of the foldaway table and slips her boots from her heels without bothering to unlace them. Slumped, Opal turns her head to look at him. But there's something different about the image. Something wrong.

'I sold the truck,' she says, quietly. He can't hear her properly at first, because her hair has been cut. It swings loose around the sharp edge of her jaw.

A well of something thick and heavy coats his throat.

'You had no right.'

Her skin tightens, making clear the very bones of her. So tense and brittle, yet he's never once seen her break.

'You are not in charge here,' she says.

Her words are a staunch blade between two ribs; there lies heavy within him the need to push back, to retaliate. Maude curls instinctively under the covers, trapping herself in the dense heat of near noon, but Denny knows better. He has never in his life been in charge of anything that didn't crumble and die at his feet.

'No,' he says. 'No, I'm not.'

It's a relief to say aloud.

'Did you,' he starts, fumbles, tries again. 'Hope you got us somethin' else.'

Opal shakes out the quilt closest to her, unearths the boy and his terrible stuffed toy, whose leg slumps down the side of the mattress and near brushes the floor.

'Got us a car,' she says with a broad and waxy smile, as if for the boy alone. 'The paint job's good. It has seat belts.'

Pa's truck didn't have seat belts, or a backseat, but it did have a bottle of old dip spit in the passenger door, a severed rabbit's foot hanging from the rearview, and Denny's initials under the mat in the well where he'd carved them with a sheepfoot blade. That was back when he was small enough to make hiding places out of a space that can now barely fit both of his legs. It's not nostalgia he feels so much as the fact of the thing – the last tether that wasn't a living, breathing person; the final nail in their swift and sudden exit. It didn't really feel like leaving, not until now.

'And the gold?' he asks.

'The gold,' she repeats, tucking a strand of hair behind her ear. 'Got a fair deal, I think. Had to use most of the money for the car, though. We'll have enough to buy what we need, but as far as accommodation goes . . .'

'Slept in worse.'

'Speak for yourself.'

This is where two ordinary people in an ordinary situation might laugh, but neither have it in them to do so.

He can make this work for them though; Maude is no stranger to sleeping outside and the boy hardly seems fussed about anything. The baby won't be a problem. He knows how to keep her quiet, and how to keep them all from being found out. It's no longer the footwell of a truck he has to squeeze himself into – they have the whole world to hide in.

Opal is already stripping the beds of their thin undersheets, balling up the towels from the bathroom – which is more likely to do with the red that stains them than any use they might have – and has taken a slightly worn satin pillow from one of the chairs; then another stuffed with feather down from the bed.

'They won't notice,' she insists. 'And the cleaners won't care.'

Opal knows this the way she seems to know most things about the world – both vast and incredibly specific. Denny's been in a room like this before, when his feet wouldn't touch the floor and his Pa's shadow was a mountain in the window, and he never noticed such things. Never thought about swapping vehicles or getting haircuts or buying things in a store where you won't be noticed. There's a rhythm to all this, and he's dauntingly out of step. He never learned what to be afraid of without Pa showing him.

The noise of the world outside, the brief glimpses of people he's seen through the motel window, is saturated so sharp and rich that it hurts to see. Once beyond the door, there will be no more hiding behind Opal, who now has to be the mother to his father – the mother to *their* children. There is a whole world of rules he has no idea about, and he will have to learn it all alongside the children hardly older than a decade. Could never do a damn thing right, certainly not by himself. Were it up to him to shepherd them from the valley, they'd have died at the crick or succumbed to despair before ever reaching civilisation. Even Pa's jewellery he couldn't take credit for – Maude thought of that one all on her own; or maybe she brought it along as a reminder, a token of what they have both had torn from their very hands by the same man who gave it to them in the first place.

Denny's heart kicks a little faster and his breath leaves him for all of thirty long seconds before Opal's muddy eyes meet his across the bare mattress and the room spins slower, to a pace he can tread against without falling too far behind. She smiles, close-mouthed and well-meaning, and they pack.

*

At Copeland, Opal makes him pull over. She leans into his space, the baby held firm in her lap by the crotch of her diaper, and flips the blinkers on. Sarge always said the lights only mattered to tell other people where it was you were going, and that such a thing was nobody's business in the first place. Seems Opal isn't worried about prying eyes, about being seen moving from the passenger seat with a baby on her hip and Pa's shotgun well wrapped in a sheet from the motel. She opens Billy's door and he slips forward, caught only by his seat belt stretched to its very limits.

'Stand,' she says. They unbuckle and lean forward in their seats. Maude's mouth is set in a vicious sulk. Beneath them, Opal places the padded weapon, then directs them to sit once more. 'Thank you. No shifting around, now. No talking, either.'

The boy can't buckle in again. Maude helps him with impatience steaming out her ears and then flops back into her own seat. But through the rearview mirror, Denny can see that the belt is biting Billy, leaving angry red marks on his neck.

'Here,' says Denny. He twists in his seat and reaches back, meeting eyes of cornflower blue that aren't a bit like Gid's – brighter and far more discerning, with a fan of dark lashes above that don't match the white blond of his hair. When the boy is settled, Denny tugs the belt forward.

'Swap with me.' Opal is standing in the open door, the baby held out between them. He accepts the exchange, because the baby is a secret joy, and slips around the back of the car lest the beam of the headlights hurt her little eyes.

Opal makes good use of the mirrors; adjusts them to her liking. She smooths her new hair down, wipes a smudge of dirt from her chin. She smiles at herself, tongue poking through the gap in her teeth, only to drop it like it hurts her to hold for longer than a minute.

Settling into the passenger side, infant in his lap, Denny regrets moving at all. Driving and its distractions had kept him from noticing the ache behind his right eye. He can't see very well out of it. It's swollen and purple, left only with a slit for sight at the hands of a southpaw. Best he keeps to the passenger side, a handful of bags between them, where he will do little else but hold the baby in his lap and trust that Opal can handle the clutch, which cuts out on her first few tries. She hisses as she jerks the stick shift back and forth.

'Maude,' she says. 'In that bag at your feet, there's a brown envelope. Could you take it out for me? I forgot.'

Maude looks on plainly for a moment, weighing options carefully. Being asked is a far cry from being told; though she hardly knows the difference. Her head disappears behind Denny's seat, and Billy's too dips curiously. It's only four miles to the border once they pass the minuscule town of Good Grief, enough time for the kids to get a good look at the envelope's contents – Maude mouthing the words aloud as Billy strains his seat belt to hear.

'James,' Maude says, the word like the whip of a bullet past Denny's ear. 'That what we're calling you now? Just like that?'

Denny's mouth falls open for an answer but nothing comes out.

'You're not calling him anything but "Da",' says Opal, glancing sideways into the rearview before focusing her attention on the road. The brakes sound awful when she begins to slow down on approach to a bleached two-story building with an overhang as wide as two lanes of traffic, a small booth tucked between them. She turns on the dome light and reaches back. 'Give me that.'

In the waning sun, Denny worries that the lights will attract attention, but there are many cars ahead with their brakes bright like the cherry of a cigarette. Queues, really. People trying to do the same as them. How stupid was he to think that you could just cross into Canada? That it would be so simple as a mark in the road; a sign, maybe, with a bright and bold *Welcome!* scrawled across the top. There is a man in uniform, hat dipping low across his forehead as he sits with one arm slung out the sliding window of the booth. He must have a sidearm concealed, as such men are known to do, otherwise his slouched and indifferent manner makes no sense.

'That's only two,' Denny says, nodding toward the identification papers.

'The kids don't need any. They're too young.'

He thinks about how to be the kind of father that's not his own, but the examples to go off are little to none. He's held a baby like this before, then a child. He can manage when Opal clearly expects so little of him. He needs to trust her judgement so that she can trust his.

She winds the window down and rolls to a stop at the booth. The man inside takes the proffered papers from her and gives them a quick glance over the top of his glasses. Hidden in half-shadow, the only lines visible on his face are the ones that come with age. His lips purse, but only as if he has tasted something that requires an extra bite for judgement.

'Chicago, huh?' he asks.

'Winnetka, really,' says Opal, with a touch of self-deprecation. 'Gave ourselves a little more leg room after I had this one.'

The officer looks at the baby, whose fat legs are likely more visible than any part of Denny from the chest up. 'What's got you in Canada?'

'My sister moved a few years back – has a place just outside Calgary – and James thinks the kids are too city for his liking.' Here, she rolls her eyes. 'Figures we spend the last few weeks of summer vacation in the great outdoors before school starts up, huh?'

At her soft, easy smile and wide, frantic eyes, Denny dips his head into view and nods. But the man isn't looking at him, not really, instead his gaze is flitting intermittently between the papers in his hands and the ragged, low line of Opal's collar where her silver chain hangs with only a pendant.

The baby starts to cry, whether from the damp of her nappy or the hunger in her belly, he can't tell. Denny turns her around, his palm taking up the entire expanse of her back, which hitches with each little sob.

'Oh, there,' he says, voice faraway and belonging to someone else. 'There, there.'

She howls, making fists and swinging wildly. She takes up all the attention, makes him a focal point in her dramatics. He whose lip hasn't stopped bleeding, keeps splitting; whose face burns a hot and swollen red, whose eye can't fully open.

'What happened to him?' The officer doesn't appear alarmed so much as confused. This is not the husband he imagined for such a charming and calm wife. Denny shrinks in his seat.

'Fancies himself a hero,' says Opal, coy and grinning. She tucks her hair behind her ear, despite how futile that is, and a glimmering, hammered band of silver beams on her left ring finger. 'James never walked by a fight he wouldn't get in the middle of. Isn't that right, honey?'

'Big man, huh?'

Denny sees the sneer of the officer, the begging in Opal's eyes. How nice it would be to string himself up through the spine and feel within his bones the strength to carry this conversation – to keep the act going exactly as she needs it. But he's never been a husband; the most he's ever been is a friend. He sees himself from above, draped in shadow and bleeding rivers from his eyes, nose and ears. Pathetic thing, holding such a treasure in his lap. The baby looks up at him with her running nose and wet lashes, and he looks right back at her, hoping she could ever understand.

'They were gonna kill each other,' he says. 'Couldn't rightly let that happen.'

Maude's foot kicks the back of his seat, but it's Opal's look that smarts worst of all. It's the best he can do, the most he can say about what happened in the valley. He won't let this thing eat her too, not when they're so far away now that there is a chance – a small, shameful chance – they can leave it all behind.

'Suppose not,' says the officer, nonplussed, near pleased by the admission. 'Can't blame a man for that.'

You can; Denny knows this down to the rattle of fist against bone.

The officer pops the trunk and runs his flashlight over its contents, followed by a quick sweep around the tires. He asks Opal another question then waves them on, and still she only looks at Denny. It's not good enough, but it's the only truth he can tell her.

July 1980

THE WASP REGARDS ITS drowning family. Remnants of their limbs hang in the syrupy water like the backs of a lady's earring. The striped shells of their bodies, the paper wings that crumble on contact, float there for the living wasp to see. It looks on, impassive, bowed legs dipping into the water as if to test the temperature. With every turn of the world comes a ribbon of yellow light; it pierces the jar on the windowsill with a terrible gold so beautiful, the jar itself could be the sun. Each morning, before heating his oatmeal on the hotplate, Denny moves it a few inches to the left, just so he can catch this moment.

His chin slides against his knuckles, his top teeth grinding on gum. It feels uncomfortable in a way that he enjoys – like when his spine clicks and settles against the flat line of his mattress after a long day below, or when his funny bone bruises hard enough to turn his vision black. Soon, he will have to go. Soon, the fate of the wasp will be in its own hands.

For now, he sits. It is nice to do just that, before the day begins in its fullness. Sometimes, when the wasps find somewhere else to build their nest of pulp and saliva, the fruit flies will swarm and fall by their hundreds. This tends to spoil the day, because fruit flies do little with any sense; they don't put stock in their kin. The wasp looks on, and it knows. It *knows* that its family is dying. Denny likes it when they leave. They get a taste for apple cider vinegar, and they recognise the wrongness. They kiss it with their tiny antennae and fly away. This usually means that he hasn't put the right amount of sugar in, which only happens when he's running low. But sugar costs too much of his time these days, and he and the wasps would do better without.

There is a smack on the door right before the wasp makes its final judgement. Denny rises, spoon clattering against his bowl; limbs stretching, joints cracking with every step he takes. Minty is on the other side, headlamp drawing a crooked line against his forehead's parallel ridges; perpendicular to his milk-white scar. Skin brown and mottled from the sun, he is already sweating in the morning's heat. His boots are covered in months' worth of muck that he has no qualms about tracking onto Denny's porch.

Denny pushes past him and sits on the rotting bench by the window. From beneath it, he draws his own boots, cleaner despite living outside, and slips his socked feet in. He keeps them tidy, keeps it all tidy, so as to make life easier. Minty likes to roll out of bed in his clothes from the night before and stuff his feet into his boots without undoing the laces. The thought of it makes Denny's breath catch.

'You miss the bells?' Minty asks, tugging at the sleeves of the overalls that tie at his waist. They're a deep blue, dusty from all the times he has neglected to wash them, and hang loose on his wiry frame.

'Yeah.'

Minty laughs like he's got something stuck in his throat, talks out the side of his mouth. 'Must be a real party in that head of yours.'

Denny says nothing, adjusting the tongue of his boot where it's bunched up against his foot. He stomps a few times to right it, heel grinding into the sole.

'Ain't even got your laces done up.' Minty drops to one knee, rips off both gloves. Denny leans back, knees rising as he curls his feet from Minty's grasp.

'Grow up, man. My baby don't whine as much as you do.' Minty presses both feet to the floor. He's stronger than Denny, with large hands and swollen joints that struggle to keep hold of the shoestring. ''Sides, we're gonna be late.'

Denny looks away as he fusses.

The dregs of their cohort sidle past, a mere hundred feet from his cabin, chewing on early morning chatter and Miss Gunn's biscuits. Where Denny has been buttoned up to stifling levels since before his own breakfast, each of them are in varying states of undress. It's the heat, he knows, but below is cooler in the summer. He can't afford to show up at the mouth like that, not with the day that's in it. He'd rather not have to go at all, sit and drown with the wasps instead. But while his presence is unwanted, his absence would be sorely noted.

'Don't have to wait for me,' he says.

Minty trusses the last of the laces and looks right at Denny when he speaks.

'Nobody else will.'

August 1981

FINDING THE CABIN IS no small feat. Denny does so within two days of them being parked out by an abandoned quarry. Hours spent trekking through dense forest, returning with little in the way of food for the children beyond some softening berries and a possum. They spit-roast it over an open fire, orange heat painting their faces. Maude still won't look at them; Billy still looks too much. The baby is content to lay back against a solid frame and gnaw on the hems of her dirty clothes. The mush that Opal bought in the gas station is dwindling; soon, the rationing will have to begin, and while the children might be able to quieten the cries of their hunger pains, the baby will not.

'Seen it up on a ridge.' Denny's voice is a gruff whisper across the flames. He pokes at the fire with a long stick, scorching the end black. 'Ain't been used in a long time, far as I can tell. Windows are covered in shit.' It's a hunting cabin, so he says. Not the kind that anybody would live in for long periods of time. 'Season don't start 'til September or even later 'round these parts. Seems to be a dirt track to it from the other direction, but best leave the car here and walk for now, lest we draw any attention.'

Opal wonders how he'd even know about the hunting season – it's not like Denny was renowned for venturing beyond the valley's bounds. It often seemed more likely that he had lived there his entire life. But there are ways he goes about things that don't fit quite right. It's his accent, for one: nothing like his father's at all, instead a botched culmination of sounds from all over. At times, there is a touch of Yank to his cadence. Yet the old man they encountered down in Bonners Ferry reckoned Denny was a citizen of Mississippi. As far north as here, he sticks out like a sore thumb.

'Have you ever been anywhere else?' she asks him, while he stokes the fire and the children sleep in the car. His chin dips to his chest and he keeps it there. She takes this as confirmation.

'Reckon I've been lots of places,' he eventually says. 'Just can't remember.' Which is a lie, it must be, because Opal can recall every single place she has ever set foot – from 54th/Cermak to the Buckingham Fountain, Minnesota Fabrics to the Vaughan's on Northwest Avenue. She could map out the world inside her own mind as a large and winding tree; branches intersecting, tangling, cutting off at abrupt ends.

The cabin is nothing like she's ever seen. It stands, rigid and rooted to the ground like a jagged boulder; buried beneath tangles of brittle branches and heart-shaped leaves, paint peeling at the brutal hands of the elements. It is a scab on the landscape, jarring and altogether unwelcome.

For Denny, there is a quality to it that lingers unpleasantly in the pit of the stomach, like swallowing the stone of a plum. He can no longer remember the feeling of home. The cord has been severed and he is unmoored. Perhaps this cabin could be a point of focus, a rock he can swim toward. Or a stepping-stone, at least, to somewhere better.

The rain creates a din of green, brown, blue noises – black in the shadows and the burrows, cavities carved by woodpeckers and kept by yellow-eyed owls. The boy is standing with his head tipped back, sandy hair painted mahogany against the dirty pallor of his forehead, catching fat drops of rain, his unfurled tongue a shock of pink against the dark expanse of trees. Opal wraps a ratty sleeve around the palm of her hand and wipes at the boy's face as the baby holds fast to her chest. But with clothes more water than fabric, her efforts are futile. Maude, with her gaunt cheeks and wiry frame, shivers in the souvenir sweater they bought her at a strip mall just beyond the border. Billy got one too – he threw up on it, and they had to soak both he and the sweater in the bath of their motel room. The boy's still freezing, though, with a thin sheet of a jacket dragging behind him like a cape. Denny grabs his hand. Milk teeth clatter as Billy's mouth snaps shut.

The handle only needs a jimmy to click open, the door swinging on rusted hinges. Denny pauses a moment, water dripping from the point of his elbow. Opal is bristling behind him, he's sure of it; longing to shelter them from the heavy rain, the relentless downpour beating upon them in sheets. The baby cries, a chorus of rattling whines. Denny ushers them all inside, catching the boy as he slips on the floor, and shuts the door gently. There is no lock, nothing to shove under the handle. The wood in the fire is damp and has long since rotted. With no possibility of going out to fetch more, Denny settles on the newspapers that sit in a neat bundle on the small counter. From the cupboard, Maude produces a can of kidney beans, while Opal wraps the boy and the baby in dusty sheets that cover the furniture. They splutter pitifully, wiping eyes and noses, but they have quietened in shelter; in the sense of safety it provides.

Later, the rain will stop. Denny will fetch the car from the quarry and park it in the yard. They will throw onions on the fire and peel apart their blackened layers. They will use the old newspapers and almanacks as kindling and curl around the hearth in lonesome little heaps. The baby – her name hidden in his heart – cradled under his borrowed shirt, skin to skin for warmth, snoring soundly at his sternum.

*

The air is sweet and heavy in the morning. Maude did not sleep well, not with the night noises and the bodies so close to her own. She made herself as small as possible, feigned rest amid her new family. Ma tried holding her and soon learned not to.

When she wakes, she bypasses the canned breakfast, the wrongness that persists in this new life. Of the many things that have changed, the trees, the birds and the clouds in the sky are all the same at least. There is comfort to be found in that.

The porch is empty; she stands there without shoes or socks. In her hand, she holds the shotgun, drags it along the floor like Billy with his toy. Ma hates for her to have it, but Ma is feeding the baby and the boy, roughly shaking bedsheets of their dust, checking the cupboards, and desperately trying to make a home of this place. So, Maude thinks nothing of propping herself against the porch railing, the gun's stock sitting over her shoulder, as she takes a breath and watches the world around her: the wet leaves glistening with the mist of rain that still refuses to let up, the shed across the yard whose exterior blends seamlessly into the bark of the trees that surround it. Along its walls, there are rusted tools, wheels bent out of shape, crates and sawn-off piping, a slumped sack of chip bark.

In the midst of this, a woman older than she's ever seen emerges, rifle in hand; hair like spiderwebs in wisps around her narrow face. She wears rubber boots and a vibrant dress under her plastic raincoat. Maude eyes her down the barrel of her own gun, keeps her in sight, hollers for Da without moving an inch.

The woman stares at her. 'You put that down!' she barks.

She is slight, but holds her weapon with the certainty of Sarge, who was a soldier and fought in wars the world over. Maude is not afraid of her, though the thrum of her heart and the tightness in her throat make it hard to speak out, to shout back and tell her to clear off. This new home was hard-won, and Maude's not about to let it go after traipsing up the country, across the border; not after everything she's lost.

The door slams open. Ma hovers over her, hands shaking.

'Maude,' she says. 'Put it down.'

'You're a damn fool,' Maude says, ignoring her. She spits out the side of her mouth the way Sarge taught her.

But Ma doesn't scold or do any soft thing that Maude is expecting of her. Instead, she yanks the gun from Maude's hands, using the weight of it to her advantage. Maude tips backward, her face warm with embarrassment. The woman eyes the exchange, hikes her rifle higher. It's too heavy for her, but lighter than Maude's shotgun. Ma checks the safety as though it wasn't already on and makes a grand show of leaning the barrel against the side of the cabin, right next to the front door. Like they are harmless, Maude thinks with gritted teeth.

'I'm sorry,' says Ma. 'We had no idea that this was your home.'

Da comes through the door, the baby on his hip in only a diaper. She has made a mess of spit down the front of his only clean shirt. She is a ball of fat and soft joints, and will only get in the way. But at the sight of her, of Billy trotting out on Da's heels with his thumb in his mouth, the woman drops her gun, lets it swing heavy in her bony hands.

'It's not.' The soft wrinkles in her face dig deeper, cutting harsh lines. 'It was my husband's place. For hunting.'

'He need it?' Da asks. Ma pinches his arm, but it's a sensible question. There's no point in letting it all go to waste if nobody's here.

'He's dead,' says the woman after a moment. Eyes like marbles, near silver in the light, drift from Ma, down to Billy, whose face is still sticky from breakfast, whose mouth gapes wide like a fish. Then to Maude; with her sunken cheeks and her dirty hair, which she shoves harshly from her face only for something to do.

'I'm sorry to hear that,' Ma says calmly. 'We thought it was—'

The woman's hand cuts through the air. 'Forget it, just— Just put some clothes on that child.' She walks across the yard, but keeps her distance from the porch. She appears to consider something for a moment before coming to a decision. 'My Leroy built this all here with his own two hands – had himself all sorts of notions about coming up here with our boys. You best put it to good use.'

'Thank you,' Ma starts, only to be cut off again.

'Don't thank me yet. This place needs fixing if you want to make it habitable.' She must not like the place very much, if her sneer means anything. 'And if you hunt, I want half of it. I don't want to know who you are or where you came from. The less you tell me, the better.' Maude's limbs vibrate with the fight that won't come. Could it really be so simple? 'C'mere and let me show you this generator. Leroy could never get it working right.'

Ma takes the baby, nudges Da and says something with her eyes that has him moving down the porch steps. He slumps as if to make himself smaller.

'What's your name?' Maude calls after them, leaning over the rail, hair quickly dampening beyond the safety of the awning.

The woman turns back, only for a second. There is kindness in her eyes, if only Maude could see that for what it is. But Maude knows kindness like she knows long division; which is to say hardly at all.

*

Mrs Schweers is her name. Margaret. Peg, to a few. She kicks a matchstick leg against the metal drum of the cabin's generator, bemoans its shoddy state.

'I can fix it,' says Denny, a foot or so behind.

She huffs with a level of derision that whittles away at his insides. On the porch, the boy is playing – legs slung between the banisters and beating against the curling mesh beneath – talking to himself and blessedly filling the silence. He is a point of focus for the woman, as is the baby. Denny is under no illusion about where he would be without them; without Opal, who made a show of leaning on Denny's shoulder and smoothing her hand down the length of his spine. Who nudged him playfully when he didn't think to follow Mrs Schweers toward the generator. Chased away or in handcuffs, maybe, red and blue lights whining. Surely, he looks the part – rough and filthy, eye still swollen with burst blood vessels; the teeth in his mouth loose and the right side of his jaw bulging. His face will soon heal, but this woman will never see him in any other light.

'You can try,' she says, like a threat.

'I will,' says Denny.

'It's the least you could do.'

'I know.'

Branches of a brittle Virginia creeper snap as Opal shoves at the bedroom window, mercifully cutting into their conversation in her urgency to air the place out. She offers an easy smile, a quick nod, a murmur of something to the baby, who continues with her cries that carry through the open window. She's due a feed, he thinks, but there's little to scrounge up beyond some baby food from their supplies and condensed milk from the cupboards that would likely sicken her. She doesn't feed like Maude did – seems a little behind, if he's being honest – but then Pa never let them ease into anything; it was the whole hog or you starved. A bath might calm the baby – if the gas tanks lined up by the peeling shed prove useless, he can heat a pot of water over the fire. The plumbing works at least, fed from a well coated in moss, under a bulbous slab of sandstone. He'd checked the level, made sure nothing dead was floating in the black water, and dug his heels into the drying mud as he pushed the slab back into place. Denny dirties himself further as he settles on his haunches, rips clumps of mulch from the underside of the generator and tosses them behind him. Once the others have bathed, he'll take his turn – no use in ruining the water when he can use what they've left behind.

'You ought to put some ice on that,' says Mrs Schweers, pointing at his eye with the gun – unloaded, he'd learned – instead of her fingers.

He hums, wondering how it is he's expected to make ice in these conditions. For all that this is a hunting cabin, he's seen no sign of an icebox to store the meat.

The faded orange and white sheet of metal nailed to the side of the generator tells him nothing worthwhile about its inner workings – both model and serial numbers have been lost to rust and grime and besides, he was never too good at all that. Back in the valley he always relied on the advice of Old Buster Chaps to lead him along the path that would best please Pa. Fix it right, and he'll have no reason to be mad.

Well, Pa never needed a reason for that.

'Anywhere nearby for fuel?' he asks.

'There's a garage about thirty minutes south on the quarry road,' she says. 'But don't tell them who sent you.'

Denny nods in acknowledgement.

'I want no policemen knocking on my door.'

'No worries of that,' he says, doing his best to assure her and falling far short. 'We're not in any trouble.'

She eyes him with a sharp squint, runs over the shape of him and then right through. Denny so rarely feels seen by others. He's not sure he likes it.

'You look like trouble.'

He was trouble – back when being a boy was all it took and the world he lived in was moulded by his father's heavy hand.

'What's trouble look like?' he asks.

Paint chipping under his nails and blood on small hands. Muscle tearing. Long hair floating on the dappled light of the crick. The belt and the switch and the knife that slides further in. A gap between the teeth.

James, falling.

Mrs Schweers' rheumy eyes stare down at him; not with judgement but something far worse. 'It looks like fear.'

*

The cabin is small and unassuming, with walls of red cedar and low ceilings that slowly bleed all light. A concerted effort has been made to rid it of this dark – half-melted candles are scattered all over and in the smallest of the two bedrooms, a wash of white coats the beams, the sills, the frames of the window and door. The larger of the two is for the children, says Opal, because she's not one for fuss. It would be easy to laugh, were this any other time in any other place – were their friends not dead – but Denny can't. Opal has *never* been one for fuss. He knows this about her, just like he knows she will offer up the bed to share between them and weigh the moment with obligation and guilt that neither of them wishes to feel. She will look at him, at the baby who exists as a soft divide, and ask him to just, for once, let her make something easy.

He could sleep next to her, turned on his side to keep his shoulders to himself. Slight as she is, Opal's limbs are long and corded; why should she have to shrink herself for the sake of his bulk? Why should any of them? He would crush the baby and the boy, and Maude won't have him, not when he's failed her so many times.

Denny's fingers shake as he gathers all of their earthly belongings into a single pile, one to be kept close at hand as he attempts any glimpse at sleep. He checks the fire, throws some papers on for kindling. He pokes at it, checks it again until it's all worn out by his own doing. Takes a patchwork quilt, chewed on by moths and stained with the flaking rust that coats the bed frames, and spreads it across the end of the couch; where it will drape over his feet and drop off the edge like a technicolour waterfall. It has to be enough, with what little they have. In their bed, the children are sweating under thick wool, kicking it off their feet to be free of the oppressive heat. But sleeping alone brings a chill he's long grown accustomed to – one he's inflicting upon Opal by refusing to bed down with her and the baby. He could hold the little thing and speak sweetness to her, only he's selfish, trapped as he is by the shame of his own shortcomings. Any search for firewood would be fruitless with the relentless wet, so he has accepted that to be in this place – to be safe and sheltered – is to be static. Though such has been his lot for the last five years, there is nothing easy about it in the beginning. To do it all over again. He's had more fresh starts than he can count, and he squandered every one of them without consideration for the aftermath. It's always easier to let somebody else decide, dictate how this version of events should play out. Opal knows what she's doing – he's lucky to have that this time around – so he is glad for her to take the reins, keep them all on track. And it hurts his pride to admit it, but she's the only one of them capable of navigating this place and the people they are bound to encounter. Except his pride never meant all that much to begin with – a deficit in dignity and a longing that backfires and smokes up the whole world, makes it so he can't see how things really are – so maybe it's no real loss. Maybe this discomfort is the sign of things, for once, turning in his favour.

The sky is murky with purples and pink, brushed clouds giving way to what stars peek through. It's late, but he can't see the moon. The trees beyond are a block of deep blue, leaves feathering the horizon; all manner of creatures fanning out across the forest and chirping happily in the night. A low creak sounds – the cabin settling – followed by a scuttle. Mice, Denny thinks, until scratching comes like claws at the door, and he is glad for taking the shotgun from Maude before bed.

He toes his boots off and crosses the floor in tense, gentle steps. The thinness of his socks catches on splinters in the woodgrain. Denny keeps the gun high, hoping that these noises mean dinner for them, and not for whatever is on the other side. He pops the latch and pokes the barrel through the small wedge of the door before his face even fits. With the screen gone, there's nothing to hide him. Turns out, there's nothing much to hide from. On the thin, rotting mat are two paws attached to long legs dappled in grey and black. A mutt. Lanky, a flop of fur between its ears bouncing against its narrow head with every tilt it makes. They size one another up, Denny and the dog, and there are no growls or grunts or urgent barks. Denny props the gun against the doorframe and hunkers down low. He puts his palm out flat to protect his fingers from the bite and waits for the mutt to nudge its head against him with the careful curiosity he knows well to expect. Neither breaches the threshold of the cabin with a foot or a paw or makes a single sound. Denny waits for the pink lick and the cold, wet nose, and closes his fingers around the muzzle. The dog stands, straight and still, paws stuck to the mat. What will it do other than need feeding? Keeping? Warmth, when the winter rolls in hard. There it is: a thing that's not worth loving. Denny plants a plum kiss on the centre of its forehead.

June 1975

Opal met James Aster in the deadly heat of a particularly heavy June, compressed into the canister of the 18:46 L train's fifth carriage. She had just finished work for the day, Mrs Goodwin having kept her longer than her contract allowed. She took liberties in that regard – with the pay, with the chores and the children – so Opal reached the Jewel at the busiest hour of the day. She held her shopping between sweaty calves, the brown paper stained to a darker shade where it met her skin. From the top poked two tall stalks of celery, white to lime green. They were accompanied by potatoes, carrots, bread, butter and cheese. She would make a pie on Sunday. Apple was her favourite: a flaky crust that, if a failure, could be turned into crumble. It didn't matter one bit, as she would be the only person eating it.

She was sweating under her arms and between her legs. It stuck her baby hairs to the nape of her neck and slid down her spine in fat drops. The backs of her thighs burned against the worn seat and she ached to scratch them but knew how it would look. There were plenty of men around, gawking at her white dress growing transparent with perspiration. Her matching clogs were nothing to write home about, but they revealed enough leg for her to be worth a look. It was her own fault, really – she'd forgone the stockings Mrs Goodwin demanded, because of the heat. It was unreasonable that the children could run around naked, Mrs Goodwin herself in nothing but a silk robe tied loosely around her cinched waist, yet Opal was to be on her hands and knees, scrubbing inside toilet bowls and mopping up puddles of piss from when little Michael got distracted. At least she could wash her knees over the bidet. Her mother would have rolled in her grave at such a sight. If she'd worn her stockings, the smell would have followed her to the grocery store, and south through the city. Instead, it was merely the stale cloud of body odour and cigarette smoke that refused to float out the cracked overhead windows.

The train rocked her from side to side, shoulders pressing against the man on her right and the woman on her left. Newspapers and magazines held aloft, elbows digging, knees spread. The man's thighs pressed her own, encroaching on the unspoken barrier between seats. Opal made a face, the kind her mother used to curse, and tucked her legs closer together, crushing the brown bag and its contents. A laugh sounded then, against the monotonous pulse of the train on its track, the din of the carriage, the air whistling through the tilted windows. Opal followed the noise, traced it to a ratty suit, a slim brown belt, a tie undone around the collar of a thick neck. She could see the laughter move inside it, a bobbing Adam's apple, scattered with sandy stubble and little red dots. Hair the colour of straw, every bit the Midwestern boy, amber grain tousled artfully in the whipping wind from above. He waved at her. She waved back.

Life was as simple as that. James made her nervous. Which is to say: he excited her the way nothing in life lately could manage. After she met him, she had little to worry about other than ballet rehearsals – he insisted she quit nannying in pursuit of her true dream. Not that Opal knew anything about her true dream beyond what urged her to get up in the morning. Which was James. Quite literally in that he enjoyed grabbing her by the ankles to drag her from beneath the sheets, but mostly in that there was someone to care whether or not she got up, went to work and came home safely. Whether she ate or bathed or opened the windows to let some air in. When she handed her notice to Mrs Goodwin, James celebrated like his precious Cubs had just won a second back-to-back World Series. He cooked her a terrible dinner and handed her a garish bouquet of red carnations that he picked up on the way home from his tentative job at Wisconsin Steel; which was a miracle and something she dared not lend any hope toward – not after the closure of the Union Stock Yards and the waves of unemployment that followed, certainly not after what that unemployment did to her late father. James talked of their future, dreamt aloud of a bigger place that Opal knew they could never afford – closer to his new job that likely wouldn't last the month, then closer to her rehearsals and almost double the rent. But Opal had never known a happy medium or compromise, only sacrifice, and while the notion of dancing for a living was fanciful and enough to make her head spin, she was no fool. Dreams were made for people who saw a world of choices and, for a time, she quite liked seeing life through James's eyes.

He said her teeth were funny with their awkward gap in the middle. The first night, he tried to poke his whole pinky finger through and wound up with a bloody nail bed. They both loved animals, though he was allergic to cats. He sang songs that rattled around in her ears for days, and soon her *petit jetés* were dissonant, her *polkas* landing to the wrong rhythm. Her kitchen was a mess, her bed unmade. Red carnations rotted away on the windowsill, wilting down to parched, brown flakes. At night, he kicked the blankets off and complained of the city's noise. He said her sneezes sounded like a car that refused to turn over. She would have followed him anywhere.

September 1981

DENNY GOT A JOB in town as a mechanic in an old veteran's garage, changing tires and replacing radiator hoses. Pure luck, offered for the sight of him on the curb outside a gas station with his head stuck under the steaming hood of their car, yanking at cables and the like with the expertise of someone who grew up with their hands on an engine. Horatio figured him a prodigy, hobbled over on his bum leg and hired him on the spot. Denny has that look about him, like he's used to hard work. The money is something, but it's not enough.

Opal spent the entire day prior fussing over the figures scratched into her secondhand notebook, and if things keep going as they are, the funds will always be left in a startling deficit. Perhaps this was the valley's only blessing: fuel had not been a concern, not for cars or generators on their last legs; and while food was bartered and sold in a currency that could never be spent elsewhere, it was plenty so long as your work was being done. James had worked hard, and after he died, Opal worked harder. She wanted for nothing in all that time, except answers, and now with those answers sitting so close she can reach out and brush her fingers against their jagged ends, they no longer take priority.

James is not her family, not anymore. In truth, Opal hasn't had a family for a long time, and the muscle had started to atrophy from disuse.

With the house fast asleep, Baby – no longer a title, but a name adopted out of sheer laziness – joining Denny's fitful slumber on the couch, the dog curled beneath them, she was free to toss and turn, play the logistics over in her mind until she could make some sense, find some acceptance, in the fact that she needed a job. It was the first step of many. Unable to settle, she crept into the kitchen and stole a rinsed-out can from the row on the windowsill. She tore the label into sticky strips, the paper balling under her fingers and staining them with ink. Sickly sweet, the scent of pineapple rings wouldn't quite wash away, clinging to her as she cut into the top half of the can on her bedroom floor. Making inch-wide segments along the rim with rusted upholstery scissors, nicking her fingers, red beading beneath her skin. She bent each strip down and over itself, meeting in the middle, leaving only a small hole that prying fingers could not fit through; that would slice on the way out. A kitty, a safe, as best as she could manage. The kind her mother kept nailed fast under the bathroom sink; that she hid from Opal's father in order to square away every last nickel. It meant little beyond a symbol to her own self of things to come. That, with time, she might forget about all the coins and small bills she'd tucked away and happen upon them some day while cleaning the cupboards: a lush wad of wealth to fall back on; or enough, at least, to start over.

She had gotten used to Baron's ways, the menial role he placed her in at the storehouse; not to create or find, but simply to organise that which others had provided: jars of preserves, cigarettes, smoked meat, freshly baked bread, fruit and vegetables from the patch. And she is a provider, at the very core of herself, for she provided love and consideration to children who had spent their lives starved of it – children who were taught gratitude for their lot but did not learn it, who were told cautionary tales of other children who did not have roofs over their heads, food on the table, electricity; children for whom love was ponies and Dobermans and a Christmas tree with hand-blown decorations from Bloomingdale's. That was a job, though, a line she drew that was thick and bold and unwavering. Opal never wanted to be a mother and now. Now, she cannot see another path.

What a funny feeling it is to widen her wingspan beyond the frame of herself, where she had built a cage of wrought iron to keep every bit safe and sound. It's a tentative expansion of the self that leaves in its wake a particular kind of ache, one she has shied from with absolute conviction since even before she knelt over the empty grave of her lover and whispered empty platitudes about how good she was at being alone; how she could stand on her own two feet well enough without succumbing to all the terrors that life had so readily thrown at her. She can still do all of those things, but now she – willingly, gladly – must do it for three others, who are smaller than she ever was when the world let them down.

The thing is, Opal has no nice clothes. She hasn't worn a skirt or a dress in six years, nor had she any need to wear high heels, makeup, or cut her hair in the latest fashion. But this isn't the big city, it's not even America. Perhaps she can afford a little bluster, she thinks, the next morning, as she blows in the door with the warm wind. The diner smells of grease, which is to be expected. It sits on the corner of Bishop and Main, though there is little distinction between the two beyond some peeling metal plates nailed to brick corners and a few spare parking spaces. It's not the only diner, but it is the busiest by a far sight, and the closest to the cabin at only twenty minutes or so on the road. It's also the only one with a HELP WANTED sign pasted in the window – which is already a great deal more promising than the grocer's, who claimed to be fully staffed, or the library, who demanded her high school transcripts when she hadn't even made it to graduation. She ignores the urge to scrape her feet on the mat – they are clean, she kicked the dried mud off them before she even set off in the car – and walks directly to the checkered counter – lined with stools and menus, patrons dotted sparsely along the way. A woman stands, unlit cigarette hanging from the corner of her lip as she pours what remains from her jug of coffee into a man's cup.

'That all, Pete?' she states. Pete nods. 'Excuse me,' Opal starts, edging around a stool. 'Are you still hiring?' This earns her a sideways glance, the cigarette flicking up on a twitch of the woman's lip.

'Well, that depends,' she says, not with malice, necessarily, but obvious displeasure. 'Have you ever worked a day in your life?'

Opal with her gawkish eyes and slim wrists, delicate hands marred by a life of hard work. Not pretty, her mother used to say. Peculiar. A thing you look at for too long, that catches your attention and sits with you. Among other dancers, she was no rarity – for they were all frail and muscular in equal measure, awkward-looking in the general sense, yet perfect for how they were intended. But Opal often felt that where all the other children were grown – cultivated, nourished with light and water – she was built. A child constructed. Made from parts that promised longevity, but at the cost of comfort and stability. She was not made for the cold of her mother's home, nor the oppressive heat of Chicago's summers; everything was wrong and yet she adapted as best as she could to the given climate; to the diner's heavy air, stagnant and burning her eyes.

She takes the folded paper from her pocket. 'I wrote it down, in case I forgot something.' Because the list is long and varied. Because she needed to, maybe, as a reminder to herself. She's been working since the eighth grade, an array of jobs that have all blurred together into one meaningless mass. But her mother always pushed for it, wanted her busy in the evenings and on the weekends; with chores and babysitting and cleaning for the elderly neighbours. As if she knew that, in only a few years, Opal would be alone and left to fend for herself. That she'd need to know how to keep going. 'Name's Opal, by the way.'

'Are you in the habit of forgetting things, Opal?' the woman asks, eyes scanning the list.

'Not when I don't have three kids hanging off of me,' she says. 'Besides, you have a little notebook for that.'

The woman smirks, closer to a sneer. As she turns to face Opal more fully, her name tag reads *Nancy Jay*. 'Where are they now? You got someone taking care of 'em?'

'Their daddy,' says Opal, quicker than the thought comes. 'He's got the day off.'

'And when he doesn't?'

There is no one else – to expand their little family to others that don't even exist would only broaden the lie that she is struggling to hold onto. It's not like they have neighbours out there in the sticks; a stray hog, maybe, a wolf or a bear or moose, even, that might crush the children underfoot. She has no idea about these things. But where Denny might know, he'd struggle plainly with the likes of this situation. Opal must have faith in her strengths.

'Our landlady,' she lies. 'She's real generous.'

'Good,' says Nancy Jay. 'Don't want any babies hanging around and doing their homework.'

Unlikely. Billy can hardly speak, let alone read. Maude is too shy, a school could never keep her. Then there is the matter of their identification, their documents, of which there are precisely none. This is a concern for later, something she cannot let herself dwell on for fear of every fragile detail falling apart.

'I'm free any day, can work long shifts if that's what you need.'

'And short shifts, they're gonna bother you?'

'More time to spend with my kids.'

Nancy Jay scoffs. 'Aren't you just perfect?' She lifts the counter for Opal to slip under and leads her into the kitchen, where a man is frying eggs on a skillet, flipping them with a caked spatula. 'Blue shirt – any you have – and a black skirt. Try and keep it as close to the knee as possible. This is a trial run, so mind you obey the rules or I'll boot you out myself. Here, you can use Patty's old apron, she's not coming back from where she went.'

Pete raises his mug in a sloshing swoop, calling through to them. 'Amen ta that.'

Opal meets the cook, Tucker – a whale of a man with a bald patch like a shiny stone on the crown of his head. He smiles at her with a few teeth missing and she smiles in return before she is led to the bins, the cleaning supplies, the pantry and the freezer.

Thrown in at the deep end, what was once dormant within her has awoken readily. She takes a moment to get rightly back into the swing of things, but the day is fairly steady until the supposed regulars work their way in for the lunch rush – which is nothing close to a rush, given what Chicago was like. It's not difficult, but it's not easy either – she's exhausted, worn down to the bone and living off fits and bursts of sleep from the night prior. After the impromptu shift, after punching out like Nancy Jay showed her, Opal tries to use what little change is rattling around inside her jacket pocket to buy a whole pie from the display; which only earns her an eye roll as Nancy passes her the pie free of charge.

'You did all right,' she says, turned away already and walking down the kitchen. 'For a blow-in.'

In the car, it takes Opal a second to orient herself properly – pie in her lap, moved to the passenger seat. Should she strap it in somehow, in case of a quick brake? She couldn't slip into gear that morning, the clutch creaking violently with enough noise to shake the birds from their trees. It's taken a lot of getting used to, driving again. Before moving to the valley, she mostly took the bus or the train and only drove when she had to go up the Ike to run errands for Mr March – which was rare, and certainly not a stick shift. Not like the vehicles Sarge kept back in the valley were prizes, either. Seems he wasn't running as tight a ship as he let on with the trucks in his garage – that or he let the men use them for drifting in the lumpy, swollen field beyond where little ever liked to grow. But beggars could never be choosers, and what little practice she got in the trucks serves her well, now.

Mrs Schweers is from a nice neighbourhood, only a mile or two away, tucked right in the corner beyond where any car would ever need to pass, unless they were looking to pay her a special visit. Opal wouldn't call this visit 'special', only something that needs doing if she is to make right all the things that seem to be falling by the wayside. The house itself has bleached rafters darkened by the light washes of rain that have blown in with the afternoon clouds, white-painted windows with double glazing and flower boxes tucked neatly on the sills in a variety of vibrant colours. There is a quaint, cobbled path that winds up from the sidewalk, weedless, and hemmed carefully by red bricks turned on their sides. Beds of roses and begonias, a birdhouse and bath perched under a tree whose branches need skimming, lest they land on the sloping roof of green slate and clip the white beams of her sheltered porch.

Mrs Schweers is out front. On her head she wears a rust-coloured wide-brimmed hat that looks more fit for a wedding than rainy-day gardening. Her dress is a green and pink floral print that hangs around her frame like a two-man tent, stretching down long enough that it almost meets the heels of her rubber clogs. She holds a pair of shears, ready to snip at something Opal can't see, when her beady gaze rises at the sound of the car's ticking engine cutting out on the curb.

Opal slides out of the seat and does her best to shut the door without slamming it. The woman has no right to look at her like that, not when she demanded their food in return for board. For all she knows, Opal has a string of rabbits in the backseat as ready payment; Denny is keen to ration what meat they have since discovering the icebox – blessedly unearthed from the smallest of the outbuildings – and plans to dole out hunks of his prize buck, which he shot back in August, on a weekly basis. He'll have to thaw it out first, though, cut it down some more and divide it into brown paper parcels; lest they leave the old woman to hack away at her supper. Now, Mrs Schweers casts her eyes to the meagre pie that Opal rescued from the passenger seat. She turns on her feet, one hand on her head as if the hat is fit to be swept away, and begins climbing the steps of her porch. There, she discards the shears and the clogs and removes the hat to press against her bony chest.

Inside, the house is far too warm for the weather they're having – heavy and gassy, clouding Opal's head for a moment and hitting hard as a wall.

'Take your shoes off.' Opal does, slipping them under the bench in the foyer, which is lined with all manner of footwear that no one person could use: rain boots in the primary colours, galoshes and sandals and a pair of white gym shoes, tags still on. 'This way.'

The hallway is long and dark, lined with blue-striped wallpaper and antique marble-top sideboards, full of ornaments and picture frames without people in them. Instead, there are floral miniatures that could only have been kept for their prettiness, filling all the spaces that want for sentimentality. Discomfort stirring within her at the familiarity, Opal shuffles along in her threadbare socks. Lamps are placed, intermittent and mostly unused, on each surface, shades swathed in cloaks of dust and silk scarves. Dressed like a diorama, there is some mail neatly stacked on a buttoned chair, the cable from a vacuum cleaner running taut around the doorframe, plugged into the wall. Each light switch is painted at its corners, with ornate flowers in jewel tones and tiny laurel leaves stretching between. She runs her fingers along the top and earns a thick ball of dust beneath her nail.

Opal follows Mrs Schweers to the kitchen. Bolstered by what she's seen so far, she is ready. Ready to make a suggestion, stand by her argument; ready to sip politely at a hot beverage and eat whatever fruitcake that's sitting, hard as a rock, in the bread bin instead of the pie she brought as a gift. But the pie is taken from her hands after Mrs Schweers suddenly turns in the doorway, startling her. Opal nearly collides with her head-on.

'Do you want to take a shower?' Mrs Schweers asks. 'Looks like you need it.'

The adrenaline that has been mounting since Opal began forming her plan the night prior swiftly melts from her body in an altogether unpleasant way. She wants a shower more than she's ever wanted anything. Dreams of running water; her skin, dry and tired, sloughed and scrubbed and smelling of all manner of things that have no bearing on how she feels within herself. Like layers upon layers of another person, lives lived that are not hers.

'Yes, please,' says Opal.

Mrs Schweers places the pie on the sideboard and leads her up the carpeted stairs, fingers gliding along the smooth banister. The second floor is dark, lit by nothing but the white light sliding between slats on the landing window. There are photographs here, though Opal dares not peer too closely at them and appear nosy. A family of five, just like her own now. They make up very little of the collection, the rest of which is devoted to landscapes of rocky beaches and snowy mountains smothered by conifers that smudge into a single drape of black brushstrokes, dense and with little room for any life. If Opal had a camera, she might take photographs of the children, to do what a mother would typically do. But what could she possibly capture that would feel remarkable in any way to them? First trip to the store? Billy brushing his teeth, petting the dog, using a fork for the first time and biting the tines to get the taste of the metal? Perhaps Maude: the purple skin under her eyes developing into an infinite black shadow. Time will make it better though and they, none of them, will be this small forever. She should hold it tighter; if she had done the same for herself, things might have worked out differently.

'Towels are in the cupboard.'

Left to her own devices, she doesn't rummage or root around in that which isn't hers – besides, she gets the sense that Mrs Schweers would know and find some terrible, passive-aggressive way of scolding her about it. The bathroom is pink like rose petals and frosting, or the particular shade that falls on the edge of a sunset. A bath takes up one entire wall, surrounded by soaps and small candles in varying sizes and shades of pastel, with small, dusty cards sitting in the hollows and the wicks standing proud. Bowls of potpourri are strewn about with splinters smattering the porcelain; fluffy monogrammed hand towels draped carefully over the edge. But a bath was not on offer, and she'd rather endear herself to the woman than overstay her welcome. They have a bath in the cabin too – though the water takes a minute to run clear and the faucets are limy and green – so a shower, with actual water pressure and heat at that, is something worth taking advantage of. She steps into the small cubicle with the frosted glass and gripping aids and flips the handle, doing her best to coax the appropriate temperature out of the sharp cold that strikes her palm. There are washcloths stacked to her right that smell as if soaked in jasmine. Tiny soaps in creamy colours, shampoo that will foam on her crown. Her shirt skims her stomach, ragged and soft. She pulls it over her head, strands standing on end where her scalp is greasy. The mirror fogs up, and she sees half of herself, shrouded: the spare skin on her arms, sagging where once she carried hard muscle.

She has nothing to change into, only dirty clothes from earlier, stinking of grease and bleach and coffee grounds – which ought to neutralise, really, but only do the opposite. Her body and all its jagged edges, the pouch of fat on her stomach that lingers, no matter the volume of food she's eating. Hips widening for children she never had – it's a convincing look, all the same, for the three babies she seemingly bore. Two girls and a little boy, wild things they are. Her hair should be greying, her breasts low and lacking from feeding them all. Six years, all in all. Billy took a little longer to wean, maybe, because of how he can be: so clingy and tactile. They loved him, hovered and simpered and made him into a precious little thing to be so coveted by the other women who walked their prams in circles around Lincoln Park. Boys do love their mothers, though fathers can often catch stray swings of this affection when it's time for bed or a bath. When the evening is long and slow and Denny is reclined on the couch with Baby in his lap; Billy laying on his arm, prattling on about the events of the day he's had, nagging his older sister, who has become *such* a teenager since her eleventh birthday. A date Opal knows well, for it was she that birthed her, of course; that birthed them all. She has photographs of all that, yes, buried in boxes from the move they have yet to unpack. These are the things that have happened to her.

Clumps of hair bunch in her palms as she combs it with her fingers. Chest flush with the heat, heady and stifling, she switches the water back to cold and grips the rail for balance. This is what she knows. And it's easy, after that, to simply go through the motions; better, truly better, for the lack of airs she grants herself and her body, and how there's comfort in the deprivation. She won't stoop so low as to half-ass it – the wash is thorough and deep, scrubbing dead skin and kneading her nails deep into her scalp. She lathers the shampoo in her palm to avoid making knots and leaves it to sit while the cold pelts her torso and pelvis. The shampoo smells of nectarines; something like the scent she used to wear when she worked in Grant Park and before she met James – borrowed from the bird-like girl who danced the Sugarplum Fairy to her Clara Stahlbaum. Her joints tighten at the reminder, knees extending, feet arching and flexing in the shower's plastic tray. The pain in her chest that's lived there happily for the last month increases tenfold. It's no reflection on the moment, but an accumulation of all the moments that have led to this point: where she stands in a stranger's shower, rinsing herself clean of all the years prior, fit to beg for childcare and any little handout she can get in order to make this life a better one for children that simply aren't hers.

Opal takes one deep breath, then another. She rinses the shampoo and covers her index finger with the washcloth, curling around her ears, poking between each toe. Upon rising, her back locks and she must twist out of it. The ache remains as she takes the hand towel from the edge of the bath and uses it to dry her limbs, her back. She lifts her breasts and pats the thin skin there, scrunches her toes on the mat; wrings her tangled hair over the drain. While dressing, the fabric sticks awkwardly to her damp skin – her trousers are the worst of it, though her socks and underwear tie at a close second – but there's little point in fussing when this is only a pitstop in her purpose. She forgoes knotting the towel at the top of her head, accepting that her hair will smack her nape and make her shirt wet, and goes down the stairs on socked feet.

There's a smell coming from the kitchen. Mrs Schweers is cooking and there are many pots and pans in action. On the counter, she has two mugs with tea bag strings knotted at their handles.

'Will I make you a cup?' she asks Opal without turning.

'Please.' She sits at the gingham-painted table, palms catching the chipped edge. Posture straight and strong, her tailbone digs sharply into the seat. The tea is poured and left to steep.

'I got a job,' Opal says. 'In town. It's waitressing, but the pay's all right.'

Mrs Schweers hobbles around the oversaturated kitchen, her spine a brutal arch covered by a thin-knit cardigan. It's not cold, but she must feel the draft in the weather's most minute changes; a whistle through the hollow of her brittle bones.

'How modern,' she says, adjusting a pot on the burner.

'Not really,' says Opal. 'Denny has a job, too, but it doesn't pay much.' Denny's going to be elbow-deep in engines, grease caked in his nail beds, sweat sticky at the back of his neck; it's filthy work and the kind he ought to be paid an awful lot more for. But the old man doesn't have the hours, nor the demand. Despite being the only garage for miles, the town is only so big and he's got other guys who have been there longer, know more.

'So, what are you going to do with those children?'

A dollop of creamer in each cup; cat and mouse, they wait each other out. Opal is not in the position to bargain – a fact of which they are both keenly aware. She has zero leverage, nothing worth anyone's time. Except for guilt – a proven method that she has little problem exploiting, not when it comes to matters of feeding the children. Despite all they have endured, they are still children.

She accepts the hot tea despite the sweat on her brow and blows on the top. 'All in all, I can't see our shifts crossing over much. So, it'll only be a day or two.' The boiled water touches her bottom lip. 'Looks like you have plenty of space here.'

Mrs Schweers takes a sip from her cup without waiting for it to cool. She swallows, loud and sharp in the charged quiet between them. Her eyes are a murky blue, coated by cataracts and a bleariness that comes with age. But there's a severity there, a quick dart of something that might slice, and Opal knows not to push further; she knows not to ask aloud.

'Is the boy toilet trained?' Mrs Schweers asks.

'Yes,' says Opal.

'Doesn't look it.'

Billy is a boy of five years, not an animal. There is nothing about his appearance that signals he might wet himself or miss the toilet. She made sure he knew how, knew to ask. Denny helps him sometimes, at her request, and she wonders how he ever managed these kinds of things when raising Maude. She is typically the one to wipe, hunched over the toilet bowl with Billy clinging tightly to her thigh. She is the one to bathe him too. Denny thinks he ought to know how to do these things alone, but he is a little boy who, until a few weeks ago, couldn't brush his own teeth, wouldn't stop eating when he became full; he hardly knew to pee in a toilet, not a bucket that soon got full and was to be thrown out unceremoniously over the back porch railings. She could always smell it, passing his father's place. That, and the waft of shit that lingered long past the smoke and the sharp sting of liquor. Moonshine, maybe, though it was a wonder that Sarge kept the supply going after all the ruckus Gideon caused; nobody enjoyed the sight of a man keeled over, crutches by his foot, having climbed halfway over the wall of the well before he gave up on the thirst and pissed all the poison out of himself. Nobody liked to think about his little boy left at home either, especially when they were told, plainly and not without threat, that he was to be left in the uncaring hands of his father. But Billy has a chance now to be a boy like any other. And he is doing so well, far exceeding any expectations she had for him when she took him that day from Gideon's porch.

'He tries,' she says. 'He's a bit of a late bloomer.'

'Is that so?'

Opal nods. 'Doctor said it was nothing to worry about.'

'Which doctor? Those quacks in town know nothing about medicine.'

'Oh, one from Chicago,' she lies. If pushed, she might manage to rattle off the names of the various paediatricians left in the address books and desk drawers. She was often the one who had to call, what with the parents of all these children typically otherwise occupied. 'You wouldn't know him.'

'Is that where you're all from, then? Sure doesn't sound like it.'

'Well,' says Opal. 'It's where I'm from. But you've met my husband – he's not exactly the most . . . eloquent influence on the children.'

'Cat's got his tongue,' Mrs Schweers says.

Opal smiles into her cup, despite the truth of it. 'That'll be Den,' she says. 'He's shy, is all.'

'That must be what you like about him, then.'

'Must it?'

There isn't much else; very little she can string into a list of things worth enjoying, for all of him is tied so inextricably to the most awful thing that has ever happened to her. But he is kind, at the very least. Incredibly kind.

'No, he's a sweetheart, really,' she corrects, easy as anything.

Fond and doting. This, she can be.

'They all are,' the older woman remarks, flexing arthritic fingers; each wrapped in a heavy ring, far too loose and yet still unable to pass her swollen knuckles.

Opal's father was not sweet, not in the slightest. He was a large and lumpy brute of a man that cared with more ferocity than his heart could handle. Ambivalence was not a currency he dealt in, and truth was a given, whether it cut you or not. Other men were often sweet and endearing enough that, when she erred on the side of caution, she felt as if she had acted impulsively and without the manners her mother had so fiercely instilled in her. Not shame, but a kind of mortification that followed thereafter. With Gideon, even Minty. James, for all of his charm, was a diary left wide open and dog-eared with colour coding and a key in the margins.

Billy *is* sweet, and he will stay just so if she has anything to say about it.

'Will you, then?' she asks. 'The little one hardly ever cries and Maude is quite good with her.'

'Is she?' Mrs Schweers asks.

'Whether she will admit to it or not.'

'And if she isn't quite good with her? What then?'

'Then, well, she's a child. There's not much I can do about it.'

'I've raised boys,' Mrs Schweers says, with little else on the matter. 'I imagine she'll be the only problem.'

It seems to Opal that most young girls are.

'We can try to pay you a sma—'

'Don't be so vulgar.' Such scorn is a blessing. 'We'll talk about rent once the checks start coming in.'

She won't get paid for another week, Denny for two; and certainly not into a bank account. What little they have has been stretched for fuel and the occasional necessity, of which diapers are quickly taking priority. Of the money they had in the beginning, only a few dollars remain. If it's an attempt at pity, it's poorly veiled. 'Thank you,' Opal offers, begrudgingly.

'I'm not doing it for you.'

'Of course not.'

Mrs Schweers' mouth tightens. She seems to weigh something within herself that is difficult to pronounce. Opal knows, quite clearly, what it is, and bristles. Her tea is finished in one quick slug, mug left to make a milky ring on the table.

'I don't know what you people are running from,' says Mrs Schweers, finally. 'But those kids? They don't deserve it.'

Opal could spit something ugly into the space between them and ruin her chances. But she's far from stupid and, though her move to the valley with James all those years ago would convey otherwise, she's not reckless either. They do deserve it: every last good thing she and Denny can offer them. Better this than what they left behind; better anything than that.

'I can clean your house on Wednesdays,' she offers. Careful as she rises, Opal takes her mug to the sink and runs the faucet to soak the bottom. 'Diners are always quiet midweek, so I'll spend two hours dusting, vacuuming, whatever you like, and you can water your begonias.'

She's good, she's thorough. Yes, all the furnishings in the bathroom are beautiful and new, but the grout between the floor tiles is darkening to a rusty orange and the damp from the shower has painted a splattering of black on the foggy windowsill. The skirting in the hall is grey in its grooves and the carpets could do with a scrub. It's plain as day that Mrs Schweers' care for her house falls short in comparison to the love she has for her garden; that, at her age, every bit of energy is spent on the latter. And while Opal's back aches and her knees click and her body is misjoined with shoddy parts, she is young; and if it is enough to sweeten the deal, to ask no questions, to make it feel worthwhile, she'll gladly do some housework.

She hopes not to offend, or to imply that the woman isn't capable, only she's not. And to keep such a large house speaks mostly of obligation. She allowed them the cabin on the condition that they keep it well, that they bring her food, so who's to say that she doesn't need some taking care of? Who's to say she has anyone at all?

Mrs Schweers only nods. It's severe, a stamp of punctuation. She carries on with her pots and pans, piling them inside a cupboard whose handle she leans heavily on, and doesn't walk her to the door. When she calls out, it's clear as a bell ringing in Opal's ear.

'Drop them by after eight,' she says. 'I won't do any earlier.'

In the garden, night has fallen abruptly and is broken by patches of yellow street lights that render everything in a murky haze so eerily similar to a life left behind. It's heavy, with enough cloud cover to trap the day's heat until dawn. So different from the valley, yet the suffocation remains.

The air in the car is cooler, though the seats are warm. Soon, her hair will dry, brittle and kinked. It may even dry before she grinds the gears and makes grooves in the logging road that winds carefully up to the ridge, to the cabin that lights her way. Bugs plink merrily against the windshield. Opal drives home.

*

Maude Rowe is born again on the threadbare carpet of a dead man's hunting cabin. Billy Bass sits next to her, his peculiar stuffed bear wrapped around him like a rubber boa, milky brown in colour like the scales she watched for in the brush when Sarge took her out to check the snares. Snakes bite hard and it hurts something awful, but being this far from home hurts more. It is that, and the knowing that they will never go back.

Billy presses the pad of his pointer finger to the ridges of her front teeth, prominent as they are.

''S a bunny,' he says, almost accusatory. She regards him: so out of sorts in a patterned shirt buttoned to his chin, spit staining the corners of his mouth with a rash that looks more like ringworm than your standard irritation. She recoils by an inch.

'You like animals?' she asks with a grimace. Billy offers his toy up to her as an answer. 'That's a bear.'

'Bear,' he parrots.

'Teddy bear,' she corrects.

When Maude used to run along down to the patch and bug Terrence Boon about those cakes of bread his sister made each Saturday while he tilled the earth, they talked about a lot of things. Toys, mainly, of which Maude had very few. Terrence liked to whine about the teddy bear his sister kept on top of their dresser, done up in all sorts of fancy things, fit for a prince or a gent of the city. *He has wire rim glasses*, Terrence used to yell, shovel pitched to swing in the air. *I can't see two damn feet in front of me, but the teddy bear has glasses.*

'You know bunnies, but you don't know bears?'

'Seen bunnies.' Billy's small hands comb across the bear's ears with a tenderness that contradicts how he bulls about the world.

'Where?' There were rarely any rabbits around the trailers, but Maude had seen many black bears and the occasional grizzly in the valley. It seemed that rats were more likely company at the rusting husk he grew up in.

'Out the windy.'

Maude's window in the valley could show her little else but the sky. A rectangle framed in pine, a slab of the world that darkened in the night and gave her no stars. But she went outside almost every single day – with Pa most often, and Sarge second. She saw many things in their home, small as it was, and struggles to fathom how it was that Billy saw so little. Bears would wander from far and wide – when the food was lacking elsewhere and the valley was flush with berries in the summer – and Pa would holler at people for letting them anywhere near the patch. One time, long before Maude was even born, a boy wandered down into the lows of the valley – against Pa's orders, at that – for some fishing. When Pa and Sarge found him two days later, it was in a mess of his own blood, both arms left floating in the frogbit. She had been warned off such creatures all her life, and yet here Billy is, holding one to his heart. He'd do better with a real one – teach him not to be so soft and whiny like that dog Da caught on the porch.

She swipes the bear from his hands, long limbs stretched between them in a tug-of-war. 'His name is Billy.'

'Tha's my name!'

'No.' Maude pinches at his ears, fatty tissue, feather stuffing. 'Your name is Bear now.'

A new being. This life is the after and not a single one of them is the same. New names, new hair and clothes, and teeth that feel new for their cleanness. A home, like the last, but better – in that the wood is not chipped away by years of swinging limbs, but carved delicately in attempted decoration. The boy has to be new too and grow fast, or else he'll get left behind. The bear between them, a sorry thing that will only drag him down. She curls it close and crawls forward to stick it under the bed – far enough that his short arms can't reach. And if he's crying, then that's life. Even Baby doesn't have a toy like that, so he ought not be so selfish.

'You have to put it away,' she says, voice hard as she can manage. 'You're big now and you can't be soft. You leave soft and small little Billy Bass under there and come be a bear with me.'

'You's not,' he whimpers, snot dribbling over his lip and down his chin. She pulls her sleeve over her palm and wipes at the mess.

'Fine. A bunny. But if you wanna be the only bear, you hafta prove it.' With a shake of his shoulders, she heaves him up. Though he's just over half her age, he's close enough in height that when she leans forward to squeeze him, her chin sits perfectly on top of his head. When they climb into bed, it's without the bear loping between them. She won't hold him for long, but she'll do it gladly until he stops crying.

'There, there,' she comforts, hand cupping his crown. 'Get all your cryin' out now, y'hear?'

A quick nod, bubbly snort; he curls his arms between them, lost without something to hold. But there's plenty to hold, with much better use than a childish toy: knives and books, food and water.

''Night, Bunny,' he says around a spit-wet thumb, his other hand gripping her sleep shirt.

'Goodnight, Bear.'

Maude's even found that, in this new life, it's quite acceptable to hold somebody's hand.

February 1976

The trailer was small, but Opal had grown into a fully formed person within the tight confines of a 300-square-foot apartment, so the transition was nothing difficult. She was used to drying laundry on the backs of chairs or, in summer, draping it across the rusted railings of the fire escape. She knew how to box things away, keep them dry and free of dust, moths, rodents. How to cook dinner in a galley kitchen that could hardly fit one person, let alone two. Opal, for all her height, could compact herself to spaces far more restrictive than this, as if she were a contortionist in a travelling circus. She was used to making herself smaller.

James, grown in the wide fields of his sprawling suburbia – his T-ball practice, carpools, carving turkeys, those mailboxes with the little red flags – paced their living room-cum-kitchen like a prisoner of war.

'I don't know, honey,' he said, hands on his slim hips with the air of someone calling a particularly challenging play. 'It's not working for me.'

'You're being funny.'

'What?' He halted by the kitchen sink, casting a vaguely miffed look toward whatever he found there. 'No. I just think, well, they told us we'd have a house.'

'Where'd they say that?' She reached for the printed leaflet that had creases in the shape of crosses from being folded over and over. '*Housing* doesn't mean a house. It means a roof and three to four walls.'

'This thing doesn't have a roof.'

'Oh, dear heart.' Opal sucked her top lip in a vicious pout. She poked at his belly and his chest, tried for a tickle under his arms. 'What's that above your head, then? You call that the sky?'

'Won't be able to hear a thing during storms.'

'*Storms*,' she said.

'They're very common here.'

'It's *Idaho*, James. Not the Gulf of Mexico.'

'The snow here is nothing to sniff at,' he said. It wasn't dissimilar to the snow in Chicago, but James had no comparison to make, as he'd never known a house without a central furnace and ploughs to keep the roads clear. He'd also never lived in a structure that wasn't a house – not for longer than the few months he spent in her apartment, anyway. 'I won't love you if you have no toes.'

Opal laughed. 'Oh, what? Doesn't "in sickness and in health" cover frostbite?'

'It's sweet that you think I'll read the fine print.'

She reached out a hand to shove at the round of his shoulder. James, despite his teasing, worried over the matter a while longer, while Opal unwrapped glasses from twists of newspaper and left them on the table for him to put away.

'Do you think my boots will be all right in the snow? The other guys have special ones.' And there it emerged:

the self-consciousness that sat on the other side of the coin to his outgoing nature. His unrelenting confrontation of the world, willingness to jump with both feet and not simply dip his toe. James sometimes needed to recover from it, needed her there to assure him of his place. Though it seemed to Opal that he ought to be the one giving the assurance; with such a length stretching between their prior stations, she still at times felt so simple when presented with his way of things. Moving through life like that, without fear of what consequences may lurk around the most unassuming of corners. Concerned by embarrassment among peers and little else. He had been raised in a different way; that wasn't his fault.

James lived scrupulously. He preferred to shower, where she had been raised in bathtubs, forced to wash her hair with water from a plastic jug. Opal had three pairs of shoes to James's ten – this presented a problem while packing, as did the crystal tumblers he had inherited from his grandfather; the twenty-one-piece Belleek tea set that his mother was gifted at her own wedding. They had no need for any of it in their new home, nowhere to keep it. Yet James stood firmly by the belief that everything had its place; from the beer mats he'd stolen out of his favourite dive bar to the mid-century rattan chairs his eldest sister tried donating to a yard sale.

'Your boots are fine. Snow's half melted, anyway.' It was a simple role to fill – one that she had practised time and time again, when little Michael Goodwin felt silly in his Sunday best; when his older brother fumbled with the knot of his tie as everyone impatiently awaited his presence in the cars. 'Now, get going.' She could laugh at the irony of it, doing the same for her own fiancé as for those children, but it was easy to laugh at everything then, when there was the promise that he would laugh along with her. 'Don't want to be late on your first day.'

James smiled in that terribly beautiful way of his, squinting against the morning light. He leaned in to kiss her. 'Maybe I'll mine enough silver to make you a ring worth talking about.'

*

In hindsight, Opal thought with absolute certainty that she didn't meet Denny so much as she recognised something in him. The precarious slope of his spine and his hands like shovels. The way he meandered through the trees with the kind of aimlessness that contradicted his vigilance. He was rarely seen eating but must have done so often for all the work he did: carting logs toward the kitchens, loading the trucks, mending fences, bringing apples to the storehouse, and pails of water from the well for her to wash them in. In the early days of James's first shifts, when she worried a groove into the floor with thoughts of him chipping away at the earth just below her feet, Denny was a constant; always there to placate and reassure. To calm the boys down in their tendency to joke and frolic and forget the reason they all came here in the first place. There were parts of him she could reconcile with parts of herself that had vanished with the passing of time: his relentless drive, the pauses between thoughts and words that were well considered and sincere. The way he kicked the browning snow from his boots and left them on the front step, took care in how he trod, bringing with him the scent of cloves and ginger; a lingering uncertainty, as if he didn't know which parts of himself to leave at the door.

In all these ways, she knew him from the very first moment she laid eyes on him. Which was her and James's first weekend in the valley: Friday night and a game of poker in the tight nook of their trailer. The kitchen sink was in need of a faucet, so the dishes had to be washed in their poky bathroom. Opal, elbow-deep in suds, kept bashing the back of her hand against the spout. Her first assignment was the following morning – to *find where she fit* – and she had no desire to wake to a bathtub full of plates and tumblers. The practical side of Opal – the one that cleaned for the wealthy, dawn 'til dusk with only Sundays off – could not simply sit in the kitchen to watch her fiancé and his new friends play games and drink. She wanted her bed. She wanted the weighty silence of a frosted night, the forest waking around her to the end of a long hibernation. Opal had never once lived in such quiet, and it seemed she never would again if these poker games were to become a habit.

'Need some help?'

She got her first real look at him, then: Denny standing in the doorway with a hand in each of his pockets, broad shoulders pulled high to his ears. His eyes were dark in the shadow of his hair, which hung limp across his forehead in a way that peeved her deeply.

'I've got it, thanks.'

Her hands were frozen. The heater stopped working halfway through the week. She ought to have asked if somebody could stop by and fix it – for as much as her father taught her about plumbing, they always had landlords for that sort of thing. Denny lingered, just as uncertain as she was about how they were to proceed. She threw him a bone, hoping to be thrown one back in the form of a referral to this place's plumber.

'So, how long have you been mining for?' she asked.

For a stretching moment, she received nothing in response. Small eyes regarded her, as if sizing her up. Opal wondered if she had been found wanting.

'Since forever,' he eventually said. 'Reckon I must've been born in a mine.'

It certainly seemed so. The minuscule craters and canyons on his face and neck were so compacted with dirt that only steel wool and elbow grease could have scrubbed them clean.

'Would you like another drink?'

Denny ducked his chin apologetically. 'Best make tracks.'

'You have a wife and kids to get home to?' He seemed old enough to have these things.

Denny slid his hands from his pockets. They too were filthy. 'Nah. Well, a kid. But she's my – she's my little sister.'

'That's sweet.'

'You ain't met her.'

'Soon,' said Opal, like a promise. Though Denny looked – as well as he tried to hide it – like that was the last thing he wanted.

'Thanks for having us, ma'am,' he said with a cordial nod, turning in the doorway.

Opal took her hands out of the water, wiping them on the damp dish towel that hung from the curtain rail. *'Jesus. Just call me Opal.'*

'That short for Opaline?' he asked.

'*Opaline* means to look like an opal.'

'So, you're the real deal, huh?' Denny was at a halfway point on the threshold. She slipped past to grab his fleece-lined coat from the hook by the doorway. Behind her, the boys were pouring shots of bourbon into James's grand-father's tumblers, goading one another into taking puffs of the cigars James had inherited from his other grand-father. Opal pushed the handle on the door to let the smoke out.

She smiled, a weak and wavering thing. 'Just Opal.'

He nodded and reached out. Their palms met in the middle. Denny did not hold her hand as if it were a baby to be cradled or kissed, but shook it, a solid and steady gesture that she matched with ease.

''Night, fellas.'

He waved to them all, her right hand still tied with his own.

'Give the princess our best!' barked Gideon. A clink of glasses followed.

Denny smiled. Something soft and not entirely tangible. Worry, maybe. 'Will do!'

Their hands parted and he put his gloves on, thick and woollen, pebbled with brown dirt. Opal looked at them, wondering if she ought to get a pair of her own. The flashlight. The boots too: steel-toed and left out in the cold – she didn't miss the wince that pinched his features when he put them on.

He caught himself. Half a step down and looking directly at her, he said: 'I'll ask Jerry to stop by tomorrow afternoon and fit y'all with a new faucet. Heater, too.' Then he was gone, vanished into a single point of light against the dark, snowy night.

*

James kicked a puddle of slush, clumps of it flying into the ditch. Gone were the worries of vague discomfort, things not being how he liked them; Chicago was a distant memory, just how Opal had always dreamt.

'You guys go hunting around here?' James asked, glancing sideways at Denny, whose long legs kept him two steps ahead as he showed them where to find the well.

'Just me 'n' Sarge on the regular,' said Denny. 'Other boys ain't so good, but they get their turn on rotation in the fall.'

'Will I be on that too?'

'Maybe.' Denny veered left at a fork in the path. 'You ever held a gun?'

James shook his head; cheeks flushed far beyond what the cold would normally colour them.

'A'right,' Denny said, his smile a sharp line, like he didn't quite know how to make it look right. 'Sarge'll probably train you up come summertime. Crew for that won't be the same as when we're below, so you'll be with Buck or Jerry to start.'

The path grew steep, but roots curled from the soil and made her grip better. Up ahead, a small shed sat among the trees. Unreal-looking, for how small it was, with a thin stream of smoke coming from its clay chimney pot, and a hand-painted sign on its door. Above it stood what remained of a tree, splintered down the middle, its bark like charcoal.

'What's that?' she asked, nodding in its direction.

'That's Buster's place.'

Denny's smile turned softer. He reached a hand out to snag at some brittle branches in passing, green buds sprouting from their ends. He fingered them as though they were pearls.

'Buster?' James asked. 'Is he a dog or something?'

'Nah,' said Denny, before playfully swiping the branch in James's direction. 'But he'll bite ya if you come too close.'

James dodged, remembering games of pick-up played in the park, when the ball was forgotten in favour of him and his friends smacking each other with towels. He spun to grin at the pair of them before sprinting ahead with their bucket.

'See that?' Denny pointed to the charred tree that stood sentry by the shed. 'Used to live up there.'

'No you did not,' she said with a disbelieving snort.

'Did.' He leaned in, conspiratorially. 'Few days here and there. Called it my vacation. Buster'd just leave me up there, tell me not to come cryin' when my fat ass broke a branch.'

'Is that what happened to it?' There were no more branches, only the serrated black trunk.

'Nah,' he said. 'Night my sister was born, were a storm that ripped through this place. Tree got hit with lightning, cut it clean in half. 'Course, it fell the other way, so Buster was just fine. Lucky bastard.'

As the sun parted the trees and finally granted them a reprieve from the grey, something had been revealed to her, though she didn't know what. Much later, she would wonder where this Denny went. But none of it meant anything to her back then, so long as today would be followed by tomorrow and she had James to meet her at the end.

Denny swung around and spared the tree one final glance.

'Only birds livin' there now,' he said, before he led her down the path, treading in James's muddied footsteps.

*

Heart aflutter, Opal kicked the snow off her front porch and waited with dwindling patience. The porch, a whole four feet square, was hers to linger on for as long as she liked; or as long as it took for somebody to come and get her. There was no lease, but a deed with her name scrawled neatly next to James's own. A sum of money far smaller than what Chicago would ever have asked of them, deposited in the palm of a portly woman in a gingham apron who gave them the keys to the single-wide, a stack of fresh linen and a hamper full of preserves in return. Sarge came by later with the paperwork – in grubby fatigues and a slick anorak, shouldering through the trailer door sideways, politely declining a drink or a seat or anything of the sort in favour of lingering on the cookware, the books, the worn pigskin, the Lorna Doones and the mahogany carriage clock that had nowhere to go but the kitchen table. He was incredibly quiet for someone who demanded such space – his broad and ruddy barrel chest was twice the width of James and three times that of Opal – and had spoken only of the agreement, gesturing vastly with his bruised hands as if that was the language he primarily spoke. But all of the work and the maintenance and the allotted hours at the vegetable patch amounted to one shining thing in Opal's mind: this was the first time in her life she had really, truly owned something.

That half belonged to James was of no matter – certain as she was that they belonged to one another in full – because even owning so much as half of something was more than she ever had in her life. Knowing how to make a home with another person did not come naturally, but Opal had made a keen study in all the time spent flitting through the houses of others, and she had learned well enough; beyond even the matching dinner service or the floral top sheets, she could make somewhere worth staying.

A speck of colour between thin tree trunks, bobbing beautifully over dips and hills in the melting snow, making a path of her own, came Liza Long. Opal had met her only twice before – during her and James's brief induction tour and once again at the well when Jerry was over fixing the faucet – and had known from the first time that Liza would be her guide. Sarge had said so, given Liza the job as if it were some high honour. But Liza seemed nice, reserved yet excitable in the way that most people in the valley were at the introduction of new blood.

What did you do out there? Did you work in an office? Were your shoes very high or is that only in the films? These were the kinds of questions Liza liked to ask her, and Opal gladly relished the feeling of being perceived as some kind of woman of the world, when before she was only ever seen as a girl from Cicero who had never set foot outside Cook County.

'I was a dancer,' she said. 'With the ballet.'

Which was a truth, just not the full of it. She had no desire to get into the nitty-gritty of waiting hand and foot on the upper classes, because then it would become about them – their lavish lives, where nothing was beyond the realm of possibility because there were always those like Opal to fulfil every whim. It was better, she thought, to be seen only in the context of one life as it existed on a progressing journey, rather than how briefly it tangled with others. She had moved on from Chicago and would likely never see any of those people again; long since accepting the fact that whatever family she had once felt so burdened by would be forever beyond reach. That whatever life she had sat so uncertainly in, smothered by distant cousins and boisterous family friends, was fine to relinquish once her mother finally passed. Those people – relatives, employers, co-workers – they never quite knew what to make of her. But that was OK, because Opal knew well enough what to make of herself.

So, she told Liza all about rehearsals with her many friends, the satins and silks and lush tulle that she swept around the stage in; the ease with which she rose to *en pointe* and leapt through the air as if carried by wings. Idyllic train journeys home to her spacious, sunlit apartment, where she and James ate dinner, followed by a walk in the park underneath a glorious canopy of black cherry trees. She built up a life so wonderful in her head that she soon began to question why she left it behind at all. But there were other things, too: the bloody feet, the long hours, Aqua Net slicking her scalp and hardening the ribbons on her ankles; the bitter cold that blew in from the lake and only let up when the summer scorched arid and she woke every morning to soaked sheets, skin steaming through long days at work; running after children to feed and bathe them; the ache that made its home in her bones, in her heart. There was the hurt, too, of contested wills and relatives who took and took when she found herself sinking into the pits of grief. Their faces found her on every street corner; stepped on the train at every station, like the city was full of ghosts she would never stop meeting. An accomplishment, really, to have been so jaded and burned by one life that she propelled herself without fear into another. James made all the difference, for Opal was completely alone and then, rather suddenly, she was not. For him, she would make anything work.

Liza led her past the so-called big house, which existed, much like a cathedral, at the very centre of the community. It was where the man in charge lived – Baron, said Liza, though whether that was a name or a title, Opal did not know. The house loomed, despite being only a single story perched on a high porch, built against some exposed rock face as if it had grown from the mountains. It cast shadows that pushed outward, separating itself from the surrounding cabins and trailers that seemed to ordinarily bustle with life during daylight hours; that, with their barrels of rainwater, leaning bicycles and draping lace curtains, were softened and lived-in. Like toys scattered in handfuls, planets orbiting the sun.

She and Liza stopped outside a long building tucked next to a clump of conifers that stood proud amid the bare, silvery bark of the forest. The wood matched – door and sills – the thin, raw slats, near-glistening in the stubborn winter glow. The sun crested carefully over the tree line but would take its time to go the full distance; crystalline on the dirty, frosted glass that was steamed white from the inner workings of what must have been the kitchen. Inside, ten or so women stood at various stations, breath fogging as if to heat the place by sheer will alone. Opal was instructed to remove her coat and scarf and hang them on a hook by the door, despite the chill that hadn't yet the time to leave her. Some women washed and peeled vegetables while others arched over large steaming pots and stirred laboriously, veins tight and thick in their chicken-skin arms.

'Where do you want me?'

A welcome wave of hands that grazed her shoulders in guidance. Opal slotted herself between a greying woman and her daughter, sleeves rolled to her elbows, and laid her palms flat to the chipped and scratched wooden countertop.

'We ain't got much,' said the grey woman. 'Bit of a stone soup situation, here.'

'But we got enough to make somethin',' said her daughter.

Together, they moved fluidly – whisking eggs in a bowl, passed off to pour into a piping-hot skillet. Opal was to collect the shells and dispose of them, giving salt and pepper and the occasional knob of butter between trips. It was boring, but it was her first day. She felt restless and hungry.

'When do we eat?' she asked.

'When the men are done and off below,' Liza told her.

'What happens if we eat first?'

Silence, then laughter; so sharp in the early morning.

'Nothing, silly!' said Liza.

Surely the heat that flooded her face was from the stove. Her question was reasonable and the answer was not, but

Opal was well used to this kind of thing from the long days she worked feeding other people and their children, eating only in the moments where there wasn't a thing to do; which was never. In the mornings, whether she had her own quarters or not, she arrived to the kitchen at five thirty and set about starting that evening's dinner, all the while ensuring Mr Goodwin's breakfast was on the table by six thirty at the very latest – newspaper opened to the obits at its side – as he preferred to leave before the children woke for school at seven.

This was nothing like that. It was a team of women, an army of them, preparing breakfast for the men who'd spend their days mining or farming or doing whatever else it was they did. Opal was not alone. And yet, comfort did not settle within her at the notion of things being precisely as she was used to. Life here was meant to be different. Stone soup, she thought, was an awful burden for every morning, every meal. It was a lesson she knew well from birth, and had little desire to repeat.

'Where do you get your supplies?'

Sarge takes care of that, they said. He takes care of us. He helps Baron with everything he needs. Good man, that Sarge. Brings back just what we need and delivers it to us all without even the slightest inconvenience shown. Sarge ate at the mess every morning, right at Baron's side. Baron never ate in his rooms at the big house because he didn't have a woman to keep them – not anymore – but he left Maude, his little one, up there to nap and fed her only from his own hand when she woke. Brought a plate made up especially by Miss Gunn – the woman with the preserves and the linens, who only ever worked the dinner shift – with extra helpings of beans and the like for her to gum on. Bizarre, but not to be remarked upon. Some children were different, Opal supposed, and she had no idea about the child's age. All in all, she hadn't spotted many children around – though she and James had been shown a schoolhouse with one room, and could make out some vague moving shapes through the mossy windows – but they could be heard, playing further afield on the patch and darting through the trees in such a blur of motion that they became no more than streaks of muddled colour in the grey and white. It was nice not to have to see them and fret that their very lives lay in her hands – to be awoken, fed and watered and bathed and put to bed – but she had to wonder.

They ate their meals at home, was what Liza told her. What Ethel and Marie and Yvette concurred. Families ate breakfast and lunch in their homes – sometimes even dinner – and the rest ate together – like one *big* family, chimed Marie. Yvette had a man and a son back in her cabin, but they liked to check their snares at this hour and would often do with simply a big lunch. She'd be back for that, but it was nice to fill the morning in this way – feeding others, chatting with the women. Awfully early for a social hour, thought Opal, but there were broad smiles stretched between apple cheeks, fond touches from hands warmed by the stovetop, hardened by callouses in a way that reminded her of her mother. Which was dispelled immediately as the door was flung open by a mousy-looking boy with burnt-orange hair slicked down over his puckered forehead.

'Don't mind me,' he said, darting between the women and generally getting in the way. As he shoved by her, Opal lost a handful of her freshly washed mushrooms from the bowl – a few portions, at the very least. And he kept on: rummaging next to the skirts of women who moved with knives and fire, without regard for anything beyond whatever it was he was searching for.

'You shouldn't run around in here,' Opal said, voice tight and restrained. 'Could really hurt someone.' The boys she once took care of acted much the same, and continued to do so unless told otherwise. Yes, this boy was far closer to being a man, but that hardly meant he couldn't be told.

Apparently, it did. Opal's scolding was met with re-sounding silence that ground down any potential agreement to a fine powder. She couldn't hold any sense of what it meant as the women frowned not at him, but at her.

'An' who in the hell are you?' he barked, slicing right through the silence.

'I'm Opal,' she said evenly, propping the metal bowl on her hip within a tight grip, guarding it.

'You're real dark. Look dirty.'

Oh, a child without doubt. A petulant little boy who knew well the words he spat would leave their mark. But he was not her charge, her responsibility.

'At least I don't smell it.'

He took one step back, then another. Face alight with both shock and glee simultaneously.

'Minnow,' said Ethel. 'Would you like a biscuit?' And he would, of course, took two piping-hot from the baking sheet and stuffed them in his pockets smugly.

'Opal,' Liza called, with a lilt to the end of her sentence that struck like a bell. 'Would you watch the bacon for me?'

That the bacon needed watching at all was a laughable concept, for there were approximately half a dozen women in its immediate vicinity. Besides all that, it had been smoked previously. But Baron liked it crispy, according to Liza. Crumbling black like soot, with a crunch between his teeth. It would taste only of ash; Opal confirmed, bitter salt on her tongue from the tiny piece she tore off. To her left, the grey woman scowled.

Breakfast came finally, well past the break of dawn. Each bite was cold and stuck in her throat on the way down. Making her own breakfast at home would cost time and credits she did not yet have, so Opal learned to grin and bear it, and when she returned to the kitchen with the other women for clean-up, she said nothing of the mushrooms that had been crushed into the floor, only scraped them up in silence with the edge of a butter knife.

The following morning, she tried again. Bid her goodbye before James showed any signs of rising from his deep sleep, with a square of his treasured chocolate melting on her tongue. Wrapped in her wool coat, hair fastened safely at the back of her neck, she made the trek through the snow and down to the front of the big house. The women were already filing in for a day of cooking, still in their house slippers and galoshes, swaddled in coats and their husbands' thick sweaters.

She followed them to the back porch and kicked the snow off her shoes, but was met on the threshold by Liza, who smiled down at her from the final step and told Opal that no, she would not be cooking with the others today.

'A special recommendation,' she said, from Baron himself. 'Isn't that lovely?'

That terrible worry of a childhood spent outside the fold, unable to find where to fit in, struck hard and fast.

Opal asked: 'Did I do something wrong?'

Liza's eyes moved to and fro with uncertainty. She hummed while Opal chewed on the meat of her bottom lip, as if she didn't already know the answer. Schoolyard blacktop rushed to meet her, with the chalk lines drawn so cleanly that she dared not cross. No partner in class, on the bus, on the train home. She tugged at her scarf, half undone and full of holes that had been stretched by the hooks of her fingers at bus stops and schoolyards.

There was no need to wait for Liza, because she had been dressed in her winter coat, ready to meet Opal and stop her from ever getting in. As she led them away, Opal did her buttons back up, cursing the soreness, the tight feeling in her fingers that wouldn't let up.

The storehouse was plenty cold for all the food it kept. Liza held the door, showed Opal where to light the lamps and keep the books. Said she was desperately needed, as the lady who worked here before fell in the snow and broke her hip. Miss Gunn would be by in a half hour or so with some hot coffee to show her how the credits worked; like she didn't already know, like she and James hadn't come down here a few days ago so he could proudly spend his first earned credits on a slab of dark chocolate.

So much for stone soup – it seemed they didn't like what she had to offer. But she wanted them to like it so very badly, just as she wanted James and his smile, his abandon and his hope. Perhaps she wasn't trying hard enough.

'Thank you,' said Opal, making a smile for Liza, turning the worn pages over to lists and lists of names and numbers. 'I'll do my very best.'

To her mother, it was always axe soup. This was like the stone, only when you got around to eating, all that was left was the blade at the bottom. Opal was too hungry, too eager. Her eyes grew bigger than her stomach and when her fingers brushed the base of the pot, they came back red.

*

There were two Kepner girls and they were completely identical. It was well into her and James's second month in the valley before Opal realised this. She was walking the long and winding path between their single-wide and the storehouse when they accosted her from behind a splintered pine tree.

There would be a party, they said. She and her husband were invited.

She danced, they said. Could she teach them?

When Opal asked who would be at this party, they simply told her *everyone*. Like it was silly to wonder, and that by doing so she had made enough of a fool of herself for them to silently retract their desire to dance with her. They were fickle, she knew well, as idle teenage girls could be. Opal smiled at the pair, wide enough for her tongue to be seen through the gap in her teeth.

'Of course we'll be there,' she said. 'Wouldn't miss it for the world. James loves parties,' she added. 'Shall I bring anything?'

'Your name's been drawn for dessert,' they said, in perfect unison, and scampered off from where they came.

So, Opal made a red velvet cake. She used the beets that were growing wild and rough among the weeds in the abandoned patch behind their home. Grated them down until her clothes were ruined, the beds of her nails stained purple. She added vinegar, so the mixture wouldn't lose its punch of colour and turn a hideous brown. There was no cream cheese, but she could make the butter stretch enough. A pinch of chocolate from the storehouse melted down on the cooktop. Sugar, plenty of it, for it seemed that the valley was in abundance. The frosting would be gritty, but that was the best part.

James followed the smell home with a wicked grin, dirt on his face and hands as he mauled at her purpled sweater. Opal made him wash and he waited patiently for the length of time it took her to wind her hair up into something less bedraggled. She wore a long skirt with thick stockings and a cleaner sweater, one of his many jackets tossed across her shoulders as the evenings still had a bite to them. He enjoyed dressing for this, she knew, though it was obvious that being covered in muck and filth with his new friends made him feel more of a man than a button-down and slacks ever could. James looked like himself, and while she was certain he never truly deviated from that, it stirred something in her to see the man she had first met. The one that only she knew, deep down.

He teased her on the way to the party like they were two teenagers headed to homecoming. She had never been, but the squeals and peals of laughter could often be heard well into the morning through the windows of her childhood apartment. Lights guided them along the twisting paths, hammered into the softening ground; leading them to the house – the big house, as it was known – where the party was being held.

On the way inside, they caught greetings with all the grace and warmth the night instilled in them. Opal looked up, where the clouded, starless sky shed no light and the world felt muffled. As if they had stepped into a bubble, under a shroud, blanketed in something that could not be bottled or sold. James felt around for her fingers and took her by the hand as he pushed the door open, and all the light spilled out.

After dropping her cake off with Miss Gunn, they found a member of James's crew, Minty, who introduced his girlfriend, Marcia. Gideon, with a glass in each hand, hovered between two seats like he couldn't decide which one to keep his ass on.

'Is Denny coming?' James asked, pushing Opal's chair up to the table with gentle scoots.

'Oh,' laughed Minty. 'He'll be along.'

'No, he won't,' said Gideon. His chin was resting on the white and blue tablecloth, and he was looking through his half-empty glasses as if they might hide him from the rest of the party. 'He's leavin' me in my time of need.'

'Time of need?' asked Opal.

Next to her, Marcia sighed. A heavy, put-upon thing that had Minty reaching for her hands in apology. 'I'm getting a drink. Do you want one?' she asked Opal, who politely declined.

'Are you sure you don't want one?' asked James, with a kind of tender concern that threw her off.

'I'll get one later,' she said, dismissing him with a wave. 'What happened?'

Minty, having seemingly forgotten about his girlfriend's displeasure, tipped his glass high to the three of them with a gleeful grin. 'Gid's gonna have himself a shotgun wedding.'

James nearly choked, fixing his hand around Opal's hip. If possible, Gideon sank further into his seat, chin pressing his mouth up into a pathetic pout. Whatever it was, Opal reserved her judgement – her congratulations – until the peculiar tension in the air was fully cleared. Then Minty raised his pointer finger from the curve of his glass and directed it toward a girl standing across the room, surrounded by the Kepner twins and one of the boys who helped with the logging in the evenings after school.

Her hair was a single sheet of yellow silk, near gold by the light of the candlesticks; woven at the back of her head with such precision that it must have been done by the hands of another. Precious and patient, getting ready for the party. A pretty dress, with a trim that frilled along the tops of her shins, to be met by knee-high socks, the kind Opal wore when she attended Orthodox School. The girl's shoes were shined and polished, and it was clear that she felt proud of them; easy to imagine how they might be dirtied on the way over – on the way to lessons at the schoolhouse the following morning – but the girl had made quite the effort. Hand on her flat belly, she glowed with it, Opal thought. How awful.

'Julie Hirsch,' Minty told them.

James laughed. Opal knew she wanted to kick him under the table, but all she could think of was Kitty Goodwin, with her show jumping and her tap classes, dancing in front of the television to *The Aristocats*. Begging Opal to rid her curls of their frizz in front of her antique vanity, or show her how to dance with boys. Once, she asked Opal what it was like to kiss a boy only to get smacked on the ears with the hairbrush. Seemed nobody did that for little Julie.

'That's not right,' Opal said.

'C'mon,' Minty said. 'Gid's known her forever.'

'Gid's pushing thirty.' Opal could feel the heat of her face, how her molars clenched tight enough to grit. Under the table, James squeezed her thigh. She smacked his hand away.

'Gid's gonna be pushing daisies when her daddy catches wind of it,' said Minty.

'Never mind *her* daddy . . .' said Gideon, and only then did he truly cower. Before, it was a game, but suddenly he was shrinking in his seat at the sight of a new guest. The doors to the big house parted in tandem and revealed a man of average stature who wore all of his bones and joints and muscles so well that somehow it seemed he was the largest person in the room. Solid and sturdy, dressed smartly in a dark blue tweed suit. He shook hands and kissed the heads of the few children. Hair white and swirling his crown like a halo, he was crisp in a way that had been lacking for Opal since she left Chicago. The colours became richer, the shadows deeper. She did her best not to shield her eyes from it.

'Built like a brick shithouse, ain't he?' said Minty.

'Got nothing on Sarge,' Gideon said, as if to calm himself. They looked toward that beast of a man: Sarge was eating a slice of her red velvet cake and licking his fingers after each bite. He was wearing the same anorak as before, despite being indoors, and had his feet planted firmly at the standard distance of parade rest – or second position, thought Opal. It made no difference: he was ready to move, regardless.

'I give you Muhammad,' James said, pointing a finger to the man. Then he swung another toward Sarge, which Minty swiftly knocked down. 'And the mountain.'

The joke fell flat, and this fact stewed happily within Opal. They did not know what he was talking about; that, or they knew but didn't want to admit to it. Not with the approach of said prophet, Red Sea parting, the works.

'Sorry to interrupt,' the man said to Opal and James. His smile was sharp. Abruptly, he asked the boys: 'You seen him?'

'We haven't seen him since punch out,' said Gideon.

'Maybe he's with your girl?' asked Minty. Which, clearly, was the wrong thing. Gideon, who sat taller than before, with his back straight and strong, turned to face away from his friend. James mirrored the action.

'My girl,' said the man, 'just got tucked up tight into bed by her daddy. Ain't that right? You think I'm twiddling my thumbs 'stead of being here with my people?' Minty shook his head. 'My girl wouldn't settle. Not with *him* traipsing around like he's got better things to do.'

'He'll be along,' Gideon assured. 'Always is.'

The man grunted in vague affirmation. He stood taut as a strung bow, tall as a tower next to Opal; the way her father might have, once. His hand found her shoulder, and she should have expected it, but the flinch revealed that she did not. Embarrassed, she fixed her face with a smile, eyes climbing quickly to meet the man's own. They were dark enough that a colour was difficult to discern, as if the light was playing tricks on her. The four of them sat still in his expanding shadow, awaiting something, anything to sever the moment into something less palpable.

'Aster, isn't it?' Though his hand still touched Opal's shoulder, he spoke to James. 'Wonderful to have you on board. I've been told you're an excellent addition to the crew, and we're always grateful for an extra pair of hands.' He squeezed the thin layer of flesh that covered the join of her limbs. James's hand moved from her hip and slid under the table to sit on her thigh, right above the knee, right out of sight. She dared not shift beneath their hold, lest she fracture; not halves, nothing so equal for the way James held her: as if she were a prize, the kind of gift a guest might bring to his host.

'Thank you, sir. Really. And it's James,' he said. 'This is my – my wife, Opal.'

'What a beautiful name,' said the man. 'And since we're using them, enough with the "sir" business. Everyone here calls me Baron. Ain't that right, boys?'

'Sure is,' said Gideon.

'That's right,' said Minty.

'Now,' Baron said, cutting across. 'You mind if I take your wife for a spin, James? They tell me she's a dancer.'

Opal thought from the moment she met James on that stuffy train that there existed a secret language between them. One that pre-empted their first encounter. A touch to tell, everything collapsing into place around their aligned ideals – despite the distance that stretched between their origins. A path that was bound to intersect, to collide in perfect harmony. The choice here was not for James, not his to take. And yet, he took it. A firm pat to the knee and she was led away from the boys and their drinking, their wallowing over innocent girls.

Baron cut through the air as if he was manipulating it by sheer force of will. He created a circle of which they were the centre. Swallowed and digested, trapped in the belly of the whale.

Fingers bunched the soft cotton at the small of her back. Opal could dance better than she could do almost anything, but already there had been a misstep. She was caught fumbling, wanting for explanation and a repeat demonstration of exactly where she was meant to place herself. Where to put her arms and precisely how to be when she could not be in her body. They floated, two rings around the sun, as if years and years had been spent in the tight circle of Baron's arms. Opal could breathe, but she worried that doing so would alert him of her presence. James's eyes found her in all the blank chaos, and she knew, without words, that he was so, so happy.

'You're a fine addition, Mrs Aster.' Baron's breath was hot and metallic in her ear.

'It's just Opal.'

Cheek to cheek, his timbre vibrated in her throat. A chuckle, with the taste of something bitter at its end. 'You were never a *just*, were you?' Opal didn't answer, how could she? Baron seemed content with this, scooping her low in a dip that had the room clapping in bright bursts.

'My first wife loved opals,' he told her. 'How they changed in the light. She could never wear them in the bath, though. They crack in the heat.'

'Lovely,' she must have said. Something pleasant and kind. He released her, eventually, though Opal could not fathom how long they had been dancing. She revelled only in the blood flow that returned to the tips of her fingers and toes; finally, she could place one foot in front of the other and carve out some space for herself beyond the airless fishbowl Baron confined her to. She should have gone with Marcia and gotten that drink, stayed talking to the other ladies about how the drying was lately; followed errant tales of gossip that burrowed each of them closer to one another as a collective unit. Rather than have them regard her now with a wariness that caught the flickering candlelight in their eyes. That was the choice she could have made, before James made one for her. She settled back into the seat next to him and folded her hands tightly in her lap.

Mindless of her demeanour, Minty said: 'You don't know who that is, do you?'

'What?' she heard herself ask, though the word was hard to place. A handprint burned at the base of her spine, as if she had been flayed. Years on, she could scarcely describe what Baron Rowe actually looked like beyond white hair and wrinkled skin. Mostly, she remembered how he made her feel.

He made her feel like she was dead.

'Well,' said Gideon, voice as close to remorse as she could ever imagine it. 'That's Denny's pa.'

October 1981

THE GRIM CHILD SPECTRE of Maude stands over her, her hair drooping forward. Woollen leggings sag around her brittle ankles; thin wrists with purple veins holding the weight of hands that worry and pick at the skin around her fingernails.

'Do you ever get blood in your pants?' she asks.

Opal kneels on the stairs, yellow rubber gloves to almost her elbow. She feels a flush high in her cheeks and ducks her head down to scrub at the thin brass line of the stair rods. The crushed, velvety indents left on the runner are far too big for the doll-like feet of Mrs Schweers, who must have been a small woman to start with if the shrinking of old age is anything to put stock in. It's bizarre to think that she didn't always live in this house alone, for how well she wears her solitude – like a pair of soft leather boots, the sole tamped thin. All in a month's work, Opal has wrecked her peace and quiet, filled her days with grimy children and animal corpses hacked to bits in the kitchen; dirty diapers and mushy food and Billy scuffing the walls with every door he slams open. She would feel sorry if it weren't such a relief. Penance can only be offered on her knees or standing on rickety kitchen chairs to swipe cobwebs from the coving. Besides, a good clean fixes most things.

So, she tells Maude. 'It's going to wash out. I've soaked your sheets in the basin.'

'I *know* how to wash blood out.' An unfortunate truth that Opal avoids with all her might. Maude knows far too much about far too little, which is expected for a girl her age in some regards, but not with the kind of clinical bluntness that she applies to most things.

Opal looks up, tries for a smile. 'Good to know stuff like that.'

She lifts her knees onto the next step, and Maude rises in turn and asks: 'Am I dyin'?'

The laugh can't be helped. She feels bad only for the length of time it takes Maude to catch on.

'No, Bun. You're growing up.'

'Will it happen to Billy, then?'

'No, it won't. But it will likely happen to Baby when she's your age too.'

'What about Mrs Schweers?'

'It stops at a certain age.'

'Is that your age?'

In her near thirty years, she's bled no more than three dozen times. Used to keep track in a little diary, mark the date, the length. Kept the details in secret, because her mother never liked for her to speak about it. Until, that is, she realised that there wasn't much point in keeping track when the whole purpose of menstruation was something she had little interest in in the first place; no matter what James or her mother, or his mother, wanted.

'Mine never happened properly – not for long,' she says. 'Some people just have it different.'

'Lucky,' Maude sulks.

'I've heard otherwise.'

The sickly smell of florals and Lysol permeate the plush rug, and Opal feels as if thrown back into a time and version of herself that she naively believed to be forever gone. This house is smaller than the ones she used to clean as a teenager, but still: things have a funny way of coming back around when you're not paying much mind. She ought to be embarrassed by the regression, or feel that she has let herself down in some way by circling back to what she had initially fled from, but needs must, and there are worse things than swallowing her pride.

'Does it hurt?' she asks, because she knows Maude won't let on.

The girl shrugs. 'Some.'

Maude's hands make tight fists – her fingernails are getting too long, Opal will have to trim them this evening – and rigidity runs up the very length of her. She stands on her lower step to meet Maude in her dark, discerning eyes; cleaning momentarily forgotten for a lasting, tangible thing that might keep, if only she does it right. 'I need you to tell me when it does,' she says. 'Or else, how will I help you?'

'I don't know,' says Maude, turning her cheek; coloured pink and clenched at the jaw.

She sees a little girl, five years younger, with a bloody mouth and no shoes. So trusting, fit to follow and hold her hand. The divide between now and then is stark. It hurts to remember. Opal hates to look back, but there are things she'd live all over again if it meant Maude might stop staring at her like that.

'It's no trouble, Maude. I promise.'

You're no trouble.

'It doesn't have to hurt.'

Not anymore.

''Kay,' says Maude. Opal wonders if it makes sense to her.

She swipes Maude's hair behind the shell of her ear, lets her hand linger there for a beat or two. Her cheeks are warm, but not swollen as they once were in that crisp, golden summer. This pain, Opal can make better.

'We'll go to the store when I finish up here.'

There's little left of last week's wages, and all of Denny's have gone toward more fuel for the generator, for the car; but this, they can spare. What was the point in getting out if not for this? She smiles with a closed mouth and steps higher on the stairs to carry on her cleaning.

'I don't . . .'

Opal waits, but nothing comes. 'You don't what, Bun? Just tell me.'

'I don't want the others to come.'

Whether shame or simple dislike, Opal can't get a read on her. Sulking is her default state – fat bottom lip and cobbled chin, a delicate scorn that resembles Denny with disturbing clarity – so to see her do it now means nothing. Opal takes another step and they are back to back, which makes it easier; to stay herself, to refrain from drifting into the imagined mind of her own absent mother, who could only ever cut deeper, even when she did her very best not to.

'They'll stay here. We won't be long,' Opal assures. With the hand that's not scrubbing, the tips of her fingers graze Maude's calf. Each touch is significant, which is a fact she cannot deny. There were no women in the big house, and even Denny was absent for the better part of her life once his exile was enforced. And though the kindest of touches Opal received in life belonged to her father, she knows well that such was not the case for Maude, who was but a shadow in the valley – the remnants of what once had all the possibility and hope of a normal little girl, but very quickly became a lump of clay, moulded solely by her father's brutal hand.

To be a child, let alone a girl, under such conditions doesn't bear thinking about. Yet there are nights when sleep evades Opal and her mind is crammed to sickening fullness with thoughts of nothing else – wishing she had tried harder, earlier; shaken Denny from his stupor and taken them both far away, further than Chicago or any ocean allowed. Knowing what she knows now, she would have done it in a heartbeat, if only to spare this girl the lonely ache of soaking her bloody sheets in secret. When compared to all that, a trip to the store is a manageable feat.

'Just you and me,' Opal says. Maude cuts a glance over her left shoulder, her dark eyes softening to wet smudges, a single drop hanging from spidery lashes. 'We'll get ahead of the pain, Bun.' It's a promise she can make, one she can keep. 'And this time, it won't hurt so bad.'

*

Bear spends the morning stuck under the porch like a dog sitting in its own grave. He likes being down there, among the lice and mice. Lately, he's been following Maude around like a filthy little shadow. It's not enough that they share a bed, but he has to live in her pocket most days too. His feet hook over the same knots and branches, pointer finger running along the same wood grain; chews his food in his right cheek, left, then right again; matches his breaths to hers in the night. Yet there is comfort in the weight of him as he leans across her side, elbows digging into the soft skin at her waist while he drags himself from the crawl space. Like the release of a single, long breath.

Bear smells of rotting leaves and rain, damp clothes and blood. Da's been teaching him how to field-dress small things – squirrels, rabbits and such – and she can tell they've tried to clean off the worst of it in the lake beyond. Last time, Bear came home and kept the sawn-off ear of his latest kill in bed between them. Maude has touched dead things before, skinned others, but she lifts both hands to cover her mouth at the memory of it. Pa would never have allowed such things; shrines, he called them, so Maude had to hide it all. Rabbit feet dyed by birch bark, little creatures carved from wood, the tusk of a boar, a doe's hoof, inky black and smooth under her thumb – she sequestered each one, like gifts, secret treasures that acted as the sole reminder for the state of her life before Denny left. Pa had his own shrine to Denny though, a collection of things to the right of the mantel that she knew well not to lay her hands on: a rosary made of oval pearls and smooth rocks for skimming, with touches of pink and grey and marbled white. The hole in the wall. There was the gun too. A pistol, engraved along its short barrel with words that she dared not get close enough to read. That had belonged to Denny's mother.

'You got a mama?' Bear asks. He heaves himself up and over the porch railing, landing with a soft thump. The chairs are his favourite – trapping himself in the tight corner made by the sloping planks. Fingers gripping the flat arms, he tries to pull himself back up.

'Yes,' she says. Maude is no fool; this is her lot. 'Her name is Opal.'

Her name is not Opal. Her name is a whisper in the dark that was never spoken loud enough for Maude to hear. She remembers a voice, a face. She remembers the feeling of slight hands and the hollow of a breast; a smell of sweat and lavender. But Maude's head has a way of building walls and towers, and she is tired. She rounds the porch, kicking chips of bark in her wake, and takes the steps one at a time. In the small yard beneath, the dog chases its own tail.

'Nah,' says Bear. 'You got one from where you came.'

'And where's that?' she counters.

Tucking his knees under his chin, he rolls back further, smacks at the damp ass of his pants. 'One that yanked ya outta her.'

That's not how it happens. She's sure of it. Prue Kepner told her that a baby only comes when the mama's belly button pops out like a smooth, brown horse chestnut. Gradually the hole gets bigger and bigger like a giant mouth and spits the baby into Doc Froy's hands. Sometimes, other hands used to catch the babies, and they'd be buried in the dirt before they could take a single breath. Maude never liked to think about that.

She knows that she was a baby once. A little thing with black feathers for hair and drool running rivers from her toothless mouth. Maybe she was bald. Maybe she came out with a full set of teeth, biting down. She has nobody to tell her these things because nobody will talk about it, and Maude never had a mama, not really. But as Bunny, she does. One who looks like the spinning lady inside her old trinket box that Sarge brought home after her wrist got broke; that she left behind in the valley. Brown hair that swishes around her sharp jaw, pointed chin. Eyes like the muddy green bottom of the riverbed, where the stones slip under your feet. She likes to watch Ma, sometimes: in the kitchen, the bathroom, going about the place as if she knows exactly where and how she ought to be at any given time. Maude doesn't know how to be, not in those kinds of ways. She knows fishing and setting snares and traps. She knows cleaning her kills, scrubbing the blood from her hands; stitching in a clean line, climbing trees to sleep in, banking fires and finding water. She knows how to walk through the forest without making a sound. But her tangled hair remains a mystery, as do her teeth and nails, and the blood between her legs that she had to hide from Pa. Ma waits and Ma listens for her to ask these things, but Maude prefers to watch. She asks when she is good and ready.

'Where's yours, then?' she poses to Bear, who is seeming mighty ungrateful. 'Must'a yanked you out and tried to shove you right back in.'

Legs fall, swishing and floating where his feet won't meet the ground. 'Gid said she done no good,' he laments.

Gideon Bass, who slammed his wooden crutches against her Pa's front porch whenever the seasons started changing. Too hot, too cold, not enough food for him and his kit. Before, when things were better than she can now recall, she bit Gideon's finger to bleeding, all for the sin of tickling her pink. That's what he told her, anyway, right before he hopped into Pa's study and demanded the credits owed to him; the credits he only ever spent on spirits and dipping tobacco anyhow.

'Gideon's got dirt for brains,' she says.

Bear licks at whatever got stuck to the back of his hand and wipes the spit on his sweater. 'Bet he's missin' me awful.'

Bet he's not, thinks Maude.

And he'd be wrong, Gideon Bass – were he still alive and his mind vacant of all but drinking and dipping – not to feel that awful wanting in his bones. Awful, truly, to be without this boy; who keeps leaves in his hair and can hardly wipe his own ass. Eats food off the floor like a starving animal. Presses the ice-cold nub of his nose to her chin while he sleeps; holds still as she bites at his fingernails and spits bitter crescents onto the quilt. He is a terror to Maude, who struggles to comprehend the way he goes about life with such abandon, without worry for what will happen. Because, for Bear, it seems that nothing ever happened. That to live with abandon was learned by example; from Gideon, who never cared about that boy a day in his life.

He wasn't Denny – nowhere near – who took her down the crick to fish and didn't get mad at her for losing a bite even once. *Da. Da. Da.* At night, she whispers the word to herself as if that might make it stick to the man that used to be her brother. Baby is better at saying it, clapping her hands and calling for him like Maude is supposed to. Seeing them together sometimes stirs a feeling she can't make sense of; one she'd rather not explore. Because Da sings Baby to sleep some nights. He never did that for her. Takes Bear hunting, not Maude – who can hunt well enough on her own. Knives kept sharp enough to slit the belly of a buck, blood to her elbows, burying the guts far from home so as to keep the predators away. These are the things that Maude knows. She was born knowing; born to men who taught her, without much consideration for what she could do with it all after. Da's hand, a soft vice around her own, a clean line from throat to navel. Make it quick, hope it does not suffer. He loved her once, maybe.

'Bun?' Bear tugs fervently on their tether, from the end that was once hers. He looks at her with eyes so wide and expectant, but words are not what he's looking for from her – because that's not the language he grew in – and she's been all out of them for a long time. At least, the ones that mean a damn thing.

So, Maude's nails, matching his own and bitten down to the quick, dig as deep as they can manage into his oil-slick scalp. She yanks, pulling his head, cheek flush with her own and so soft in the early winter bite.

'What planet you living on, huh?' she hisses. 'We got one mama and one daddy because that's how the world works.'

'You hurtin' me, Bun.' But Bear is not surprised, which is a double-edged sword she refuses to handle. She would never hurt him, not really, not when he has tied himself to her at the root, joined by clumsy and clumped knots. But this is their lot, and she knows he can't understand – not with the way he grew: hunched and starved and crawling across a wet mattress – but she is doing her best to help him. Ma and Da, with their girl and boy and baby. Ma and Da, who are all that will ever matter. Gideon is nothing. Gideon is a sack of organs slumped across Pa's floor. Pa is *nothing* too, even when he is all that has ever been.

'Good,' says Maude. She flicks at Bear's ear for good measure, releasing his head so he can tuck into himself and pout something awful against the inside of her elbow. 'Go back into your hole.' She points to the dank, webbed thing beneath them; not a place that he likes, simply one he knows well enough to fear going without.

'No, t'ank you.' Snot glues to the skin of her forearm, round cheeks heating her down to the bone. 'Wanna stay with you, Bun.'

And she supposes he will have to. Lives that started completely apart, forced together into a single room, a single bed. Soon, Baby will be old enough to join the fold and then Maude might not feel so at odds with the idea of being somebody's older sister. Because she never learned how to care for something, either. Never could figure out how it was they made the plants at the patch grow, only knew to pick apples from the grass beneath the trees and check them for brown spots or worms. But she can watch Ma and learn how. She can watch Da, too, even if it smarts like a burn. Bear doesn't fear it or shy away from the good things – he has no words for what they are, but seems to know what is right and wrong by feeling alone; how to be a person without anyone ever explaining.

Many things were explained to Maude when she was even younger than Bear, and she did them well. There wasn't a choice, and oftentimes she will try and convince herself that she could have run from it the way Denny – Da – did, but she remembers then that the first thing he really, truly taught her – that wasn't brushing her teeth and hair and how to wash in between her toes – was how to hold a knife.

Bear is in no need of a knife, because he has her. She will be the knife and the fist too, the hand to hold. Thicken his skin before it can be split and tarred. Better to feel the sting and know how to cope with it than have your pain sitting in someone else's hands.

'We're a family now, Bear,' she says. 'We're safe.' Though neither can be sure of what that means, she can decide for the two of them.

Ma says it doesn't have to hurt so bad, but she's wrong, because Maude can see it: through the mountains and their dips, through the sky that stretched above the valley in a wide and unwinding ocean, hurt is all that keeps.

*

Mrs Schweers lives up the ways a bit. Maude could walk it by herself if they let her, make no mistake, but the younger ones hold her back something awful. Ma says it's too far and they've got to take the car. But Maude used to walk the mountains with her Pa for days on end. They would set up in a blind that Sarge had dug out and wait for a buck to stroll by. That was Sarge's secret spot for hunting deer that he only told her and Pa about. It was special because Sarge had dug it like foxholes from his war and liked to sleep in it from time to time, when things along the valley got too tense or dramatic for his taste. Which was a lot. Maude knew all about it, more than she ever wanted to, but she couldn't run off to the blind when things got tough; she couldn't go anywhere without her Pa's say-so.

Mrs Schweers lives in a house. Prior to their move across the border, Maude had never seen a real house. One with windows that stack on top of each other. A roof of slate with gutters and eaves. Foundations that run deep enough for a basement to fill with boxes of old photographs, drawings, pieces of paper that mean little to her beyond how funny the names on them sound when they roll off her tongue. Mrs Schweers got mad at her for poking around down there once, said she was fit to smack her ass with the wooden spoon she uses for mixing up Baby's applesauce. Maude can't help it, though, and ventures down every time Mrs Schweers takes Baby upstairs for her nap, whenever Bear dirties himself in the garden and needs a bath. The faces are what she likes most. Maude's seen herself in a mirror before, but people look different in photographs, is what she's learned. Mrs Schweers looks nothing like these other versions of herself – where her jaw cuts the same on both sides, her eyes rest higher and her brows lower, thicker. Maude wonders if, side by side in a photograph, she would look like her Da. She ought to, and the fact that she might not troubles her greatly.

It always smells in Mrs Schweers' house. It's the Crisco she uses for pie crusts and the goose fat she keeps in small jars for her roast potatoes. There is a tang in the air too – it is sharp and burns Maude's nostril hairs. Vinegar, she knows well, a basin full of it on the kitchen counter. Maude left it there the day prior, grubby crystal soaking in one cup of vinegar, three of water, with the hope of a sparkle, the glint of a rainbow, as promised by Mrs Schweers. This, like most things that Mrs Schweers tells her, feels like the stuff of storybooks. There is little she can coax herself to believe of these people and their lovely things. Maude knows it's all just fluff. She's seen plenty of rainbows in her short life, stretching across the valley and landing in the mountains like a long smile on rounded cheeks. Some fancy glasses can't show her anything more promising than that, not when she last saw them coated in dust and the fine webbing of dwarf spiders.

'Have you come to finish up?' Mrs Schweers hands her a pair of thick yellow gloves. Maude hates how they feel between her fingers, but they're worth it to avoid the stink of the vinegar. She nods, and Mrs Schweers raises a single, thin eyebrow in response.

'Yes, ma'am,' says Maude. 'You think they're ready?'

They leave Bear and Baby to sit on the carpet, playing with the decorative stones from a bowl on the table. When they first came to visit, Maude thought these were chunks of amber, but Mrs Schweers bought them in the store, and they smell of rotten fruit. Mrs Schweers buys lots of things in the store: flowers and vegetables, smelly soaps, clothes and picture frames and makeup that gets stuck in the grooves of her wrinkled face. She's beautiful – Maude knows this from the photos – but she always tries very hard to be.

Mrs Schweers leads her to the kitchen, where yellow and orange tiles, like squares of plastic cheese, line the walls from floor to ceiling, broken only by a pine picture rail that matches precisely the trim of the counter. She has a stove and a refrigerator, a microwave, a toaster oven, and a brown electric heater in the corner that burns bright orange through steel bars. In a clear bag by the sink, there are round wedges of some kind of marrow – a zucchini, Mrs Schweers tells her – coated in flour and breadcrumbs. On the skillet, a knob of butter sits, cold and hard until Mrs Schweers turns the gas burner on, and it slowly begins to sizzle.

'What are you making?' asks Maude.

'Just a little thing the Jews taught me.'

Maude doesn't know who the Jews are. Mrs Schweers talks about them a lot, said they knew her Leroy, so she reckons they come from fairly strong stock. Dozen or so children, has to be, for how often Mrs Schweers will point them out while they're working their crops a few fields west of her back garden. Maude's never seen the same one twice. Must be nice having a family so big and not being stuck with a choice of four. At least if she had more – some her own age, especially – she might find a real friend.

'Has your father fixed that pump yet?' Mrs Schweers asks. She uses a fork to pierce each slice of zucchini and drop it in the pan.

'Workin' on it, I'd say.'

Maude's gloved hands remove the individual pieces of crystal from the lapping bowl. She wipes them with a cloth for drying, then sheets of old newspaper for shine, like when Ma cleaned the upstairs windows last week. Mrs Schweers says: 'You better not be using dish soap on that pan I let you borrow.'

'We don't have dish soap,' says Maude.

'Just hot water – that's all it needs.'

'Don't have that neither.'

'Jesus,' says Mrs Schweers, eyes to the ceiling. 'Well, you've got water and a stove, don't you? No excuses. Please tell me they're bathing you children. You'll catch all sorts of nasty things if you don't wash enough.'

Maude never has her baths with Bear and Baby. Not with anyone at all. Ma says that sharing a bed with someone is enough, and she ought to have her own privacy. At first, she didn't quite know what to do with all that space and time, with the water and the bar of soap and the jug that was left on the lip of the bath. But ten or so minutes passed, and Ma returned like that was what she intended to do in the first place. She made suds in her palms and worked the knotted strands of her hair through her fingers. She removed her shiny ring when it got caught in a tangle and asked Maude to wear it while she worked. Maude slipped it onto her pointer finger, but it was too loose and swung around like a lasso. A soft hand flat to her forehead and not once did the soap get in her eyes. She likes baths now; has them as much as she's allowed.

'I know. We wash plenty,' she informs Mrs Schweers.

'That so?' Maude nods. 'How often is plenty?'

'Every day.'

Mrs Schweers laughs like she's got a sickness in her throat that she can't catch in a hanky. Sometimes, Maude reckons she needs a good and hard smack on the back, but fears that her ancient and curving spine would collapse under the force of it.

'That's a nice little ditty you're spinning there, Bunny. Are you going to tell me that you brush your teeth too?'

'Are now,' she says. A drop threatens to slip from the base of one of the bowls; she catches it on her glove before it can land on the waxy tablecloth.

Maude thinks of last night, standing at the sink with Bear on a chair next to her so he could see himself in the mirror. Even though it wasn't on the list, Ma picked them some new toothbrushes and toothpaste at the big store. In the valley, Maude only had a wet brush and some baking soda, if she was lucky; a wet cloth if she wasn't. This time, instead of the usual mint toothpaste from the drugstore, the one Ma bought tasted sweet like fruit candies and the bristles made her gums bleed – Bear tried to swallow the whole tube.

'I got one tooth left to lose,' Maude continues. She bares her teeth to Mrs Schweers, finger so close to the smallest of them that she can taste the vinegar in her mouth.

'Oh, you'll get a whole dollar for that one,' says Mrs Schweers. 'Maybe even two.'

'Why?' asks Maude. She tongues the offending thing, but to do more than that – to even look at it in the dusty mirror of Mrs Schweers' powder room – prickles a horrible sense of foreboding in her gut. On the skillet, the slices sizzle and some are even smoking slightly at the edges. Mrs Schweers looks at her with such a flat expression that she's certain she must have said something wrong. That she's about to get a smack for the trouble of it.

'What do you mean, "why"?'

'If teeth are going for dollars, then why's everybody got so many still?'

She rears back at the bolt of laughter that cracks from Mrs Schweers' throat. A wheeze, a little cough. 'Oh, Bunny,' she says, and peels her top lip up to reveal her own row of perfectly straight teeth; hollow-looking, gums that are far too pink. There is a slip, a shadow just beneath her lip. 'I cashed in a long, long time ago.'

On second thought, she'd rather keep all her own teeth, every little part of herself where it's supposed to be. She scoffs. 'City folk.'

'I'm no city girl. You ought to know that by now.' Mrs Schweers out with her cane, beating the apple tree; splitting timber, tilling the earth to plant her flowers. How she hollers and swings her rifle around to aim at the whistle pigs in the field beyond her house; how she once aimed it at Maude herself, when she caught them all breaking into her dead husband's house. 'I'm just like you, Bun.'

Her heart warms to think it, but her head knows better. Maude isn't even like her own Da, and he was her brother in a life long ago. Cut from the same cloth and stitched so tightly, only to have the seam shredded. She can't fit with another person like that – not with her edges so frayed – and though Bear is a better fit than most, there are things that he will never understand in the ways that she does, which is a blessing more than not. But Mrs Schweers has a history like Ma's that Maude can't quite put her finger on, and though she watches and waits, observes so keenly and tracks each movement as if she is waiting for a possum to spring a trap, there are things she will never understand too. Because of how Da raised her, and how Pa ripped it all apart.

So, when she is finished with the crystal and Mrs Schweers has the zucchini plated up, when Baby needs changing or soothing and Bear is preoccupied with playing pretend, Maude will creep back down to the basement and look at a life that's made a house where all the rooms are safe, where food is plenty and every hand is a guiding one. And Mrs Schweers will meet her eyes across a black cup of Sanka with a knowing so deep Maude will have to look away. They are not the same, but that's what makes it so easy to see. Like the moon on a clear, dark night, or blood in the water.

March 1976

DENNY PICKS AWAY at the drift started by Minty only a week prior with a jackleg drill; makes holes in the cavern walls, dead centre of the squares he'd drawn in chalk. He stops for a moment to catch his breath and relieve his shoulders of the weight, to sweep his eyes over the boys: Minty, who fills the stopes left in Denny's wake, and Gideon, who swings his pickaxe back and forth like a pendulum, testing the balance. They're digging in the wrong direction, doubling back the way they came and then across – perpendicular to the mine's adit that stretches down a 1,500-foot slope – just like Pa said. Denny's got the map Sarge drew up in his pocket so the boys won't see, just like Pa said. He fields any questions and talks about the Noxan Line, the Lewis and Clark, says that's what they're digging for because none of them know a single thing about it, anyway. They just know what Pa tells Denny, what Denny tells them, and seem quite happy when that's all the knowing they need to do. Which is a mighty burden, the fact of which only occurs to him when James joins the fold, posing all kinds of questions that fall away from the usual script, causing Denny to clumsily play catch-up with his own lies.

His headlamp flickers, needing only a tap to reflect the peppering of silver, iridescent veins cutting through infinite black. Beams of calcite like fatty strips of bacon skim above their heads, the air so dark and humid, like a heavy cloud that dampens all feeling. Down here, it's quiet. It's comfortable. Nothing works how it's supposed to, but it never did, so he feels no loss. Skeleton mine, Pa called it on the first day – bones of their forefathers, for them to build stronger, better muscle around – left over from the twenties, when everything went bad and the workers had to head south.

'Can I try?'

He's kept James on the sharpening for the most part. Three to a crew is the way it's always been, so finding things for their spare wheel to do has been hard, but Pa's keen on ramping up productivity and never turns away a man who's willing to get his hands dirty. James can use the cup wheel just fine, so Denny passes off what needs sharpening and hopes that will keep him occupied.

'Trolleys are easier now,' says Gid, chatting idly. Bragging, mostly, about how established he is to the new kid. 'Electric, generally. When me and Den was younger, they used to make us run 'em up ourselves. We was the ore runners for this whole mine.'

Denny makes to start the jackleg again, then pauses. 'Was not,' he says.

Back then, they threw rocks and hoped for treasure at their cores. Tumbled around in sagging overalls, tripped over rails and generally got in the way. Denny paid the price for every little bit of fun, and kept along anyway. Work and play both yielded the same result.

He straightens his knees and comes to a full stand. The bandana Maude picked for him this morning gets pushed beneath his chin. From his flask, Denny takes a sip of water and watches with keen eyes the way Gideon puffs up, preens under the attention of someone who isn't used to his tall tales.

And yet, the cart is hardly hitting the halfway mark. They've been at it all day. Clumps of ore sit by the wayside, eyeballed by Gideon's alleged expertise and deemed unworthy.

'Looked all right to me,' says Denny, with a nod to the steadily growing pile of waste.

'Light as a feather,' says Gid. He's such a big man these days. 'I'm not here to waste my time.'

'How can you tell?' James is clumsy with the grinder, but there's learning in him yet. He's eager as a pup, the whites of his eyes near blinding in the dim light. Pa has taken such a liking to James that Denny can't quite understand it. James, with his boyish way of talking, his lean frame, his soft hands that he is careful not to cut or burn; all of this, Pa hates. Denny's hands are coarse, baked in dust and dirt and smelling constantly of saltpetre. Down the middle of his left palm, there is a scar that runs a white river across all the creases, making a valley of his flesh. He closes his fingers around it.

'Look, rook,' says Gid. 'Even what we got in the cart is pretty subpar in terms of what Baron is lookin' for. Once they smelt that down, you're talkin' a few grams, at most.'

'How . . .' James starts with uncertainty. 'How do you guys even make money off this?'

Even Minty, who has so far remained outside the conversation, looks away from his work and to Denny at the question. Gideon is silent, gauging. There's no correct way to answer that they know about, because Pa's not their father. Because Gid's been around since the beginning and Minty came not long after, but they don't carry the truth like he does – a stone in his pocket that sears his fingers each time he tries to handle it the way Pa wants him to. By now, he figured it would feel easier, but it's not the lying that's the problem – Denny's good enough at that – it's the truth that wants to pry his lips open from the inside and wrack a violent mutiny on the order of things.

'The tunnels are wider out under the patch,' he says, rote. 'The boys are there while we're here. Product's richer, more output – that's why the soil above's so fertile. We're just doin' research off the main adit.'

'Exploration division,' chimes Gid.

'You dug all this on the off chance there's more?' asks James. There's a pull to his brow, the first sign he's shown since arriving that he might be a little bothered by something. It rubs Denny the wrong way.

'Well, Pa has a map,' he says, and presses his thumb against the jagged line of silver white instead of looking at James any longer. 'So, there's no "off chance". More is around us. More is under the patch and the schoolhouse and under your very own home, James. We ain't goin' on a treasure hunt here – this is a business.' He's never said so much to James, and the thought makes him worry some. Pa says that too many words can spoil a lie, and that's why Denny's always been so good at it. Pa says it's not really lying, anyway, because the valley's got the highest concentration of silver on the whole continent, they just need to reach it.

'God,' says James. 'This is going to take us *forever*.'

Gideon throws a perfectly round rock at the wall and watches it split in two, containing absolutely nothing he deems worthy. 'Would it kill you to have some patience, rook?'

'I just want to *see* some, y'know? Get my hands on it. Make my girl a ring.'

Opal doesn't seem the type to want something precious. Pretty, maybe. Polish the silver to a high shine and hammer it into dapples that land like drops of rain in the crick. Buster made a brushed pair for Minty and his girl when they got married by Pa's hand last spring, and Gid's been bothering him for another set so he can give one to the little Hirsch girl, but last he asked, Buster threw a flathead at him and said to never set foot in his workshop again.

'Good luck seein' any,' Gid huffs.

James has altogether abandoned his sharpening. 'What do you mean?' he asks.

'We don't see none of it,' says Gid. 'Gets sent off for smeltin' elsewhere.'

'Where?'

'Elsewhere,' Gid repeats.

'*Really?*'

'You callin' my Pa a liar?' Denny snaps. 'Get back to work.'

The chalk in his hand shakes as he draws lines on the tunnel walls: here is what they're going to cut into the following day and the day after that. Everything Pa outlined, measured down to the millimetre, with a margin of error in case the drill slides, and room for supports. Something to soften the rough lines and make it into a space that can be passed through easily. If Denny can bring his crew close enough to the original deposit from the twenties, Pa won't have to bother with the cage or the shaft at all. If Denny does this right, Pa might look at him like he's a thing to be proud of. Like there's something in him worth keeping.

In answer to his wish, a whisper of a ring sounds, rushing down the adit until it strikes them in the echoes like the lapping of waves.

'Hear that?' says Gid with an almighty groan.

'Them's the bells,' sighs Minty – first thing he's said all day. 'Grub's up.'

October 1981

THE SINGLE POINT AROUND which Denny's entire universe once revolved has been sitting in the dirt yard of their new home since morning. Small stones grounding red welts into her kneecaps, a single, rotting leaf in her tar-black hair. He can recall very little of his life before, but Maude he remembers with harsh clarity: once a baby in his lap, now in her twelfth year. It's as if he has taken one lengthy step into the future, and what happened between then and now doesn't mean a single thing.

'No coat?' he offers into the space between them. Miles of it. A decade of time lost to their father's brutality. He can't parse it; talk to her in the ways he used to, back when her main concerns were paper dollies and the state of her supper. Now, there is a look to her eyes that screams knowing. A distinct incision that separates the before from the after. She is no longer his little Maude, dolly dancer, moon child, Princess of the Silver Valley and Lady of the Coeur d'Alene. She is a girl with the buck teeth of her dead mother and a new pet name to match.

'Got the tree.'

A single muddy finger points to the sugar tyme crabapple above. Denny hates to look at it – fruit soft and brown after the year's first frost. Opal figures him a walking farmer's almanack and had been short with him all week about his inability to predict the weather. Not like there were signs of it; the birds were still singing their dawn chorus, and there was no winter coat on the stray cat that leapt through the bathroom window one morning – starving and with a ring of mange around her neck where a collar used to be – and made its bed in the bath. Nothing of note but the clouds blowing across the milky skies on a cool wind that rattled their windows in the night and woke the baby.

'Maude,' he says, a conscious effort. 'A hat, at least.'

She scowls, the shape of her mouth so different from his own. Often, Denny wishes that he and Maude looked more alike. Then, at least, things would be obvious to her.

'I don't like it,' she says. A new line from Billy, used to divide the world into categories that make sense. Opal encourages it, despite the fits it inspires. Billy's got more words in there, he's just not ready to say them to anybody but his new sister. Maude's about bursting at the seams, and with each passing day that she refrains and restrains, the unspoken builds between them into something that Denny can't face.

'Mrs Schweers made that 'specially for you. Don't want to offend her.'

'Mrs Schweers isn't going to *evict* us because I won't wear a hat.'

'I'd reckon she's done more for less.'

Maude flicks a rotten crabapple in his direction. 'Ma's right.'

Denny ventures one step closer, shoulder leaning against the splintered porch beams. ''Bout what?' Two peas, they are, nowadays. He knows that they discuss things he will never be privy to; as a man, now a father. Opal has a way of handling the kids: she pokes and prods, asks all the right questions, where he flounders for the correct cues. It's a minefield he poorly navigates, no foot in his mouth because he has no damn feet left. Maude can tell, cute as she is. Leaves him to squirm before sparing him an awfully delayed answer.

'Ma said you're *sensitive*.' Blunt as she states this, a quick twitch to her right cheek that conceals a smile.

'Ain't.'

'Said you'd deny it too.'

'Your Ma says a lot of things.'

'Like what?' she asks.

Like: a lie hurts more than the potential pain of truth. A lie of omission is no better. If only the words would leave his throat. 'She says dinner's near ready. C'mon and wash up.'

Maude rises, fingernails flicking at the stones that have embedded in her skin. 'Yes, Da.'

A wall of heat overwhelms the pair upon entering the cabin. Dinner is not quite ready; vegetable peels litter the basin, fat and gristle clumped on the countertop to be thrown to the dog, standing sentry at the back door. Baby gums on the butt of a marrow. Maude grabs it from her sticky hands and chops it plainly into circles.

'Thank you, chef,' says Opal. 'Wash up.'

She whacks her wooden spoon against the side of the skillet, wipes her hands on her jeans. Maude follows her orders and makes for the sink, picking at the grit that has collected under her nails. The heat of the stove has Opal's cheeks flushed, irritated by the wisps of hair that stick to her face and ears. The cool air that the door let in has dissipated now, lost to the fog of the windows and the steam that feels as if it's rising from the crown of Opal's head.

'Crack a window, would you?' she asks. Denny blinks at her request, but with a grunt, he obliges. She hates how the hinge creaks, the rusted handle leaving flakes of mustard paint on his fingers as he latches it onto a stiff, metal notch. She hates how he lingers, too; acting like he's been knocked out of place. They all have, one way or another, he's nothing special.

Room has been made for him at the table, right beside Baby, just how he likes. Between the chairs' legs, Billy crawls and barks at the cat like he's seen the dog do, licking just about anything he can get his tongue on. The cat hisses and hikes her legs into arches, claws sinking into the once varnished pine chairs.

Denny kicks his feet out as a set of teeth hooks around his ankle. 'What you doin' down there?'

'Me'phis,' Billy says through thick denim. A growl and tug. Denny shakes him off.

'Memphis never bit me like that.'

'Memphis doesn't ever bite,' says Maude, hands cupping together to scoop heaps of raw meat onto the pan Mrs Schweers lent them. 'More pussy than dog.'

'Memphis not a pussy cat,' says Billy.

'Wash your hands again,' Opal tells Maude.

'Why?'

'They're dirty from the meat. You could get sick.'

'Never threw up in my life,' she claims.

Denny laughs, that's what does it – a rare thing that cracks through the atmosphere like a whip for its proximity to Baron. The only evident likeness they shared; down to the rasp, the quick smile that reveals a row of perfectly straight teeth with pincers either end.

'Biggest lie I ever heard,' he says. Maude glares at him.

Opal would urge Billy out from under the table, if not for the shelter it provides from the oncoming storm. On the skillet, slices of burgundy venison sizzle, kernels of pepper cracking a foot high. With a fork, she pierces the flesh and flips it, but the edges have stuck to the cast iron and torn chunks from the meat that already seems so meagre for four people. They've stretched the buck as far as it will go; the freezer is once more empty. Opal's worries never cease.

'And you'd know?' It's Maude's turn to laugh, a disturbing mimic of his own and their father's in turn, as she wipes her greasy hands on her shirt and down the length of her trousers. Opal frowns. There won't be another wash done until Friday, and Maude only has one other pair.

'You're a liar,' the girl spits, knuckles flat to the table now. 'You know me 'bout as well as you know him.' She emphasises the final word with a kick. Under the table Billy whimpers and scrambles out to his feet, latched to Denny's side, his small and grubby fingers curled between leather and denim, tugging at his father's belt.

'Da knowed me,' Billy defends, though his eyes are low and shuttered, the thumb of his free hand stuck in his mouth.

Denny should say something, but he won't. What ground has he to stand on when Maude is looking at him like that? Her little heart is broken up over all he failed to do, and the gaps he left have only grown wider and darker around her, leaving no safe place to tread. Opal could say something, but she won't. Maude has a way of weaponising what little information is given to her and turning it into a heavy-artillery assault. Times like these colour the whole house a murky grey, encroaching on the stove's warmth, and stomping out any small joys that may be collected to keep them going through the night. There is no fixing it. The image is warped, overexposure has leached it of all colour and left them to fill in the blanks. Where Opal might recall the moss-green water of the creek, where Denny might only see red on white under the cloudless sky, neither of them sees what Maude sees. Neither of them will ever truly know how it was for her.

'You're just ...' Maude tries. Her little fists curl up and flex. She clears her throat, forces the words up. 'You're a *liar*.'

The meat has burned, caked to the skillet. Opal turns the stove off, laments the cremated dinner. Billy is still at Denny's side and pets the waxy sleeve of his jacket in consolation. Baby notes the heavy silence, the severity in tone, and begins whining in inevitable upset.

'Maude,' says Opal, dinner forgotten. She approaches the girl – her *daughter*, whose side she must always stand on – and touches her shoulder. 'You go on to bed and I'll bring something in later, yeah?' It's not a question or a suggestion, but it's better offered as one.

Silence is the only answer, followed by three distinct stomps on Maude's journey to her and Billy's bedroom. For once, the boy doesn't make to follow, thoroughly bruised by his sister's contempt. He watches Opal, waits to see what she will do. There's no clear way to proceed, for as much as Opal would like to pretend that this has nothing to do with her, there is a moment that started it all, and that terrible thing – the hole that was dug in her life – happened to her too.

'She was fine earlier,' Denny says. Distant and solemn, he is somewhere else entirely.

'Yeah, well.' Opal shrugs the tension from her shoulders. She takes a clean knife and begins scraping the meat of its charred skin. 'Maude may not be able to hate you herself, but she can do her best to make the rest of us.'

July 1980

DENNY DARKENED THE DOORWAY of the storehouse with his looming, overgrown shadow. Opal ignored him for as long as it took to jot down all the credits it cost Liza Long to get a damn apple, then decided to let it linger a little longer so she could push the snap on her Trapper Keeper and file it all away. He jumped at the noise; sweating, hair sticking to his forehead, framing his face in a crooked square. Little flicks like bat wings, it was longer than she had ever seen it – which was still shorter than what most men elsewhere would call *in fashion*. There was something about it that skewed on the side of off-kilter and stirred discomfort in her she was loath to feel. Denny looked *wrong*. Where, in past summers, his entire head would have coloured an even shade of burnt brown, now his face and scalp were a shocking white.

'What's wrong?' she asked mildly.

The bell above the door rang once more as he shut it. The slight breeze that followed the afternoon was gone, and the heat in the air felt like something solid pressing against her chest and back, fit to squeeze. The day's shift below was over – the other, louder bell told her so – and typically the miners passed the storehouse by without much thought, heading straight for a drink in the back end of the big house, so she wasn't expecting anyone this close to dinner, least of all Denny.

'Hm?' he asked, removing a pair of gloves coated in a mucky, flaking crust of dirt and slipping them into his back pocket. He sidled forward, the tips of his fingers bouncing experimentally against the wax seals of the preserves that lined the centre table. She wanted to tell him to quit it and shoo him from the store altogether, but there weren't many places that Denny was allowed to be anymore besides below and his home. Robbing him of one more felt like a further weight she could not carry.

'You're hovering,' Opal said. Her palms pressed flat to the counter, forearms rising at ninety degrees.

He sniffed. 'Ain't.'

'Are.'

'Just here for some sugar,' he said, eyes landing on every little thing in the store but her own. A rapid flit across the scales and their weights, bags of grain slumped against the countertop – right where Sarge left them, too heavy for her to budge alone – a crate of filthy carrots shrivelled into nothing after too long in the dry summer heat.

'That's what all you boys say,' she tried. She always tried.

He flushed to the tips of his ears. ''S for my wasps.'

'You still got it bad, huh?' The walk she took each morning from the cabins to the storehouse passed right by the gap in the trees that led a long path all the way up to Denny's place. Through the pines, she could see the flaking edges of the wasps' nest clinging to the shack's pale blue wash. She could hear them too, a violent cacophony that lived in her ears for the rest of her day; softened only by the vibrant play of the little boy that haunted the crawl space of Gideon's decrepit home. 'Why don't you try some peppermint?'

'They don't like it.'

'That's the point, Den,' she said. There was nothing good about a wasp; a bee pollinated, made honey that she could seal into perfect golden jars of varying shapes and sizes with the help of Jeanie Specker. Did they wake him in the morning, she wondered, in that crumbling shack, tipping the edge of the ridge that loped down into a canyon? How did he sleep with the noise of them? There was no mark of stings on his skin – none that were visible, anyway. He had his usual criss-cross above the brow, and a white line that dragged through his bottom lip and ended at the tip of his chin; the bumpy nose bridge and uneven jaw were a given, the welts on his hands that swelled at his knuckles and made every minute movement a clumsy gesture that he quickly hid in his pockets. Denny had been marked by many things, but a stinger was not one of them.

'Will you not call me that?' There was a brittle snap to his voice. He forgot himself. The dismay was so clear and painful to witness. Opal was not blind to the way Denny could be, how he was still so tangled up in the roots of this place despite being exiled to its borders. Unlike her, he was from the valley, and likely hadn't left in his whole life. The trees that swallowed them up were what the sky was made of most days. In the winter, there was a clear view of nothing but bloated clouds that looked fit to spill over and flood the whole valley. She couldn't imagine seeing nothing but that forever, but he deserved none of her pity. Not when the world still turned beyond their borders, where people lived and thrived and suffered and died. He chose this place. Leaving was not an option that had been taken from him, despite what his father would have him think.

'Fine,' she said, changing tack. 'You've been avoiding me.'

'Ain't.'

A bold-faced lie. His inability to spend more than ten minutes in her presence was something Opal had grown accustomed to in the four years that had passed since the accident. She was well aware of his discomfort, his guilt, and was not going to alleviate him of that when he refused to engage in any discussion about what exactly had happened in the mining shaft. But his most recent avoidance of her was unrelated to that. She could feel it in how he shied away from the challenge in her gaze, switching paths when they crossed one another between the rows and rows of trailers and cabins that lined up in a tight collective, so separate from his own. His father's presence was a valley between them, and Opal had no means to get across. She wasn't entirely sure she even wanted to; not when Denny seemed content to just live like this.

'And I'd rather you went right back to it,' she bit, taking an empty jar from beneath the counter because he clearly hadn't thought to bring one with him.

'This is where the food's at.'

But there was food everywhere. The valley was his to reap from. What his father would have them all believe was that the land had been the property of the Rowe family since the pilgrims came across to pillage it from the Natives. Yet Denny sat in exile for his crimes, straddling the line between his home and the world beyond, never fully setting foot in either realm for fear of what it made of him.

'What happened to your hunting?' she asked.

He looked away, somewhere over her left shoulder. 'Snares ain't turnin' up what they used to, else I would've brought you some.'

Opal fed burlap through her fingers as she unwound the elastic cord tying the sack together. She produced a clean, dry cup measure and shoved it into the sugar to loosen the grains. Her hands curled protectively around the rim of the jar to prevent any fallout.

'Hunting and setting snares aren't the same thing,' she told him, filling the jar to the exact amount his few credits would allow. It was a sad lot.

'Rabbit's rabbit.'

'Are you catching bucks in those little traps of yours now?'

'Stop.'

Opal slapped a wax seal over the top of the jar and tied it off with a length of twine; tight, a double knot, a snip that frayed at the ends. 'I don't know why you won't just go out and hunt what you like. You used to be gone for days tracking the same thing, and you were always better for it.'

After these days, Denny would return with a pink flush to his cheeks, a wicked gleam to his eyes, as if he were a young boy who'd been kept inside too long and finally got to live under the sun for a spell. He'd never been so alive as he was in those moments. Her first summer in the valley, after weeks of trails gone cold, traps empty and reset elsewhere, he came back from his hunt with thighs bruised and beaten from getting the drop on a boar he'd been tailing for days. In the night that followed, they all crowded around the pit between the mess and the big house and spit-roast it over an open fire. Like the Fourth of July, James had said, as if Denny hung the moon above. Sparks spitting into the air, each face painted golden under the cloudless night. Baron carved up the beast, gave everyone a helping from his own hand; a fond touch, a smile, he fed them and boasted of his boy. Held his drink high and the moonshine sloshed around like liquid gold; higher again past the heat of the fire and it cooled. Two dozen hands in the sky, he made stars of them all.

'He won't *let* me.'

The greater truth was written in every jerky movement Denny made, as if he could erase the words he had just spoken by scrubbing harshly at his face.

'And what will he *do*, Denny? What will he do if you go anyway?'

Anywhere at all, to a world he had never once seen in its fullness. Whatever glimpse he'd caught was tainted by colours far darker than any one person could cope with. The point was not the food Denny hunted or what it would do for the people, but the control that it kept. Denny was only kept for digging around in the dirt of the mine, emerging as a man made of dust who must retreat to his home. Alone. Like a dog on a collar, and the leash only stretched so far.

'Denny . . .'

There was nothing they could fix, nothing to heal; to leave and start over was their only chance. Yet neither of them found they could do it; step outside this place where death had made its bed. It was easier to get up every morning in anticipation of the same thing – the same walls and windows and faces, trees that grew taller with every year that passed, shrouding the colourless sky – than to worry about the kind of danger that change could bring. Whatever darkness lay in the valley scared her far less than what existed beyond. She could live in this feeling, as she had done for the last four years, so long as the hurt never grew larger; only deeper, where her eyes could no longer see, her heart no longer reach.

But she reached for him, as she always tended to, the jar of sugar easily forgotten – for he too was dependable, static and rooted as one immovable point on the near horizon. A mirror in that dark room they shared. Who was she to judge him, when neither could find it in themselves to open the door? When was the last time somebody allowed him this understanding? When was the last time somebody held his hand?

Denny did not return her reach. He shook his rotten head, wiped at his nose with the mottled back of his hand. He turned and he walked away, the bell above the door ringing behind him.

*

He hears murmurings of discontent, of plans to be made down in the canteen, while clocking his card and tucking it back into the slot with his name marked in faded yellow pen – *D.B. Rowe 012*. A night at the bar is no rare thing, yet excitement trills through the room as if this time it's an occasion worth marking. Everyone is sitting in the steaming heat, dust on their hands, eating sandwiches carefully packaged inside tin lunch boxes. Their ladies made those – salted ham, butter thick as cheese, folded lovingly into brown paper and tucked beside an apple or a pear from the trees beyond the patch. Denny makes his own when he feels the want to. There are days he'd rather keep going until the job is done: chip away in the dark tunnels, get the ore fit for shipping to the smelter; or whatever else Buster does with it lately. Eating is a waste. He's had breakfast and he will have dinner; why split the day into another segment that needs wading through? Minty came to fetch him again this morning. Denny did not miss the bells, but Minty came regardless; sweating and half-dressed in that leisurely way of his. When they walked to the mouth, they walked together.

Maybe that's why he's included – why Minty is spending time with him now, after all these years. A mark of change. But, as far as Denny can tell, nothing has changed. Drinks, says Buck. Like always. Watering away their sorrows, soaking and steeped in spirits. Talking over the bar that Denny built with Sarge when he was fifteen about things that he is no longer allowed to understand.

'You coming?'

'Huh?'

Minty's talking to him, dead on. Eight pairs of eyes turn to do the same. It's disconcerting, in the dim artificial light. 'Sarge got that shit you like, when he was in the city. Goddamn paint thinner,' he says. 'You should come on down.'

The men laugh. Some of them are too young to have any idea what Minty is talking about, but they laugh regardless. Did Minty ask Sarge to do that – for old times' sake – or was it a coincidence? Did Sarge feel bad and decide to take things into his own hands? All these things seem unlikely. And yet, despite the unease that sits in the pit of Denny's hungry gut – and has done since the start of summer – he nods dutifully.

Denny, out of practice with the art of it, returns home following punch out. Hunched over his small basin, he wrings out a cloth and scrubs at the grit on his face, the sweat drying around his nostrils. Drags it down his chest and under his arms, air drying while he roots around the dresser for a clean shirt. A cotton thing, well-worn and washed, smelling leafy and dry, and faintly of the peeling paper that lines the drawer. He unbuttons, slips his arms in, and buttons once more. Rattles a finger inside each ear, finds black dirt beneath his nail and scrubs it away with a brush. Hands wet again, he musses his hair only to slick it flat to his head. It's not right – he hasn't worn it this long since he was a boy – and he suddenly becomes all too aware of the way it curls around his ears and tickles at his tacky skin. He changes his shirt. With a knife, he makes another notch in his belt, cinching it tight around wide yet bony hips, missing the buckle a time or two when his gaze tracks dutifully toward the windowsill.

Without a touch, he recalls the shell of a wasp between finger and thumb, hard and smooth. He's never been stung – not even once. They buzz around his head in the night-time and swarm his sheets in droves, a mass of dark brown flecks that glint gently under the wedge of moon-light. In his ears and the very recesses of his brain, which has lumps and bumps and canyons; fissures and swings like oxbow lakes floating serenely in seas of plum red. It never hurts. Cast under a blanket shadow, arms and legs in their thousands. They coexist in perfect harmony, living inside the same shell. But when he wakes, the room is always empty.

Denny blinks and the light has changed. Burnt orange makes sunspots in his vision, dappling against the walls and pushing all else into darkness. The boys will be waiting – with a head start, no doubt. Despite his exile and isolation, it's been a long time since he's touched a drop of anything. It costs too much in the storehouse and the bar out back of the big house is the only other place to get it. What was once a familiar path – the most familiar in his life – is now entirely different in its dips and cracks. The gnarled knot of an exposed root catches him halfway; grit and bark has been shovelled in heaps to fill a hole that regularly made puddles and soaked him as far as his knees.

When Maude was little, he used to hook his hands under her arms and haul her across it with a good five feet of distance either side, lest she get any ideas about splashing and ruining her clothes. It was fine for him, caked in mud and all sorts from his work below, but she was his to keep clean and tidy. Above his head now – just as his feet pass a lump of lowbush blueberries – is her bedroom window; so high up that the only things to see from the inside were the clouds and a snap of the sun once it passed noon. The loss of her strikes him so suddenly, his teeth vibrate with it. So afraid of what lingering might make him do, Denny rushes past, rounds the corner to the bar room. More of a lean-to than a room, but there are doors and windows that Denny salvaged from empty trailers and a rotted-out cabin deep in the bowl of the valley. He used the dregs at the bottom of paint cans to coat the flaking edges in black, spruce it up nicely for all the hard-working men – a prize for all they'd done toward the betterment of the valley. Never wired, the bar relies on oil lamps and candles for light. It glows like a click beetle and paints the dimming evening a mossy yellow, deep and malignant. The dirt path out front is in shambles: chunks torn from the soil, boot prints and tire tracks from ructions in the night. Bottles buried under plants and hedges; green and brown and black tossed into the makeshift ditch on the far side of the house. None of it's his doing – he hasn't been around to do any damage – but he still cringes at the sight of it; how it's aged with him into something drab and tired and altogether lifeless.

He pushes down on the handle, but it won't open. Inside, the boys yap on about something or other that has them bursting into bouts of raucous laughter. Denny put that door in himself, and there was no mechanism that had it locking automatically – it had to be done manually. He then added a deadbolt for emergencies, but there's no clear emergency in sight. He tries the door again and it won't budge. He knocks three times, peers through the window: at least ten people are there, all resolutely looking the other way. Except for Minnow, who flushes beet-red and dips behind the bar. Minty is there, sipping at his usual, legs swinging back and forth. He's got his gear on still, shoved down around his waist; back and arms covered in streaks of grey and black. None of them have washed. Denny, in his clean clothes and shiny shoes, a pillar of uncertainty and discomfort. He tries the door again and they can hear him, they must. The music is low and the chatter is softening. But nobody comes. He settles on his haunches, head in hands, and waits; waits far longer than dignity allows.

The dark is solid now, flattening around him and meeting the earth. His face feels hot, burning down his neck. There is a laugh in his chest somewhere, ready to spill out and save face if any of them come looking. He could cry, but he won't.

One time, when Denny was twelve – and suffering greatly through a spell of confusion and mounting rage that could only be outwardly explained by the onslaught of adolescence – Pa took a trip away with his new pal, Sarge. Denny was left, for the entire day and the evening that followed, in the unfamiliar and filthy hands of Old Buster Chaps; who wasn't that old in the way of looks, but in the way that seemed like something might be eating away at him from inside his own chest. The valley was young, then, with only a few meagre travellers at its hearth and the promise of more to come once Pa returned. That day – with snow pelting down in inches, then feet, then freezing over again in a thick, solid layer that made each step treacherous – Denny spit his oatmeal back into the bowl at breakfast and refused to tidy his dishes. He tore all of the pages from his favourite book and left them on the floor of his bedroom like the rotting, wet leaves beneath a blanket of winter; hid the keys to Buster's shed and hauled himself through the window that only he was small enough to fit. He yelled and screamed and tossed things around with abandon he had never once felt in his short and entirely blank life. He took a carabiner and some stretchy rope, an oil lamp and two fat cigars and marched out into the white night, parking himself in the biggest tree he could find. In all his haste, he forewent a hat or scarf or gloves to warm his hands, left any and all food or water behind; he had only the heat from the ends of his stolen cigars – a heat he knew all too well – and what little flicker the oil lamp kept.

All the while, Old Buster Chaps did nothing, only sat and watched.

Early the following morning, Denny came down with a vicious bout of sickness. Pa did not come. Noon passed to afternoon to early evening, and it soon became clear that Old Buster Chaps would not climb the tree to retrieve Denny, no, he was merely waiting for the moment he would inevitably fall. When it happened, he carried Denny back to his shed like a baby and unlocked it; force-fed him broth stinking of garlic and did not rise to the bait of vomit down the front of his shirt or Denny's cold sweats sticking to his only set of sheets. He read from a book about birds, then from a pamphlet detailing the inner workings of a BCI group size 29N 12-volt battery. Denny slept and when he did not, he sat and watched Buster right back. It was easier to be around people who weren't Pa after that.

Now, Denny marches, just as he did in those early days, down the bare path to Buster's shed. Wiping at his face, he does his best to rid it of the ruddy tinge; the obvious upset. He raps lightly on the door. Once an affirmative sounds from within, he steps inside and kicks his boots against the frame to knock any muck off. These are his good boots – a pair that once belonged to James.

Buster has all his hearing, so he knows Denny's there, he's just not one for reactions. He must sense something in the air, because he spares Denny the shortest of grunts before folding back over his wheeling tray table, lamplight strapped to his head, painting washes of white against the gadget in his hands. Denny swings himself onto the wooden workbench. It has a clamp bolted to the side, holding in its vice a book without binding. There's a picture painted along the spine – sandy cliffs and sea columns plastered with foaming white waves, a dapple of small birds flying in formation above. Denny's never seen the ocean except for his dreams, but he can smell it all the same.

'Don't touch that,' says Buster. 'It ain't dry.'

Denny retracts as if burned. His hands are shaking, still, so he rests his palm flat against the smooth grain of the bench, pinky touching a cool metal flask. There are several of them arranged neatly in a row, labelled in blocky red text; the ink still wet.

'Don't touch that neither.'

'Touch nothin', you mean?' Denny counters.

'Don't get smart, young Rowe,' he says. He's not young Rowe, and hates to be called such. 'It's poison.'

'Well, I know that.' The hand-drawn hazardous waste markings say as much.

'It's cyanide, you know that?'

'I can read.'

'I had no idea.'

Denny smiles carefully, turns away before it takes over. Buster must have taught him, in those early days, or else Pa did in the year or so they spent on the road. Before that, there's nothing. Not that he can recall the day when the before stopped and the after began. He was not suddenly born into the body of a child who could walk and talk and tie his own shoes. There are other things, merciful blanks. It's a kindness, really.

'What you messin' around with all this for?' It wasn't here last time he visited – over a week ago, now. He would have noticed.

'Sarge brings me my books,' says Buster. 'I give him lists – magazines, journals, newspapers.'

Denny snickers. '*Magazines*.'

'Scientific, like. And I sent him off to find that, some way or another. Not like Froy can write me a prescription for it.'

'Is there not a store where—'

'No.' Buster sighs. 'There's not a store where you can just walk in and buy yourself some cyanide, Newports and a Coca-Cola. You got sand in that head of yours?'

'Ain't come here to get scolded.'

'You come here 'cause you got nowhere else to go.'

'I got places to go.'

Buster looks over the wire frames of his glasses. 'Like goin' botherin' that Aster girl again?'

'She bothers me,' Denny grumbles. Lies, really, because Pa told him to stay away from her and it's been a hard thing to do. 'Pokes her nose.'

'And what's she to do when you're walkin' around all pathetic like?'

'Ain't pathetic.'

Buster hums with a quick shift of his shoulders, his gaze pulling back to the delicate work in his hands. 'Why are you here?'

'I'm always here.'

'Why?'

Denny shrugs. Buster never lets up with this kind of talk; he's worse than Opal in that regard.

'You got me, you got the storehouse. Got Sarge when he's not scamperin' around after your daddy, but even he's not a sure thing. You want more, don't you?'

There's enough in the picture frame of his window view that stretches pleasantly over the wide maw of the valley. The food in his belly and the air in his lungs. He ought to be grateful – he was *taught* to be grateful. That too is a kindness.

'You work for Pa.' Just like Sarge, like Opal. Has he truly got any of them?

'We all work for your Pa. Ain't news, bo'.'

Nothing is news around here. All tired and rote, same thing over and over. But while Buster works maintenance with Jerry, he'd be hard pushed to let anyone boss him around. Hardly works down with the ore at all, instead sitting up here and turning his ideas over and over until they're something worth handing to Pa on a steaming platter.

'Well, I s'pose Pa knows what he's doing,' says Denny.

'Yeah?'

'Yeah. Pa knows what's best and sees to it happening.'

'Does more than seein' to it.'

Denny's not stupid. No flies on him, Sarge says. 'What's it for?' he asks. Buster looks at him over crooked eyeglasses. 'The cyanide,' Denny says. 'Why do you have it?'

'For the silver,' says Buster, whipping back to attention – alert, fixated – glasses climbing the bridge of his nose. 'It's a process for extractin' it from the ore. Works for gold, too, but we's not dealin' with that in these parts.' Denny's dealt plenty for Pa. Trading metal for metal. 'Sarge knocked it 'round too much in the truck, compromised the compound stability – weather ain't helping, this heat.'

'You got enough in this?'

Buster doesn't complain, so that's not what he's doing. It's purely fact – indiscriminate, he likes to say. His put-upon sigh is anything but.

'With them deposits of late, I'll need as much as I can get.'

It's nothing bad – certainly not as dire as Denny had feared. The boys go about their days as if the ore's infinite, with walls of solid silver beneath them. Yapping away about all sorts and lounging on their lunch breaks when they know it's the kind of thing Pa gets real wound up about. Only Pa's not acting wound up – nothing to let on that their supply is dwindling, that the land will expire and no longer be of use. Denny's supposed to keep that between them – a secret that only he can be trusted with – but clearly Buster knows enough. He must, for Pa to have him rooting around these alternative methods.

'Gonna toss it out now, don't you worry. Ain't nobody want to die that way.'

Denny has read about cyanide poisoning. Bright red breaths that scrape the bottom and bring up silt – foam and choking and damned noises. There is a point where the poison makes everything inside stop, but it is a slow and grinding halt that can sometimes carry over days and nights and well into dreams that melt in reverse. Boiling stomach, heart, head. There may be worse ways to go, surely, but none that he fancies thinking of.

'I can toss it, if you want. Got nothin' better to do.'

Buster waves a hand. 'Best not. Toxic waste.'

'My skin's hard as leather.'

'Leather's still skin.' Denny could swear he's smiling, but it's hidden by his wiry beard. 'Now git, bo'!'

Denny fusses about the bench, palms the cyanide container, moves things around to make it look as close to before as possible. Buster has time for him, but only so much.

'Catch ya later,' Denny says, shutting the door softly.

The dim light fades behind him as he steps onto the main path; the contents of his pocket rattle on the turn. Maude's bedroom window is a blip in the distance he ignores. It's shameful, this walk; as is the thought that the women might see him in his retreat while they peek through curtains, waiting for their husbands to come home and tell them over pillow talk how they left him out in the dark. Why? Because Minty said so? It isn't in his nature surely. But Denny is no real expert on the things that people stand firmly for. Minty just wanted somebody to drink with – that's all he's really wanted, so long as Denny's known him.

'Penny for your thoughts?'

The night-birds fly into a frenzy. Pa's voice is a bullet through the air; it catches Denny like a gutshot. His father is parked up on the front porch of the big house, rolling paper curled against the railing. He's loading it up with tobacco and hash, a healthy heaping of it. Sarge did well on his trip to the city, it seems, but really all there is to show for it is some drugs, drink and poison. Is Maude in her room, reading her stories alone while Pa is down here smoking? Denny knows not to ask, but the urge to do so near overwhelms him, until his father's eyes find his and sit there, heavy and expectant. It's an invitation, good as any. One he can't reject. Denny stands next to his father, about half a step back, and waits.

'What you gettin' up to tonight, huh?' Pa asks. He lights a cigarette and passes it to Denny, who takes a single drag – deep, he holds it – and gives it back.

'Nothin', Pa.'

'That's right.'

The evening air hums violently. Denny never gets moments like this with his Pa, not anymore. But today's been different – every day leading up to summer's end feels charged with it, and he can't fathom what he did wrong this time around. The thought unfurls and slips out into the space between them. 'Boys asked me for a nightcap earlier.'

Pa smiles, a white bright vacuum that draws in all light. It warms Denny. 'That's right. Gid mentioned it.' Gideon wasn't at the bar, not that Denny could see. Was he invited too? Did they do the same to him?

'You were up with Gid?'

'Sure was.'

Denny's pocket is heavy, stainless steel still biting the tips of his fingers as he cradles the capped cylinder. 'He doin' OK?'

Clouds have rolled in overhead, quick and low. There's nothing for it, but the rain may come. It'd be a reprieve from the weight of July. Pa lights up again and does not offer Denny a puff.

'Good as can be expected,' he says.

'He still drinkin' like that?'

Pa does more than seein'. When he looks at Denny, the plates start shifting. He can't plant his feet fast enough to work out how he's supposed to stand.

'Now,' Pa starts. 'The man can drink however he damn pleases. Way I see it, *he's* got nothing to be sorry for.' Because he knows what's good for him, Denny doesn't breathe a word. 'Seems there's a lot worse he could be doing to the likes of you, only he ain't got the strength yet. None to raise his boy either, starvin' down in that there shack without a mama to nurse him.' Pa lets that sit right on his windpipe, linger for a long moment. 'Suppose I oughta thank you for that one too.' The upset bubbles up in Denny, but it's nothing close to indignation – never has been. Pa knows just what to say, even when they both know well it's not even true. He hardly spoke a word to the girl in her life; which was far shorter than his own had any right to be. Denny spent near his whole life doing his best to keep Gid and trouble miles apart, but there was nothing he could do for Julie Hirsch – not once Gid had set his sights on the slightness of her.

And he hasn't seen Gid in a year – not since the seasons changed over and Denny was out beyond the patch with a pail, pulling plump apples from the tree to haul by Miss Gunn's for stewing. They'd go to Opal, then, kept in jars with their wax seals and counted meticulously in her notebook. Denny was doing it just to be doing something – to pre-empt the request from Pa, which he knew was steady coming like the sun in the sky. He liked being beneath that sky, even in the greyish light of day, searing his eyes with the sheer pallor of it all. Children played around him, but never too close, and he knew none of them well enough to offer greeting. Gid had no problem in that regard – hauling up on his crutches, shouting and hollering about all the things Denny was and is, like it even needed saying. None of it made a difference: weepy bastard who wouldn't have lasted a day in these mountains without Gid showing him what's what; *murderer, coward, liar.* The canister of cyanide is cool in his pocket; he clutches it like a lifeline. What's a thief, now, in the grand scheme of things? A murderer two times over, if it meant never feeling this way again? *What will he do,* Opal had asked him, as if Denny could stand up, fight back, run away. As if what Pa could possibly do to him was worth finding out. Opal's always right, but Opal can go back home whenever she wants. Denny's got no home other than the one right in front of him, and he can't go anywhere without its say-so.

'Naw, Den.' Pa's hand moves up to his face, to cradle the back of his neck. 'None of that, now. I won't have it. You're a man serving his time and that's all there is to it. Them boys ain't ready to look at you just yet and they can't be blamed for it.'

Pa looks at him, though. Denny's not real if Pa ain't looking at him. He oughta go on home and let himself be swallowed whole. Sit in the shack's dark belly and feel the swarm, the high and forever drone in his ears. He oughta take the container from his pocket and down its powdery insides like a shot of rotgut. Fritz about on the floor until Sarge comes looking for help with the shitter or the lug of scum at the bottom of the well, only to find him coiling around himself over and over, lungs capsized and slick with tar, clumps of soil, the taste of decay from the collapsed shaft and James's last breath a quiet whimper that catches the back of his throat.

'Will you give 'im mine?' he dares, voice low, eyes low; all the way down to the dirt between their shoes.

'Speak up, son.'

'My credits. Got plenty of 'em and I'll work up plenty more.' He likely won't – not at the rate he's paid. But he's only one man going it alone in a cabin, when Gid has a boy to feed and no means to do it with one less leg than the rest of them. Denny's got it luckier than most, he knows, who'd have been knocked right out on their asses and sent to the city after an incident like what happened five years ago. Pa, without needing to be told as much, nods in wholehearted agreement. He passes the butt to smoke and Denny sucks it dry.

'Got that heart that killed your mama,' says Pa. He leans in to kiss Denny's cheek, even though he's blowing smoke and sweating through his nicest clothes. Even though his eyes are red and his hands shake and he was only just fixing to put cyanide in his tobacco.

'I'll sort it for you, Den,' says Pa. 'Don't I always?'

Mountains split down the middle and the wind howls through the valley. When Denny was fifteen, he had to re-break all of the fingers in his left hand before he set them, so they wouldn't heal wrong. This feels something like that.

November 1981

AT WORK, OPAL CAN FEEL the past pressing in on all sides. Main Street is framed at each of its corners by small bundles of browning slush peppered with grit and salt. It snowed last night – took its time, Mr Wells tells her over his morning coffee. She had tried her best to dress for it – Chicago, coupled with the valley and her mother's early life in a desert tundra, trained her well – with thick, woollen tights that don't fit her crotch right, sagging in the middle and needing to be hoisted over her hips every ten minutes. There had been something decidedly uncomfortable about sourcing her undergarments from a dime store bargain bin, but Opal has paid far more for far worse. A pair of Denny's socks act as a second layer, doubled over to protect her ankles. They ache terribly in the cold from the damage done in her hurry to dance *en pointe* all those years ago, but what had she expected? There is rarely a safe outcome to rushing such a commitment.

Nancy's halfway through a pack of squares by noon. When she sucks on her most recent cigarette, the hollow cut of her cheeks draws Opal's eye to the green tinge that paints the taut skin of her temple; a thin coat of powder and a heaping of blush does little to cancel it out.

Or maybe it would, had Opal not known to look for it; were she not left idle. But the day is quiet, perhaps the least busy she's been since she started working at Frank's in September. It's the weather, most likely, the wind that cuts through the diner with each ring of the bell above the door. The customers are huddled around their cups of coffee, some black, others swirled with dollops of creamer. Sachets of Splenda sit sticky and forgotten in their chrome canisters. The grill offers some heat beyond the thin sleeves of her maroon, moth-eaten cardigan, but she hates to get in Tuck's way, eager as he is to busy himself in any capacity. When another customer finally arrives, her chance at a reprieve from the boredom and the cold is snatched away; by Nancy, who had only lit up a moment prior.

'I'll get it,' she says, stubbing the butt out on a novelty ashtray. Opal tidies the order wheel and crumples each slip into a single ball. As she tosses the ball into the wastepaper basket, she sees him. Denny comes in and wipes his boots on the mat. It slides under his feet. Nancy smiles good-naturedly and leads him to a booth in the far-left corner. They talk, though Opal can't fathom what about, and he takes the paper menu that Nancy hands him. Opal could order for him – she knows his likes and dislikes well enough by now – and he'd probably thank her for it, but it seems he's humouring Nancy, letting her tell him about the specials when Opal knows for certain that he will like exactly none of them.

She stacks a wad of thin, white napkins in one of the spare dispensers that's lined up along the counter. Pinches the menus by their metal corners as she tidies them. Nancy swishes back toward her and hooks the order onto the now empty wheel.

'Your man's here,' she says.

'Thanks.'

It's not that Opal resents this notion, nor is it that she feels Denny is not her man. He is. She is his woman. There is a string by which they are connected, a tenderness that was not chosen and couldn't be helped. Both ripe and raw at the same time, more of a bruise than a wound; one that she cannot stop pressing her thumb against. It helps that there is nobody to remember what happened but the two of them; it confines their world to exactly what they make of it: the children, feeding them, ensuring that history doesn't repeat itself in a vicious cycle. It's a relief that it is him she must do this with, despite all her grievances. She fills a large cup with water and brings it to his booth.

Denny sits with his back pushed right up against the plastic seats, fingers clutching the silver rim of the table, regarding the rest of the patrons with nothing short of resenting suspicion. His hands are heavy with welts, the permanent black dirt caked into the split grooves of his fingernails. Opal hands him a napkin from the chrome dispenser.

'Thank you,' he says.

'You're welcome.'

She stands at the table, both hands stuffed into the front of her apron, ankles crossed on the sticky black and white tile, a pitiful third position. Denny looks sideways at her in that suspicious way of his, but there is nothing much to it. He's nervous, as is she – this is not something they typically do, nor is it something they discussed beforehand. In the months prior, he had only ever lingered on the pavement outside once Horatio let him off for the day, chain-smoked until her shift ended and she joined him for the walk back to the car. On days where she worked and he didn't, he'd drop her off with nothing but a closed-mouth smile and a promise to return later. This is certainly more than that. A statement, perhaps, or a challenge.

Dry skin flakes around his nose, red from where he tried wiping the tickle away. If he were Billy, she'd simply grab him by the back of the head and pull him close, yank it off like it was nothing. But he's not; things are decidedly different between them in a blurry kind of way – there is a certainty to him, sure, a solidity that she can reconcile with the man she first met: dependable, kind, loyal to a fault. These inherent qualities are something she can look to in the times where it feels like they're floating in the unknown, holding hands on the water's dark surface.

'How's work?' she asks, if only to lighten the thrum in her chest.

Denny shrugs. 'It's fine. Cold.'

'Busy?'

'Chains on tires, mostly. Had to knock a dent out of some lady's station wagon, but it won't look the same as before, no matter what she puts in my pocket.'

Opal hums quietly. Outside, short and sharp gusts of wind threaten to knock down the butcher's specials board, the chalk already runny from the morning's sleet showers. She asks him: 'Why are you here?'

'I not welcome?'

'It's not that,' says Opal, careful with her words. 'It's just, well, you never come here. I packed you a lunch.' Generous to call it this – dried meat and a tin of peaches, more than what she brought for herself.

'Too cold for that.' She can see it in him where it was never before present – Denny's not coping with the weather like he used to. His lips are cracked, with pinking skin that will soon give way to blood. He's gaunt, hollow around the cheeks and, though he still refuses to sleep in the bed with her and Baby, coming here is trying. She imagines some of the men from the garage ragging on him about his waitress wife the way Nancy rags on her, and he, hunched over his lunch; blood from a stone, retreating further into himself. But Denny was boisterous, once, and could dish back what was given to him tenfold. Maybe some of that colour will return and she need not fret so much over what is beyond her control and entirely within his. He is choosing to spend time with her outside of the house – time he could spend on himself, relishing in the absence of an alleged wife and children – and to some, that is the bare minimum, but to Opal it is more than enough.

Nancy returns, tucking in beside Opal to give Denny his plate; heaped far beyond their usual servings. She is flattered at first, but the feeling is soon lost at the sight of Nancy's hand – smoke-yellowed fingertips sinking into the fabric covering Denny's shoulder.

'That'll warm you up in no time,' she tells him.

Denny flushes. 'Thank you, ma'am.'

'None of that,' says Nancy. 'I may not look like I'm being chaperoned at the school dance, but I'm not old either.'

Opal could hiss and spit and act bothered by the comment, the implication. She could stake her claim with a kiss right on the mouth, crawl across the booth and into the lap of her husband, leaving no doubt in anyone's mind. There exists a part of her, far younger and more alone, that would see no other option. But Opal has no need for this assertion of their relationship. So, she waits patiently and pleasantly for Nancy to depart and announces that she ought to take her break – lest the afternoon pick up and she have no time for it. Then Opal leans against the edge of the bench, arms crossed over her chest while Denny holds his cutlery with a bizarre kind of delicacy – swapping hands to cut the meatloaf, pointer finger flexed against the top edge of the knife. His bites are measured and polite, which has always been something of note in comparison to how the other men would feast on Sarge's spoils, or whatever delicacy could be cooked up from her lot at the storehouse. Even James, with his Sunday-supper manners and no elbows on the table, ate like a man starved.

'That nice?' Opal asks, though she knows the answer.

Denny grunts in the affirmative. 'You want some?'

She slides into the space to his left. Tucker is listening to the radio, and Nancy is smoking in the kitchen. The plastic leather seats chafe against the backs of Opal's thighs, itching through the wool of her tights. She accepts the fork he hands her, loaded with meat and mashed potatoes, dipped in gravy. It's quite the mouthful, but enough that she can chew. Her cheeks are full when he looks at her again; he hands her back his own dirty napkin.

'I won't come again, if you don't want me,' Denny says.

It's not about the want – he has a way of catching her off guard. The sum of her feelings for him combines in a grand contradiction; Opal does not want him here, but she's glad that he is. She can't trust that he will stay away simply because she asks him to, but she knows that Denny wants whatever it is that makes her happy.

'I don't care,' she says.

Denny huffs. 'Whatever.' He takes another bite, chews for longer than he could ever need to.

Opal shrugs, picking at a lump of ground meat. 'What do you think of her?'

'Of who?'

'Nancy.'

'That your friend over there?'

'We're not friends.' Opal has never been friends with a co-worker, she's not about to start now. 'Besides, we don't have those.' Not anymore. This fact sits heavy between them.

'She seems nice,' says Denny.

'You could talk to her, if you want. Her shift's up before mine.'

Denny shrugs. Opal presses. 'Her husband's a piece of shit.'

'Terrible.'

A customer comes in the door, Nancy's got it. Opal shivers at the sudden gust of icy wind. 'Should I give you my jacket?' Denny asks.

'No. I can't wear it over my uniform.'

''Kay.' Denny looks away, bites at his lip like she scolded him. Opal is hunched over, elbows in her lap, twirling a thin, browned carrot on the plate, when she feels a heavy arm drape across her shoulders. 'This all right?' Denny asks.

It doesn't feel any different. There is no grand realisation in which Opal comes to the conclusion that Denny touching her is something novel and worth noting. There is an air of inevitability to it that she dares not inspect with too sharp an eye. Mostly, Opal feels grounded; tethered to something in a way that she can't recall ever being certain of. There was James, and there would always *be* James, but Opal is not naive enough to think that she can only be made whole by the first man she gave herself over to, even if he was her best friend. Denny is not any of those things to her; nothing but a husband now, a man, a figure and a role to play. They don't share a bed, nor do they share kisses. Though she rejected his jacket, she will often wear his clothes over her own, when the morning air is biting, and the grass is damp with dew. Slip her feet into his unlaced boots and wiggle her toes for warmth. Fold the sleeves of his sweater over her palms and grab a bucket of feed for the two chickens they bought from a local farm almost three weeks ago. Gather eggs in the felt pockets of his coat and duck into his collar when her breath makes clouds in the pale sky.

Opal doesn't answer him. She dips her head back, neck resting against the cold leather over his arm. Under the table, the tip of her shoe brushes his boot. They sit like that for a long while, until the silence is broken by the ring of the bell and they both get back to work.

*

The black plastic bags feel dry and chalky in Maude's hands. Mrs Schweers had tossed them down, little care for where they landed. Maude tears into the plastic with such ferocity that the edges turn grey, then white. Inside, everything is dirty and scrunched up in a manner that doesn't quite reflect what she knows of Mrs Schweers. There are fabrics of all different textures and patterns – very little black or green in the piles of clothes that she unearths, which is what has become typical under Ma and Da's rule. There are pink flowers stitched haphazardly onto blue and white checker, but the clothing is fit for a baby – Baby, specifically, whose pile is mounting far higher than anything she or Bear could ever achieve. Yes, there are T-shirts that say things like *Camp Toadie, I Sailed the Powell River Race in 1962!* and *GAP*, but they're far too big for Maude's slight frame; boyish as she is in comparison to those girls at the big store, or the ones she sees on a rare visit to town. She holds the smallest of them to her chest – a dusty, faded, purple *Indy 500* – and it hangs almost as low as her knees.

'Beggars can't be choosers, Miss Maude.' Mrs Schweers tuts.

'Like I'd beg.'

She'd never. Don't beg and don't kneel – that's what her Pa used to say. Rowes are stronger than that; but Pa made her brother beg. Made him kneel on the carpet in the big house and kiss the muddy toe of his boots. Kicked him like a dog. She hates to think about that and those times. How maybe she should have begged too.

'Did you get that mouth from your daddy?' Mrs Schweers asks. Like it's any of her business. Maude dumps the most recent bag down to Bear's prying hands as Mrs Schweers descends the ladder. She's too old for things like that. Frail and spindly, all her strength is hidden. But Maude knows it's there – because of the moving she does, the stirring and carrying and wheeling; because of how she's already well into her day when Maude, Bear and Baby arrive at eight o'clock in the morning.

'Got it from *his* daddy,' says Maude. Because that's the truth now, and she can't find it in herself to be resentful. Not anymore. She thinks again of the begging and the place she used to hide – when Sarge wasn't there and the screams were loud enough to make her ears ache. Tucked inside the wicker trunk that belonged to her mother, splinters poking the bare skin of her arms and legs where blankets could not cushion; blankets of all different colours: squares with flowers, stars, other, smaller squares inside. One had her name embroidered, and the year of her birth, done in golden thread that shone in the light that came through the slats. If only she could smell the lavender now and feel its dry sprigs between her fingers. But everything in these sacks is loose and worn, smelling of musk and mothballs. Mrs Schweers has no chest from which she can unearth treasures – ribbons and frills and golden threads – Maude already checked. So, she rips into the final bag and sucks at her bottom lip, knowing that it will likely yield no more luck than the last. She schools her disappointment, because Mrs Schweers is hacking up dust from her trip to the attic. Maude ought to make her a cup of Sanka.

'Enough of that,' says Mrs Schweers, a catch in her throat. 'It's lunchtime. We'll get back to business later.'

Mrs Schweers doesn't like for Maude to carry Baby down the stairs, but the alternative seems worse. With each step, Maude thinks that Baby will slip from between gnarled hands and tumble down onto the patterned floor below. Bear scoots down on his ass, as always, various pieces of clothing tucked under his shirt. They don't need this – the thrift store was just fine – but Mrs Schweers insisted, as she does with most things, and it would be rude to deny.

In the kitchen, she makes them cheese sandwiches. They could do without these, also, but again Maude is pressed by the reminder from Ma that manners are a vital part of their new life, and that she must use them if she wants things to run smoothly. She holds the triangle to her mouth and takes a small bite. Bear has deconstructed his sandwich into lumps of butter and peels of cheese. He rolls the bread's soft centre into balls and shoves them into his mouth all at once. Baby cries a little, over nothing, and Bear tries to give her one too. Maude smacks his hand away before he can make their little sister choke.

'No fighting,' says Mrs Schweers, dusting off the serrated knife with a dish towel. She's not even looking. Maude is being good like she was told to, and still she gets berated like she broke something or said a bad word. She sticks her food-loaded tongue out at Bear, but he doesn't bite. He slips from his chair, nearly knocking his head on the table as he goes.

'Finished!' he yells. 'T'ank you.'

Withholding a sneer, Maude watches as Mrs Schweers delivers a fond pat to his overgrown hair, piled like straw atop his large head. He plays underfoot of her while she scours the sink with steel wool, putting things in the pocket of her apron. In his wake, trails of socks and shorts fall from the belly of his shirt, from the leg of his trousers. He crawls across the tiles toward Baby, who's sitting in a homemade cage that looks more like a fire guard or the kind of thing you'd keep a dog in. She's gnawing on her fist, drooling on the filthy bib that's buttoned around her fat neck. Maude wipes it all away when Ma tells her to, but she figures Baby ought to learn to do these things herself, or she'll never grow up. Bear pokes his fingers through the bars and pulls at Baby's socked feet.

'Quit!' Maude hisses – they'll lose another, and Da will be upset, because tiny socks aren't easy to come by in these parts. Not if you don't knit them, and Ma's never been inclined toward such things. Mrs Schweers would, but Maude reckons that Baby's gotten enough from her. Bear too, once his spoils are scattered across the floor like a rug. Mrs Schweers hunches over with a click to her hips, knees, spine, and just picks up after him. Maude scowls into her glass of milk.

The kitchen window, stretching across the entire length of the counter, fogs up from the heat of whatever Mrs Schweers is cooking in her pot. There's always something boiling, stewing. With the heater on too, the kitchen is stuffy, stinking of lard and onions. Hot air in a compressed canister, door shut tight. The milk is warm. Bear scuttles across the floor like a creature of the forest and turns his attention to the humming heater, which he knows well not to touch. It's large and metal, the size of the television in Mrs Schweers' good room, the one she never lets them watch, no matter how many times Bear begs to see the snow on the screen. The heater is painted brown, with a metal smile and teeth that glow yellow when Mrs Schweers turns the knobs that make it go *click, click, click, click*. It's very hot to the touch, and Maude knows this because she can feel the heat from all the way across the room. Sturdy, a sound investment, Mrs Schweers said. It's suffocating. Baby claps her hands together and chews on her sodden sock. Bear reaches out to touch the wired, amber teeth, glowing terribly in the kitchen's steaming air. He likes the colour, beams back a gummy smile to match. He looks for Maude, eyes like morning glory searching hesitantly. She smiles at her little brother and, without waiting, he presses a single dirty palm to the searing metal grate.

The flesh sizzles, the smell rotten and joining the acrid air. A howl, followed by hot tears that glisten against the alarming red of his cheeks. Bear is so small and silly; he doesn't think to take his hand away. It's Mrs Schweers who does it for him, fussing in a terrible panic, and she hoists him under his armpits and forces his hand under the faucet.

'Mama!' Bear cries, and though frozen to the floor, Maude's lashes grow damp. He reaches for her with his one free hand, but she can't help him with this – what is she supposed to do? Mrs Schweers struggles with the weight of him, at his attempts to break free of her hold. Bear doesn't want *her*, he wants their Ma.

'Why didn't you stop him?' Mrs Schweers asks, vicious and accusing.

Maude pushes the cage aside with the tip of her boot and hoists Baby onto her hip. She kicks happily and babbles; a pat to her ass confirms that her diaper is damp. Maude shrugs, bending easily to retrieve the missing sock. 'He won't do it again,' she says, opening the kitchen door, letting all the air back in.

September 1976

Julie Hirsch gives birth to a baby boy on a wet and miserable morning; the very morning the leaves turn to the world in a bright gold and summer is left forgotten. He is born with a caul on his head; the veil of a mourner, a cloud obscuring his features and trapping his cries, shrouded in glory and something sinister that she cannot yet understand. It's disgusting, and she spends hours weeping in her mother's arms, unwilling to hold him for the slime that coats his skin; that came from between her legs and hurt so terribly on the way out.

Baron Rowe himself comes to smear the child's forehead with the dirt of the valley and kiss his cheeks the way he often kisses her; cradle him close and speak of what the boy will become with such an omen bestowed upon him. Strong lungs, strong heart. Nothing from his daddy but the eyes, maybe, every bit Julie and a little sprinkle of something else sweet. Gideon's not sweet, but plenty others are. They crowd her on her first walk along the vegetable patch, offering congratulations and condolences in equal measure. Nobody will touch the child – they only stare, picking him apart with their eyes, remarking on the strength of his chin, his proud ears. This walk soon becomes part of their daily routine, the pair of them, as she is no longer allowed to go to the schoolhouse for daytime lessons. Baron says she is to attend to her man, to her boy. And Julie always does what Baron says, even when he is heavy-handed or wound up over something or other that she has no idea about, but pays for regardless. Being that she is a young girl, he says it stands to reason that there are things he must teach her. And, well, Julie takes to most things like a duck to water, so it's a pity that she can no longer do her math, her science. Read her books. Mrs Jeanie never did get around to giving her lessons about babies, and while most other things do tend to come easy, that is not one of them.

Because little Billy is red and stinking. He gawks at her with a gaze so muddled and strange that she's convinced he must not know her at all. His mother! Who kept him inside her belly for almost ten months, waddling about the valley like she had been pumped full of water. Unable to do much else but hunch over a basin and scrub clothes against the washboard for hours on end. She must be a monster to him, hovering over his little body and poking at his wrinkled pink skin. A giant head to eclipse the sun, no longer golden as she once felt in the light. Mostly, Julie feels tired. Bone-tired in a way that her fifteen mild years could never have prepared her for. She is no longer fit to jump to the very airs and whims of others; being eager about anything is a chore. The truth of it is that Julie aches somewhere deep down – perhaps so deep as her heart – and she reckons when that little thing broke from between her legs and came into the world howling bloody murder, that he took something with him.

She hopes that she will still get to play with the Kepners, with Beaver when he's done his lessons and his logging. She loves her friends, but she can't love this baby very much. Not yet. Not least until she knows him a little more; knows what it is that he took.

November 1981

WHEN MAUDE DREAMS, she dreams in circles. The world is a ball so small that it fits in the palm of her hand, cupped close for warmth. She blows on it, and waves crash, gusts of wind send the leaves far from their trees and into a spiral; a tornado or a hurricane, she's never known the difference. A twister is what Pa calls them. Pa's not dead in her dreams, he comes and goes like the moon; waxes and wanes, commands the tides, eclipses the sun like the hole in his head. Because there is no sun, nothing will grow. No flowers, fruits, trees, vegetables. The animals are gnarled and exposed, bone-white with eyes black as night; predators preying on predators, gnawing at her own ankle to break free of the trap. She runs when she can, but the running never ends without a fall; a tumble over the cliff's edge, no kind slope to ease her descent. The wind whips her across and into a straight plummet, and there's always a moment, a sad little moment, where she thinks she might reach the other side. But she never wakes before she hits the ground.

Lips to her forehead, the scratch of stubble – Maude wakes, eyes wide and unblinking. Above her, Da stands with Baby sleeping on his chest. Her socked feet swing loose around his hips as he sways above Maude – a shape she'd know in any dark. Little by little, her heart slows.

'Were havin' a nightmare,' Da whispers.

'Weren't.'

He smiles, pats Baby on the back. Maude can't recall the feeling. The mattress dips as he sits sideways, though not close enough to touch her.

He's so quiet all the time, keeping every little thing buried. She can't reach where he goes. Never knew where that was in the years that passed, never knew *why* he left her – the answers in Pa's dangerous silence, Sarge's stories of the weakest children being left out in the cold to perish. Only the hands that held her were anything but weak. Once, when she was far smaller and the world far bigger, Denny made up every inch of it. He was the sun and stars, the whole sky and every cloud in it – mackerel, grey, crisp blue infinity. She had missed its light on her face.

'Where did you go?' she asks him.

Baby's nose makes a gurgling sound. She's had a river of snot running down her lips and chin the last two days, and no amount of hankies will fix it. Her cheeks are bright red from the steaming Ma gave her over the sink earlier – how she screeched at the burn of it – but she's no longer as cranky as she was when she threw Bear's picture book across the kitchen. On Da's chest, she sleeps peacefully as if nothing is the matter at all.

Maude wonders if this is what they looked like: when she herself was a baby and he, hardly twenty, together under a single roof where he fed and bathed her, tucked her lovingly under blankets, never again to be so close. When she was little, Maude feared the dark. Sleeping next to Bear has taught her that she's not alone in this, but tonight he is in the other room, until his hand throbs less from the scorching. Sometimes Ma will leave the lamp lit for them, let it burn out before dawn. But the dark never felt all that bad with Denny – not when she could turn over in her cot and know he'd be there: the shape of him so clear to her in the black, a forgotten book open flat to the spine on his chest that rose and fell with every slow breath sleep allowed him. In the night, he looked safe.

'Had to go, Bun,' he says. 'Would'a stayed if I could.'

Gone in a blink. For days, she had thought him simply asleep in his room, trapped by some sickness or other that made it impossible for him to even crack the door and share with her a smile or a gentle kiss. But his name was gone from the house, from the mouth of their father and Sarge and anyone else who came to pay visits; old and serious, they told secrets to Pa and acted nothing like Denny's friends. In fact, not a single person acted as they had before, burdened by some baffling sorrow, and those who seemed to stay the same maintained such a distance that they never saw her wave through the window, never heard her call across the patch. Maude began to think she had dreamt Denny, only to see his slumped shoulders slouching between the pines, dressed in his work blues with his dirty face and hidden eyes. An imaginary friend, a name Pa laughed at, scowled at, lunged at. She knew to keep him away, then, in the furthest reaches of her heart.

'Why d'you call me that?' she asks.

'What d'you mean?' Da looks off out the black window. There are no stars and the moon is hidden behind a copse of trees and some smoky clouds, but she can still feel it there.

'Never called me that before.'

There were other names, few she remembers. They used to call her a princess, a lady. His friends would sing and laugh and poke at her belly until she turned red from the short breaths of laughter. Never liked it much, and he always made them stop. Held her close as if he was hers alone, and they didn't have the right to her purely because her father did.

'Because your brother came up with it,' he says. ''S nice.'

'You're my brother,' she says.

'No. I'm your Da.'

And though Maude wishes to argue, to defend the history he so readily forgets, she cannot find it in herself to do so. She's so tired of pretending to hold off the hurt.

'Go back to sleep,' he says, one hand under Baby's butt, the other reaching out. He pulls the blanket higher, smacks the pillows. Maude doesn't flinch, and it's nice that he knows she won't. 'I'll be right outside with this one.' Baby's Da, Bear's too. He was always *her* Da in any way that mattered. Like a dream you don't quite remember – the worst kind, maybe. Maude never wants to have it again.

*

'You want some?'

Denny is holding a day-old loaf of bread to his chest. Cradled in a gingham dish towel, flour all over his fingers. It's from Mrs Schweers, sent home with the children. She bakes on Saturdays. Denny doesn't bake bread. He won't buy it either. He might, if Maude or Billy asked, but it's not the kind of thing he'd think to get, not when the land seems to suffice. His diet is so packed full of meat that it's a wonder he stays standing on the days where they have to go without. Which are few and far between, now that they're in the swing of things, in the rhythm of this new place, and buying meat in waxed paper from the grocer's deli. So, Opal nods. This bread is not something they have to store away safely – it will soon grow stale and be of no use to anyone – may as well enjoy it while it lasts.

'It's always better on the second day,' she says, retrieving the largest knife from the block before he can tear the loaf with his hands.

'Yeah?'

She places the knife on the table between them. 'My deda said best not to have it fresh. Won't sit right in the stomach.'

'What's a deda?'

'My grandfather,' she says. 'You ever have one of those?'

'Reckon so.' He cuts her a jagged piece first, bigger than the slice he starts on for himself. 'Think the kids'll want one?'

'A slice?'

'No, a deda.'

'Oh.' She tears pieces from the dough and rolls them into tiny balls between her forefinger and thumb. At her feet, the cat yowls. She tosses it a piece – another mouth to feed. 'No, I think they'll be fine. Not like they have much choice.'

'Your daddy dead?'

And he is, but that doesn't mean Opal won't wince at the reminder. The look on Denny's face is that of regret. 'Sorry.'

'It's OK,' she says. 'He died when I was nineteen.'

'We don't gotta talk about it,' he says gently.

Her mother: unable to set foot outside their home, leaving Opal to make the arrangements. It was good practice, in the end, because burying her mother the following year came naturally by then. 'It was a long time coming.'

Denny favours the chewing of his bottom lip over the bread. He nods heavily, keeps his chin dipped low.

'Do you remember your grandfather?' she asks.

'My mother . . .' She is surprised by the formality – he says the word like he's tasting it in his mouth for the first time. Chin up, his eyes flit across Opal's, catching hook, line and sinker for all of a second. 'She used to teach me songs on the piano and we'd play 'em for him. My feet couldn't reach the pedals.'

'Do you still play?'

He turns away again. 'Nah. Don't know much about all that.'

The floury crust of the bread coats her fingers. She sucks her thumb thoughtfully, stalling in the hopes of coming across a way she might be able to ask him what she wants to without scaring him off. But this new life of theirs is a chance at going about things differently, and there's plenty they can say to one another now without fear of who is listening.

'What happened to her?' she asks.

Her question shakes him from whatever reverie he had been soaking in. He holds a piece of bread against the inside of his cheek, mid-chew, and looks away as if she has committed some vicious betrayal.

'It was my fault,' he says, and suddenly, she can't tell what they're talking about anymore.

But Opal had bathed him in the river with her own hands, dressed him in her dead lover's clothes. This should have been a kind of benediction. A rebirth and baptism, cleansing the soul of everything that had blackened it, dragged it down through cold tar. But months have passed now and still, he struggles to meet her eye across their small kitchen table. He looks at her hands, her shoulders, temples and forehead. Sometimes, he looks so far off into the distance that she must call his name as if he is miles away.

'Denny,' she releases in a single, tired exhale. 'You don't have to—'

'Pa wasn't one bit happy with her,' he says.

In her mind, she imagines a woman who makes up all of the softer parts of Denny that Baron's bruteness can't possibly account for – he may have his father's jaw, his rough voice, his eyes, but the long lashes that frame them, the pitch-dark of his hair, all belong to someone else. Funny, Opal thinks, that the features which distinguish Denny and Maude from their shared father are what further connect them to one another.

Maude carries Baron's presence in other ways: with her coil of anger, the wound-up fists that clutch her blanket and the collar of Billy's pyjamas while they sleep. The night they left the valley, Baron must not have been happy with her either – for she came running toward Opal, unbridled and silently pleading, pockets filled with jewellery and a promise of Denny on her tail – which spells a far worse feeling, one that stirs something awful in Opal's gut. Maude may have been there, borne witness to her father's final breath, but she is too small to understand what any of it meant. Denny knows, she can see it in the way his hands shake as he cuts another piece of bread; the knife nearly slips to slice his finger, but he catches it before blood can spill.

There are times she thinks Denny might take every little thing he knows to the grave.

'We don't have to worry about him anymore,' he says, with confidence he wears like a poorly tailored suit. 'I took care of it.'

November 1976

NEVER ONCE DURING HER TIME in the valley did Opal's heart long for home. Not in those early days, where the warm weather yielded winding, bright nights to be filled so completely by drinking and dancing. Nor when the afternoons grew cool and sharp, flurries of snow drifting down from the north, and they all gathered wordlessly in the bar built on to the back of the big house.

She liked a drink as much as the next person – and when the next person's arthritic hands were permanently fixed around the narrow neck of a bottle, it turned out to be quite a lot. Her mother had been a drinker, and her mother before her, the way that women were in those days: a glass of wine or sweet Miodula by the sink, stem slick with suds, only moments after Opal was tucked lovingly into her bed. Her father had been a drinker too, but in a way that was different and no less painful. He went teetotal on Opal's tenth birthday and likened any form of alcohol to the heroin that chewed up their street and the surrounding ten blocks, yet saw nothing wrong with spending all his time and money on the dogs. Opal had no such problems – that is, she knew *enough* like she knew shredded beer mats, trains home at sunrise in her best dress, the stained and silty bend at the bottom of the toilet. *Enough* made her the kind of person not worth being around. So it was that she kept it in her sights and never toed too close to the line. She took one sip for every three of James's, and watched as he swung about the place, relishing the constant company, the belonging that this place and these people granted him with such ease.

She cringed, though at the shape of him: arms draped over the shoulders of his fellow workers, utterly unable to tamp his eagerness. Gideon appeared to enjoy it for the most part, perhaps for the role reversal it offered him; a reprieve from playing limpet. Minty, on the other hand, could rarely hide his disdain: facing off to the world with such brash selfishness that it made him honest, trustworthy and inexplicably charming. Because of this, James rarely shied from the grumbling, the never-ending cache of complaints. He took it as begrudging affection – the likes of which he had experienced from the siblings he left behind in Chicago. The youngest of four, this dynamic suited him. With a slew of faces to look up to and rely on, he was content to sit back and be at the helm of nothing. Opal could see the attraction, the simplicity in carrying little on but a family name. Even that, lucky for her, hardly mattered – his siblings had their careers and their children. James was the one who got to play around – be the dreamer among the doctors, the businessmen, the paralegals. There was pressure to do more, of course, but not enough; this fact was made obvious when she tallied their savings to a tentative total and there were discrepancies she couldn't account for. A surplus nearing the thousands that made all the difference for their big move from one state to another. It seemed James's parents thought it easier to let their youngest son run wild, and be rid of him, than to try and change his very nature. Which was right in the end, if the glee that lit his face at Denny's sudden appearance through the door meant a thing.

Denny had sidled up to them, one arm slung across the back of Minty's chair, the latter making plenty of room. There was a smear of black dust across his forehead, which he wiped with a fine linen hanky – *Dufresne*, it said, in royal-blue cursive stitching – dirtying it beyond any further use. He watched her watch this and tucked it away into his coat pocket for better keeping. For shame, she thought, with a winsome smile sent his way.

'Pa's wantin' to talk to you both,' he said with a nod to Gideon and Minty. 'Regardin' the shaft.'

'What about it?' asked Gideon.

'We're goin' to try sink it again.' Before, they had only ever taken to the earth at a gradual descent, an incline so subtle it seemed most of James's exhaustion at the end of each day came from the hitch of his chest at all of the laughter he let out. 'Goin' to rig the cage to the back of the big truck – y'know, the GMC – and ease us on down about five hundred or so.'

'Is it even functional?' she asked. Every bit of the elevator she'd seen was jagged and brown, metal grates with water pooling beneath and a terrible stench all summer. At first, she hadn't even known what it was for, only that it was deep and dark and could likely fit no more than five men at one time. But Baron had taken the time to give them what he had dubbed 'The Grand Tour' – show them what's what, where things grew and where they died and were butchered, the relics of his family's alleged past up in the Silver Valley, before they were run out of it by locals and competition. The mine works were meagre, and certainly not the kind of set-up she'd considered when James pitched the Silver Valley to her last Christmas. Yes, Baron's slice of the valley was the deeply rural, close-knit mining town James had promised her, but its facilities did not match the lustre of this belonging. Despite a rough start, she had grown to appreciate the sense of community that blossomed around them, but the thought of James entrusting his life to that fragile cage made her want to take it all back. To bank on the whole thing holding to a truck with some chain or rope felt like tempting fate, or worse.

'Pa knows what he's talkin' about,' said Denny, eyes harder and less inclined to meet her own.

'When are we going?' James asked, and Opal could hear her heartbeat in her ears.

'No way,' Gideon scoffed. 'You're too green, rook.'

Minty nodded thoughtfully, and she ought to have nodded along with him. 'That machinery's temperamental.'

'Your Pa comin' down with us?' Though looking at Denny, Gideon held an arm out behind him, swinging playfully for James with every attempt he made to merge into the conversation.

'Nah,' said Denny. 'He'll be off with Sarge on a run.' Nobody asked where they were going, nobody even *thought* to. 'Reckons we can handle it.'

'Big boys now, Den.' Gideon grinned, lips thinning as his mouth widened.

'And that's regulation?' James asked over his shoulder.

Minty's disdain increased tenfold. 'Regulation,' he scoffed.

'What?' James cast around the group. 'Isn't he supposed to go too? None of you have used that equipment before.'

'Neither has he, kid,' Minty said, chasing it with a sip of something light to soften the blow. 'We're on the edge of a new frontier.'

Denny did not laugh with the others; he did nothing, only let his arm fall from the back of the chair. Opal held her own steady, hooked over James's shoulder, leaning and utterly still so as to stop the worry from shaking right out of her.

When Baron finally made his grand entrance to the bar, he was not alone. In his arms, he held his daughter – though for all the familiarity between them she could have belonged to anyone.

'Who's all here, little Maude?' Baron asked, his tone playful, but his eyes made of crystal-clear glaciers that cleaved the crowd into compartments and pushed them to their corners. Some kept drinking in their quiet content while others folded inward as if to form a cloak around the man who moved mountains in their eyes, and dug down to their very core. It reminded Opal of a story her mother would often tell, when the Chicago winter was at its most ferocious peak and winds shot across Lake Michigan. A warning, really, as her stories typically were, about how the danger of hypothermia was not in the cold, but in the heat that flooded the body from dilated vessels – a last-ditch attempt at survival that made men strip to their skins and die of exposure anyway.

'Miss Maude!' rang in a swift chorus, jovial greetings toward a child who passed no heed of anyone at all. She was soft and rumpled by sleep, half the sweeping length of her unbrushed hair stuffed into the collar of her shirt; flimsy for the weather they were having. Her inky eyes scoured the room twice over, back straight, hands limp at her sides rather than holding tight to her father. She caught Opal both times, who fluttered her fingers in return. This was met with a steady wariness, a rigidity in her posture that Opal couldn't quite parse. When Maude found Denny, she slouched and swung her little legs and smiled broadly, bending toward him like a flower in the sun.

To watch them with one another felt intimate and intrusive, yet she couldn't look away. Denny didn't dare smile in the company of his father, not in any genuine way. They were nothing alike, down to the darkness that shrouded both Denny and Maude – underpainting of olive, sickly even – where Baron boiled close to crimson. He was bright and bold, lighting the entire room by virtue of constantly existing at its centre. The people flocked and gathered, willing him to listen to any drab little detail about their day and, were Opal not seasoned in the trappings of such men, she might have found herself among their number. Because there was something warm about him too – something that sparked like a powder keg, tinderbox, a lone match in a room flooded with gas. Denny could only fill what little space remained.

Baron hoisted the child on his hip, which lacked any grip for the roundness of him. He made his greetings and slapped a few backs. When he spoke, the world snapped to immediate silence. His daughter flinched.

'My boys here.' He drew a picture with his free hand, so bold and blue, purpling his grip. Opal watched intently, chin resting on her palm. 'They're the best we got. Goin' to be headin' up some especially vital work in the comin' weeks, and I just know you're all fit to rally right 'round them *every* step of the way.'

Someone poured him a drink, another put it in his hand. A tall stool was placed beneath him, where he sat and propped Maude against the bar – the seat of her pyjamas sticking to the liquor-wet surface.

'We couldn't do any of it without Denny,' said James, above the chatter. His voice was loud in Opal's ear and made her jump. She had forgotten he was there. 'Hear, hear!'

She raised a glass, they all did, and at the very centre, in the focal point of this perfect scene, Baron held his son; the hook of an arm fastened around his neck in a game of affection. Even worse, she thought, to bear witness to such a closeness: Denny's knuckles turned white on the bar's edge, and his breaths drew short and sharp. With the stilted smile on his face, it might have been laughter.

'My boy,' said Baron, while Maude hung by the wayside; clinging tight lest she fall off. Denny, beet-red and squirming, looked away from his father and to his friends instead. They found the sight unremarkable, it seemed, and Denny smiled wider to bolster that notion. Because it was all in good fun, really; nothing unusual about a father hugging his own son – in fact, such a sight would seem refreshing – yet Baron didn't hug so much as tighten the noose.

'Now,' said Baron. 'That's some real strong support you're showing, James. Real loyalty.'

James, flushed with drink and embarrassment, said: 'Well, I just call it like I see it, sir.'

Baron hummed, patting Maude's rear in a rhythm that coaxed the wanting and waiting for what he might say next. Opal did not want to know. In fact, she longed for Baron to look away and not see James at all. He was not made for that kind of looking – to be picked apart and dissected of all of his moving parts – and could never quite figure how to face up to it. All of his conversations with Baron had him staring at a fixed point over the man's left shoulder, unable to truly meet him eye for eye. Baron made him nervous, made him want – all kinds of things she never knew him to want for.

'How's about you join them?'

What?

'Really, sir?' asked James.

'Well, what d'you think?' Baron said. 'Are you fit for it, or are you still finding your feet?'

To pose such a question in front of near twenty people was dangerous. It was tempting. James's pride never ruled him, but being a man did.

'Reckon I can do it,' said James, grin spread ear to ear, drink forgotten. Opal's nails dug into the denim of his pants. She tried to communicate to him the apprehension she felt, the terror that swirled darkly beneath it, but his legs were bouncing enough to throw her off. He was giddy with belonging.

'Worthy of some celebration, I'd say.' It was too much, too soon. 'Drink up, little one.'

Without a single remark being made in retaliation, Baron tipped his weighty glass back into Maude's mouth. Her little hands clutched the base, breath fogging up the insides. Opal shot up, hovering an inch or two above her seat, shoes bent around the rung.

'Pa, c'mon,' said Denny, as the little girl leaned further and further away. Her bare toes curled and her feet kicked out, and the world was silent of all but the chortling of her father's cohort. 'She don't like it.'

'So you drink it,' Baron said plainly.

'Gotta check them snares real ear—'

'Any left and little Maude here might drink it.' Another pat to her behind. 'Thirsty girl, she is.'

Opal waited for the laughter, for the joke to land and dissolve the awful tension that culminated around them, but it never came. Denny dipped his head back and swallowed it in a fast, single gulp. He coughed into the back of his hand, coughed again as large palms landed all over in praise and congratulations. Baron poured him another. Again, he drank it. He did not stop drinking it until his father stopped pouring, which kept going long past when the room's temperature shifted to a dangerous degree and Opal's heart began thudding wildly in her chest.

Stop, she longed to say.

You'll poison him!

But she could not, so she fled – hardwood to powdery snow as she burst out into the night and breathed slow. Exhaled the horrible thing that swelled inside of her, that threatened to poison her too. James's laughter through the crack in the door was grating, it was too much, and grew worse as the door flew open once more and spat the frantic form of Denny out onto the snow. The shape of his shadow so familiar to her by now that she ached to reach out and touch it, but she didn't – not the scrabbling creature he made of himself on the cold ground; heaving the contents of his stomach, coughing with such a vengeance that a white-hot worry lanced her heart at the thought that he might be choking on something.

'Denny,' she gasped, palm finally settling flat between his shoulder blades. Making a home there to rub soft circles and attempt comfort despite not knowing how. That is, she knew well how, only there seemed a peculiarity to the air around them – the sense of what they had just escaped – that made the upset that bit worse. She could have cried, then, for the feeling of his spine arched and taut beneath her fingers.

''M fine,' said Denny.

'You're not.'

Hissing like a cat, spitting, he kicked at the snow with his boots and covered the mess. Her hand stayed, sliding higher to curl around his collarbone, fastened tight. With the way he shook, she prepared for another set of convulsions in the dark and belatedly noticed he wasn't wearing a coat.

'You must be freezing,' she said.

'You too,' he said. She was – in only her wool sweater and jeans. Neither sought to remedy the fact. Instead, Denny stood straight and slipped from her hold. He walked around the far side of the bar – to the outbuildings that stored all manner of machinery and equipment that she was not privy to – and cracked open the lid of a rain barrel. The drainpipe above was frosted and glittered in what dim light cast through the bar windows; kerosene lamps and stacks of dripping candles that were scraped off the bar's sills and melted back down with Jeanie Specker's beeswax. In the dark, Opal stood next to Denny; leeched off what little heat he radiated as he hacked through the layer of ice in the barrel with the butt of his buck knife. Were it slightly warmer, he might have been able to push it down like a dinner plate, and let the water flood between his fingers, but the nights were growing colder with every passing day; they were well on their way toward the dark winter. In that moment, she felt rather suddenly the certainty that she was not prepared for everything to come. She was built for it, yes, but not under such cruel conditions. Not when it felt much better to be there – on the outside, in the burning cold – than inside, where all manner of things felt so far beyond her comprehension or control that she saw it better to freeze. Denny splashed his face with water, swirled it around in his mouth, and spat it out at his feet. Opal did not cringe, she did not move an inch. He swiped at his mouth, his eyes. He looked to her.

'C'mere,' he said like an apology, and led her to a log on its side near the inky tree line. She sat, mindful of what might wet her trousers, and he sat closer. A foot between them, give or take, so far from touching and content to sit in the cold dark, side by side. It was calm and his earlobes were dripping water onto his downturned shoulders; like a diamond earring in the half-light. He could have been so elegant, with his cheeks drawn high, eyes sharp; nose broken both ways, almost straightening itself out.

'Will I fetch Maude?' she asked. And she would. Fit to dart for the door and swipe the child clean from her father's hold.

He shook his head. 'Sarge'll bring her back to bed. Pa's— He's done with her now.'

A fear previously unknown to Opal took over – distilled down to a point so fine that, were she to touch it, the feeling might have gone unnoticed as it pierced her skin. She could see in Denny what it meant to have your heart welded to the palm of another; to have no choice in the matter. Because sacrifice was a choice, but where was the choice in loving your own father? No, such a thing only ever tallied to a loss.

Drink after drink, why didn't he stop? Denny, a grown man – with more height and muscle on him than most – rolling over to reveal his soft belly underneath. He allowed the knife and the twisting; he met it with each mouthful swallowed. And the alternative a bluff, surely, yet Opal knew by the frantic manner in which Denny drank every drop that there was no option, no ultimatum – it was do as you are told or have your still-beating heart crushed in the palm of his hand.

Her own heart ached at the thought. Denny smiled as if he knew, and she caught a dart of red at the corner of his mouth; drying down to maroon where the pink of his lips met stubble.

'There was blood in your sick,' she said. 'Denny, we should—'

Hand to her wrist, loose and gentle, he stopped her. ''S not what you're thinkin'. Busted a tooth out a few days back.'

As he spoke, she saw it herself: the void where a molar should have sat snug. Immovable. *Busted*, he said, yet there was no swelling, no damage to the surrounding teeth. So precise. Such a thing to have lost in a fall, even in a thump.

And Opal recalled another tooth, swallowed clean in the summer, verdant moss floating around small feet in the shallow water of the creek. Denny's ruinous eyes, and how they had been so filled with the very same concern she was now showing him. A black dread settled deep within her.

Pinching the thick wool of her sleeve over her fingers, she dabbed his chin with every ounce of tenderness she possessed; she dragged her thumb carefully up the curve of where a smile ought to be, but never seemed to quite fit. Denny sat utterly still in the snow as if he didn't know how to be, and she worried that she had crossed some invisible line between them that neither could see beyond. *This is a trap*, she thought to herself. *This is a place you cannot be.* But Denny was only looking – deep, dark eyes swallowing up all the light of the vast cobalt above as if the stars existed within them – and she, looking back. Stripped clean to the bone, an exposed nerve; it was not the cold that did it, but another beast entirely.

This, too, was quite enough.

December 1981

IN THE DREAM, her wicker heart beats in threes. It creaks to the point of splintering, full of apples from the day's harvest. There are plenty, picked at the most perfect time by delicate hands that held them as if they were eggs, or the soft skull of a child. Their stems pierce the gaps in between, each a pinch and a tug that weave themselves into the tapestry of her heart. The fruit will rot within her when the time comes.

But time does not come in this place, nor does it move at all. The sun stays high in the sky like a ball of melting butter. It weeps down into the lakes and rivers and feeds the salmon in their wide-open mouths. Hunger scrapes her insides, but she can only watch as the fish leap in wide arcs of light, landing with ripples that sound through the mountains in beautiful song. They are so loud that she fears in her heaving chest that they might cause an avalanche.

The mountains rise and fall, and she stands regardless. So, why is it that her knees tremble when the tumble of powdery white approaches? They miss her, she knows deeply – back in the valley, where she will always be welcome. She was born there, she ought to die there too. This is a certainty to find solace in – she feels her father's swollen, knotted digits form a vice around her wrist, her throat. The people watch on, and they rejoice. They thank her for her service to the valley. The sun melts down upon them in gratitude.

She can't meet her end in the snow. Not alone. Not with these – these strangers who took her and who want to *keep* her. A cold corpse – violet lips and veins, lashes frozen solid all the way to the root and into her—

'Bunny.'

A musical whisper, a calloused finger swooping down the bridge of her nose. The tip is cold to the point of numbness. It's Ma. Her dark brown eyes are amber in the morning light, with black flecks like insects trapped in honey.

'I saved you some breakfast,' she says.

Ma's chin sits on top of her folded hands. She's at a level with the mattress, her feet curled beneath her on the floor. She smiles at Maude who tries to give her one back, but she can't feel her mouth either.

Maude's feet touch the thin rug through her thick woollen socks. The cold reaches her bones before she has the chance to flinch, but Ma sets her right with a pair of slippers; bent at the knee still with her head bowed. Fingers tangle with her own and she is torn from the bed, toward the room with the fire, which is lit, and Baby, who is laughing.

'Oh, you're just hilarious.' Ma waves in the vague direction of the cot they got for cheap at the consignment; pale blue and peeling, with Bear's stick drawings along the planks.

Baby makes some noises that are high and sharp, then swings low into snot-filled grunts. She sounds like the pigs back home.

Baby can look like a pig too sometimes, when her face is all screwed up and red from crying or exertion. She's about as useful when it comes down to it.

'Has she eaten?' Maude asks.

''Course she has,' Ma says lightly. 'She'd have let you know otherwise.'

Maude thinks of all the nights prior – Da's quiet cursing at the screeching from those tiny lungs, letting Baby gum his fingers up with spit and snot. Maude knows what it's like when children grow teeth.

On the stovetop, a plate of flaky fish steams a white cloud, caught from the lake only yesterday. Ma serves it up on the crockery they found at the same consignment store – a set of dinner plates, side plates, soup bowls, cups and saucers, a milk jug and a sugar pot; missing one entire place setting with every second piece chipped or scratched with grey lines. The plates have orange and yellow flowers at the centre, hemmed by navy curving leaves.

'Great,' Maude says of the fish. At her feet, the cat cries in envy. 'Again.'

Ma shrugs. 'Da likes it.'

Maude can't imagine Da ever announcing that he likes anything. Ma's just hearing what she wants to hear.

'It's OK,' she relents. She picks at the fish with her fingers, the heat of it burns. It's dry on her tongue and struggles on its way down. For a fraction of a second, she wishes to be back in her terrible dream.

'You shouldn't do things just because Da likes them,' she says. Ma must know this. She's been in the wide world far longer than Maude. Maude's only knowing it now because it took her so long to see in the deep dark.

Ma's bright gaze wavers for a moment. Her fingers sink into the knots on the old table and, behind her, Baby cries out at the lack of attention. Maude moves to quiet her while Ma stands frozen. The cot is close to tipping on the floor with how Baby leans against its side. She's nowhere near standing on her own yet, but she's growing stronger and fatter by the day. Soon, her knitted clothes will stretch beyond their capabilities and leave large holes behind to thoroughly freeze her in the winter. Awkwardly, Maude manoeuvres Baby onto her hip and walks back over to the table.

'Did I say something wrong?' she asks, remaining at arm's length.

Ma shakes her head, slowly, as if trapped in a daze, and then furiously. Her gaze lifts from the plate of rapidly cooling fish and arrives at Maude.

She says, 'It won't be like that here, Bun. It will *never* be like that. You understand, don't you?'

There is a severity to Ma that often lands when Maude is least prepared for it. It arrives quickly, a strike that makes you bleed before you even realise you've been bitten. In times like this, she wishes she could ask Ma to hold her.

'Yes.' Maude nods. 'I understand.'

Ma smiles, teeth flashing bright. She sends Baby an indulgent, open-mouthed laugh and a small wave. The child screeches in delight, bouncing with such strength in her limbs that Maude struggles to support her, but tries her best anyway.

*

The boy can't lift his legs high enough to clear the snow. His trousers are soaked as far as the knee, small hands red-raw and frozen around the handle of the buck knife Denny gave him when they set out that morning. He holds it like he's wielding a sword, straining with the weight of it but wanting to keep it anyway. Opal thought it was too dangerous. Opal doesn't understand. Denny's been hunting and skinning animals since he could put one foot in front of the other; long days that are a blur to him flash by like they've been distorted by the smudge of a spit-wet thumb. Blood in the water, the knick of a gem against his cheek; cutting teeth on the curl of a fist. He missed that shot five times over before the consequences came about. No boots for the journey home – calluses and thickened skin amounted to nothing against the elements that tore his soles open to hot and swollen infection. Pa held his boots in one hand, cigar in the other, and paid no mind to the way he cried. Served him right for making a creature suffer so much, for not being able to put it out of its misery. Only Denny tried, lined the shot up real nice, for Pa to

203

nudge and shove and throw him off. For him to stumble back to the big house, tail between his legs, leaving little red footprints in his wake.

It's time that Billy learn – led by a hand that's gentle and coaxing – even if he can hardly walk right on the best of days. He's not slow – not by any means – but he's a child in the way that none of them were taught to be.

'Bun said if we don't find no food soon, she's gon' eat my fingers.'

'Ain't much meat on 'em,' Denny says. 'Better off goin' for your toes.'

Billy regards his booted feet with heavy consideration. They're in dire need of replacement, but Horatio isn't paying Denny for another five days. There are other things too: diapers for the baby, flour and corn and gas to last them through the month. Opal makes lists and Denny tries his best not to look at them, for how long they stretch.

'My foots sure is cold,' Billy says, bending the nose of the boots until they crease. Denny shrugs, weaving through a tight burst of trees, Billy on his tail. He holds the bent branch of a spruce aside for Billy to dip under. Powdery clumps of snow fall onto the boy's woollen hat; he shakes them off like a dog.

''S all right,' says Denny. 'We'll cook 'em up over the fire. Nice 'n' crispy like shrimp.'

The boy stumbles. Denny rights him with a grip on the hood of his coat.

'What's shrimp?' he asks. This was not something readily available back in the valley, as there were no large bodies of salt water to scoop them from. Even if there were, Gideon would never have bothered – he hated things that were *different*: like shampoo, clementines, olive oil. Anything that was unfamiliar, or came in fancy packaging or plastic, with cigarettes and hooch being the exception.

'Little boy's toes that grow at the bottom of the ocean,' says Denny.

Billy nods sagely, then pauses. Face bunched up in a rosy frown, he asks, 'What's a ocean?'

'It's where all us people grew our legs,' he says without thinking. 'Underwater. With the fish.'

'Fish ain't live in a ocean. They in the rivers *and* cricks.'

'Salmon can live in all of 'em, though there ain't much livin' in a crick – too small, see.' The voice of Buster Chaps rings like a bell in Denny's ear. 'That's what the ocean's for. So damn big they can g'on live happy wherever they want.'

Smug and smirking, Billy nudges him like they're in on a secret. 'Like us, huh?' All Gid suddenly, with the familiarity, the endearing snark.

'Yessir.' Denny grabs him under the arms to lift him over a rotten log that is piled high with snow. It falls in drifts around these parts; heavy and sculpted, a smooth and curving wall. 'You best catch something if you wanna hold onto your toes, so.'

'Yessir!' The boy parrots.

Bright red berries have been crushed underfoot of something. The snow makes it easy to track, muffles the crunch of fall leaves with the soggy blanket of winter. Billy moves

205

through it all like he's waging war on the world, storming into a battle or marching at the head of a parade. To him, it's a big party. Denny hopes it always will be.

They make it to the lake without glimpsing any further signs of life. It's more of a pond, half frozen with flat beds of rock on the shore; tufts of heather frosted by silver, a wispy frame, gilded gold by the emerging sunlight. Whatever they've followed here is long gone, but the hedges that curl around the water rustle with the promise of food. Surprisingly, Billy notices this too, and instead of launching toward the movement like Denny expects, he takes three steps back and hides behind his legs.

'It's comin'.'

'Don't think so,' says Denny.

'I heared it.'

Denny settles on his haunches, so that he and the boy are eye to eye. With a gloved hand, he nudges a brittle branch aside to inspect the underbrush.

'You 'member that snare we set yesterday?'

A chore, really. Maude took to these things much faster when she was Billy's age, but that was to be expected – she knew how to twist the wire around a twig and leave a two-inch tail to make an easier catch as the animal passed through. She could spot a rabbit trail from a mile off. Billy had gotten distracted as Denny made a funnel of the foliage around the snare, shovelling clumps of dirty snow into his mouth like he'd spent forty days in the desert.

'Under the leafs?'

Denny nods. 'Well, I'd bet you it caught somethin'.'

'Ta eat?'

'Yeah, ta eat,' he laughs. 'We ain't gonna keep it as a pet.'

'Do I hafta eat Memphis?'

'I reckon Bun will if we don't nab somethin' soon.'

Her patience with the dog is wearing thin – Denny wishes she'd see what he sees. But she was wired different, got it all crossed somewhere along the way. Memphis is no good for hunting, and pisses on the floor when it storms hard. Maude hates when Denny pets him, feeds him from the table, throws sticks out in the yard for him to chase into the tree line. Pa treated dogs and people much the same, and that was the problem.

Denny lifts the branches high so Billy can see under the hedge too. The boy's mittens curl around the shelf of his shoulder, a cloud of white from his mouth fogging up his vision. Trapped in the snare, there's a tawny rabbit with wide eyes, dark and vacant, tiny breaths and twitching whiskers. He knows that Billy won't watch this part. For some reason, he is glad for it.

A snip and a slice, blood in the snow like the berries they tracked, like the footprints his dreams follow.

'It go sleep?'

'Yeah,' says Denny. 'You can look now.'

Billy's cold nose is pressed to the nape of his neck, eyes no doubt squeezed shut like when he doesn't want to eat his vegetables. Denny should make him look, grab him by the scruff and squeeze with the threat left unspoken. If he sees all of the terrible things now, his mind might protect him. He might not remember. But there are times too when Denny wishes so desperately to remember, because truth might be found in the pulp; in the blood and dirt between his fingers.

''S dead, Bear.' A sigh of relief is shared in the press of Billy's chest to his back. He stands up, catching the boy as he stumbles forward without something to lean on. 'C'mon,' he says, tying the rabbit to the boy's belt. He needs to grow used to the weight of it. 'We gotta dice up half of this for Mrs Schweers. Then you can take the rest home to your Ma and sister.'

Billy looks sullenly at his new accessory, the colour of his lips fading to a dull pink. Denny curls a finger beneath his chin, forces their twin eyes to meet. So many times, he has been at the receiving end of this touch – fit for scolding, knowing that every bit of him is wrong; because he was scared, and only small. All things are meant for dying, some sooner than others, but it's no sin to be sad about it.

Denny smiles, wide and true. 'A bunny for Bunny.'

Billy grabs Denny's hand in both of his own and the terror falls victim to a squeal of delight. The noise sounds a song into the mountains, and echoes far further than memory will ever reach.

*

The car's engine buckles to a stop in the drive. Someone's come along and grit the paving for Mrs Schweers – Denny would have, if only she'd asked. Billy doesn't get out of his seat yet, because he knows quite well not to. They're only flying by, no need to do any more. The children have been welcomed time and time again into the woman's home, which is enough giving. Denny loathes the thought of imposing. He takes the steps made of brick, with twisted, cast-iron railings. The welcome mat is painted with faded cursive lettering, and there is a boot scraper in the shape of a smiling hedgehog to the left. While he has wrapped the rabbit in some burlap, to simply leave it on the front stoop feels tactless in a way that he is trying so hard not to be. Surely, Opal has a special spot for the game some-where. Or she passes it directly into Mrs Schweers' frail hands while the children run out to the car. Denny has no exchange to make, only a deposit. So, he rings the bell and feels far smaller than he ever remembers being. It chimes prettily in the silent evening. There's a pause, the weighty swing of a moment forgotten, then he turns. He's down the steps and halfway to the car when the front door opens. He does not stop, carries on as if he hasn't noticed she's there – it's the polite thing to do, surely. Then her voice calls, loud and hoarse, across the drive.

'Are you a dog?' she asks. Denny stays put, eyes on Billy and the car. 'Bring that boy of yours up here and carry my dinner into the house.'

*

Bear kicks his muddy feet, out-in-out, bouncing on the spring of the soft bench. He has to wait for Da to sort the buckle, that's the rule. Da's no dog; no cat neither. Cat

209

leaves tiny, baby mice called shrews at the door; all cut up and dead against the screen. Da would never – says all the time that there ain't any use in killing the small things when there's nothing to eat from them. Bear knows Bun wasn't going to eat his fingers and toes, but he knows she likes to eat small things – like worms and bugs that Gid would have smacked him around for even touching. Sometimes, Bun will hold a rat up by its tail, screeching, just to watch it break off and scramble down into the leaves.

Missus didn't smack Bear around when he touched the hot metal. She was angry, and she yelled, but when she touched Bear, it was only to give his steaming hand that was red and sticky a soft kiss. Run it under the faucet until the cold won out. It hurt a lot then, but on his insides too. Bear cried like Baby always does, and couldn't rightly stop until Ma came in the car with Da to pick them all up. Bear spent hours and hours tucked under Missus' arm, nose running and wetting her purple cardigan. She smelled of soup and flowers, and she told Bear that he could keep all the new clothes they found up there in the attic. Every day now, he gets to wear a new shirt; different colours, big and small. He's wearing one under his winter coat, under the sweater that he shares with Bunny. Da tucked the sweater into his pants before they went on their hunt, but bunches of it are slipping from the band as he lifts Bear from his seat and drops him onto the ground; even more falls out and swishes around his legs when he runs for Missus' front door, for the spiky thing where he's meant to clean his boots. He holds the railing with each step, because Bun said it will stop him from falling, and scrapes his boots on the spiky, even though he's going to take them off inside the door anyway. Da does the same, watches where Bear sticks them under the bench, climbs on it to hang his winter coat on the hook that's special, just for him.

'You can put it with mine,' Bear says of Da's coat, because Da doesn't have a hook.

'Thanks,' says Da. They go to the kitchen, but there's no more heater where Bear burned his hand. It's gone, and the plug holes in the wall that he's not meant to touch either are empty. After his burn, Missus showed him all of the things in her house that he must stay away from.

'Da,' says Bear, yanking on his sleeve. 'Did you knowed not to touch the plugs?'

Missus smiles real big at this. Da pulls on Bear's ear. 'Had no idea,' he says. 'Thanks for tellin' me, bo'.'

'You're welcome,' says Bear.

He climbs into his chair, the one with the yellow cushion, and turns on the seat until he's close to the table. There's some newspapers there, like what Missus uses to clean the windows, and some glasses for her face that help her see. Da looks at the newspaper that's open, sometimes; he reads stories to Bear from the almanack and Bear gets to ask questions after about things he doesn't understand. There are lots of things he doesn't understand, not yet, but Da is very good at explaining.

Missus puts a tin cup of milk on the table. It's warm, but not hot, so Bear knows he is allowed to touch it. He blows on the top like Ma told him to, and takes a very small sip – because a big sip will make him sick, and there is always more, he is only to ask. Da doesn't have milk, but Missus asks him if he wants a cup of Sanka.

'What's that?' Da says.

'Ain't nice,' Bear tells him. It's brown and burnt and much too hot. 'Have some milk.'

'Coffee,' says Missus, tapping Bear on the head. 'Special decaf. Get it shipped in from the States. Wholesale.'

Da makes a noise like the car when it rumbles. Bear likes the feeling of it against his ear when it's Da's turn to put them to bed and he carries Bear like he's Baby. He takes a sip of Bear's milk and lifts the cup in thanks. 'G'on then,' he says. 'I'll have a go.'

The cup is on the table again, right in front of Bear. Maybe Da didn't like it. That's OK, there are lots of things that Bear doesn't like and Ma says it's no problem at all, so long as he has manners about it. No spitting, swiping, smacking. *No thank you*, she says and he copies back.

'I'll have a go,' Bear says to Missus as she pours Da's cup, because he wants the Sanka too, even if he hates the taste.

'You don't like it,' she says. 'I'm not wasting it on you.'

'Please.'

Missus makes a frowning face. 'Billy, don't be ridiculous.'

'Y'all said I was only to ask.'

'No back talk,' Da says and Bear jumps in his seat.

'Yes, Da,' he says. 'But I was only to ask.'

It was something they had to drill into him after finding rotting food under his and Maude's bed. Opal sniffed it out, made Denny come and look under the guise of helping her with the fitted sheet. It was no animal, no skin left from a hunt that hadn't been cleaned – Maude knew better – but heaps of rotted fruit and blue spongy bread; half a loaf that went missing a few weeks prior and the dog lost his supper for. Candies in their wrappers and a furled-up bag of potato chips with some stale crumbs rattling around the bottom. His bear was there too, soaking in it all. They cleared it: dumped the trash and steeped the bear in baking soda and boiling water, then left him to dry in a sack of used coffee grounds from the diner so as to banish the smell. Billy howled something awful and tore at his hair until it seemed fit to peel from his scalp.

Denny slides his mug across the table. 'Take a sup of mine.' Mrs Schweers cuts him with a look he can't solve. Billy's stubby fingers pinch around the cup, feet swinging happily under the table and knocking Denny's shins now and then. He will sip and screw up his face and, like clock-work, tell them both *I don't like it*. Sure enough, things go in precisely that order. Denny takes it back and finds, unsurprisingly, that he also doesn't like it. But he swallows each mouthful gladly, ignoring the burn, the bitter grit.

Billy is given another cup of milk. Cold this time, but clearly plenty. There's a space for talking that needs filling, but Denny doesn't know what to put there. He used to be better, but that was in a world of his father's creation – not easy or seamless, but with people making the effort where he lacked. Mrs Schweers has no such obligation, no Pa to intimidate her. *Nobody* to intimidate her. He feels the painful draw backward into himself, and holds the mug with both hands to give the impression of intent. Mrs Schweers tracks the movement with the weathered eyes of a hunter, who could make the hit and land it but, to his careful surprise, chooses not to. The egg timer saves him, ringing shrill like screaming; enough to move him in his seat. Billy bounces too, with a delighted trickle of laughter, and stands to lean over the back of the chair and eye up what's been cooking.

'What's this here?' he asks. Denny places his foot on the rung to stop him toppling forward.

'I'm steaming a pudding,' says Mrs Schweers.

'Like pie?'

'No.'

'Like ice cream?'

'Can't steam ice cream,' she says. 'It'd only melt.'

'Oh.' Billy slumps, knees bent. Denny places a second foot on the rung. 'What's you steamin' then?'

'A pudding.'

Billy's curls frizz and expand in the heat of the kitchen. His face is flush as he lets loose a screeching laugh, swinging forward to pull at the back of Mrs Schweers' cardigan.

'*Duh*,' he says. 'I knowed that.'

'It's a Christmas pudding,' she says. 'There's fruit in it.'

'Oh. Yum,' he says, licking his lips. The skin around his mouth is red raw from how often he does this, and the bitter cold only worsens the stain. 'I'll have a go.'

'Billy,' Denny scolds.

'*Please*,' says Billy. He rubs his round tummy, where it pokes out through the thick wool of his sweater. 'Oh, it smells just *lovely*, Missus.'

It does smell lovely: sweet and sharp, like lemon cake with cherries and syrup. Peppery cloves and cinnamon, a hint of something that spikes like a dig to the ribs – rum, maybe – and is only made stronger by the steam that wafts it around the kitchen in a heavy perfume. The feeling runs away with him, out the window and well into the trees where the animals lay sleeping for the long and violent winter. Other houses with other doors and windows; flower boxes and hanging baskets emptied for the cold and replaced with sprigs of holly, Lenten rose, winter jasmine and poinsettias that hardly last the week. Inside, everything is bronze, glazed walnut, black and white marble tops with family portraits in gilded frames, everybody smiling on snowy slopes in matching clothes. A woman sings, high and keening, fingers on ivory keys. The turntable spins and threatens to unspool the thread; the candles flicker and flash white.

'Da, look!'

The water is no longer boiling. Mrs Schweers has wrapped the pudding in a red and white dishcloth, fastened in a knot at the top to keep the heat in. Billy holds it in his arms like a prize won. Like a Christmas present. Denny smiles, feet slipping off the rung of the chair. He reaches out to pat the boy on the back, hand lingering between his shoulders for closeness at the upset he feels press so readily against his breastbone.

'It's too much,' he says. 'We wanted to give you the rabbit.'

'And you gave me the rabbit,' says Mrs Schweers. 'Now take the pudding.'

'But it's too much.'

'Oh,' she says with a frown. 'I think it's just the right amount, hm? About ten pounds of pudding there, which is plenty to last you through Christmas.'

They don't have a stitch for Christmas – Opal never mentioned it. Is she working on something that she hasn't said to him, thinking he'd be no good at it anyway? The pudding would be soft enough for Baby, though the taste might bother her. And Maude, well, she would love it. Billy already loves it, even if the loving is just at the thought that he can store it under his bed.

He says, 'I'll get you another rabbit. Two.'

Billy beams. 'I will catch it.'

Mrs Schweers' purple-spotted hand falls softly on top of Billy's head. She musses his hair and smiles down at Denny, who can't move, not really, for how uncertain he feels.

'Two's a deal. But don't leave it at my door this time,' she scolds. 'Don't need an invitation when you took my other house without one.'

Denny flushes and comes to a stand, prepared to apologise when her look slices the words right from his tongue. 'Yes, ma'am.'

Billy looks up at the pair. 'You Ma too?'

'Oh, Jesus!' Hands over her eyes, she shoos them down the hall and to the door. 'Go home, the lot of you. I want two rabbits.'

'Two rabbits,' says Denny.

'Two bunnies,' says Billy.

'Oh, no,' says Mrs Schweers. 'I don't want to see hide nor hair of that girl until after the holidays.'

'Yes, *mayum*,' says Billy. Denny nods. He holds the pudding while Billy slips on his shoes and they swap over when laces have to be tied and coats buttoned. The boy cradles the pudding to his chest, despite the weight and heat of it, and vaults down the front steps, boots skidding on the grit pavement.

'Billy!' Mrs Schweers wraps her cardigan tight, yells at him from the doorway. 'Mind you don't fall.'

'Might do him some good,' says Denny.

She hums, looking at him out of the corner of her eye while they watch Billy run circles around the yard, kicking up tufts of snow from the grass. 'How do you mean?'

'Means . . .' He falters. 'Means that he'll think twice about getting hurt again. Be more careful about where he treads.'

'I think you'll find that children rarely think twice,' she says. 'So, you do your best to make sure there's good, solid ground under his feet.'

'Yes, ma'am.'

She nods. 'Go on home, now. I'll see you all in a few days.'

'Thank you,' he says, though the words will never come close.

'Don't mention it.'

Denny opens the passenger side door and puts Billy on the seat, pudding first. His cheeks are rosy red from the cold and with his bright curls glowing in the darkening daylight, he is an angel. He looks up at Denny and smiles with gapped teeth, all gums, legs swinging in the footwell. Without thinking, Denny leans over and presses his cold nose to the boy's crown, planting a kiss to his curls.

'Good day?' he asks, hoping with every bit of him that it was.

'Good day, Da.'

December 1976

IT WAS THE COLD that saved Gideon: slowed the flow of blood, froze the mangled stump; but it came at the cost of coal-black flesh. Doc Froy cut away segments of dead tissue until what remained was little more than a slim, white thigh, covered sparsely by hairs and smudgy, violet bruising. Denny sits with Gideon all those days, fed only during Buster's lunchtime checks: temperature, a finger drawing lines Denny's eyes must follow, made to eat a bite or two and sip water from a canteen like he is once more twelve and entirely helpless to a terrible sickness of his own making.

There is a welt on Denny's head the size of an egg, weeping blood down into his eye; it dries to a thin crust across his skin, sticky and flaking onto the clothes they gave him. They're not his, nor are the shoes on his feet and the socks beneath. He came from the mouth in something else and they burned it, he knows. He remembers the smell, and little else after that but the residing ache. A terrible weight and Minty, hurtling forward on all fours, dizzy from a knock to the head and vomiting on the snow. Gideon carried on his aching back, a single foot dragging tracks behind them in a line unbroken. Denny would have carried him forever if that was what it took. He tried to carry them all, but could hardly take a step.

Gideon's girl won't come, fearful thing that she is – said it would upset the baby, whose colic is worsening by the day – so Denny fulfils the role as best he can: mopping sweat from Gideon's brow, wetting his lips with a damp cloth. The sheets smell stale, sharp like spirits and scabbing. There isn't much to do but wait, though nobody knows what for. Doc says that the risk of infection is high, that more of the leg could be lost; that the other limbs aren't necessarily safe. He says that Minty's got a grade-three concussion and two broken ribs. That James took a long time to die, by the sounds of it, but that he need not be sad, because it could have been much worse.

In what little sleep he can grasp, Denny dreams of birds in their flocks, cutting fissures across the sky; fingers sunken to the knuckle in loose, dark dirt; James's eyes, clear and bright and empty, holding his own. Concentric circles of beaming silver. They keep dying and he sits comfortably in the grave. The earth falls on his hair in powdery clumps, it compacts and takes all the air away. He sees himself as a skeleton, curled tenderly around blank spaces and corpses. He sees himself with friends.

Each time, he jolts awake, a creak in his neck from the strain of the chair. His ass has long since numbed, joints stiff and tight, hands tucked into fists that refuse to loosen. Ivy could climb the trunk of him and root him there for eternity were it not for the shaking; the rattle of bloodied and muddied fingers, the tick of his jaw. The very world vibrates in his vision. The sun never quite makes it through the window, never quite passes the pallor of their skin. Gideon is a few pounds of flesh covered in white sheets; if not for the sharp whistle of air through his nostrils, Denny would think him dead. He reaches for Gideon's hand, takes it, but something awful creeps upon him and he must let go. He rights the edges of Gideon's comforter, pours water from a jug to a glass that Gideon cannot drink. A touch of skin to skin finds him a fever, a flush of infection that Doc Froy warned against. Maybe Sarge will drive back to the city and find some better medicine. Maybe Denny will, for the first time in his life, if only he can get his hands on some keys. If only Pa would think it worth the hassle.

But Denny is of no use to anyone in his current state: shaking, fragile at the seams of himself. He hasn't seen hide nor hair of Maude, who he is desperate to lay eyes on, but fearful of. He cannot be what she needs in this state. There's no room for thoughts of now when he dreams with eyes wide open of decades prior, of a time when bad things meant bloody knees, a slip in the snow, a holler from Sarge, a smack on the ear from Mrs Bass. A precarious winter adventure, a joy for two boys of only twelve, looking for the steepest of hills to sled along, to rip down in quick whips that burned their cheeks red. They came across a hole in the ground like his Pa worked in, a mouth where the snow had melted, warmed by a lick of flames, by those inside. Gideon threw rocks at the people when they came to gather snow into buckets; he said they were lurkers on the mountains, stealing their lot. But Denny reckoned there was nothing to steal, not from the earth. The snow was going to melt anyway, it would be a waste not to drink it. And besides, if there was more silver, Pa would already know something about it, wouldn't he? He, at least, would have gone looking. Denny hoped that Gideon would not blab, that he might keep this to himself. There was no need to drag Pa all the way out here for some people warming themselves by the fire, drinking some melted snow. What was the harm in that? Plenty, turns out. Pa said those Indians had no damn right to camp out in a place that didn't belong to them. But did any of it belong to any of them? The mountains would be there long after Pa was gone, long after Denny and Gid too. After Maude, and Gideon's baby. Pa just likes a fight, is all. The break of skin under a fist, a blade, a bullet. Pa's not afraid of what it looks like for all of the insides to come out of a person.

But Denny is, turns out.

And sure, they found silver, plenty of it – Denny was given brand-new boots and a buck knife the length of his arm for his thirteenth birthday – but attacking those Indians, driving them away with the threat of gunfire, amounted to nothing in the grand scheme of things; Pa is still running out of ore. He got greedy, mined too much too fast. Going down the mining shaft – situated in a clearing well beyond the big house, a relic of his father's family legacy – was a last resort, Denny knows that. And still, he can't help but wonder if he and Gid hadn't found the Indians, hadn't reported back, would Pa have been forced to use the shaft sooner? Would he have sent Denny down with only Minty and Gid? Would he have gone down himself with Sarge and Buck? Would the cage have held their weight long enough to make it back up again without snapping from its cable, plummeting all the way down and shredding the earth in its wake? The thing is: there is silver down there, plenty of it, but now James is too, and neither will ever see the surface.

Denny feels the rumble of footsteps as familiar as his own shadow. His Pa and that Midas touch. Waiting days to clear the threshold of the infirmary as if his presence were a blessing to behold by his own son. And yet, Denny finds his gaze lifting toward the sun, a gentle tilt of his chin by a crooked finger and it is all too bright. Too much. After days in the dark, it blinds him.

'Dennis,' says Pa. 'You come along with me now.'

Thick, knotted hands hold his own for the first time since childhood. Denny is led away from Gideon and out under the distended clouds; birds flitting between the treetops, trilling the dawn chorus. One foot after the other, stumbling along in Pa's shadow and oh, how safe he feels there. The early morning light cannot touch him, nor can the black lines of winding branches, so crisp and pointed against the moving sky. Denny watches his father's feet as they trudge through mud and snow, keep in time and do not drag. Purpled hands like a vice, curled around the jut of his swollen shoulder.

He fears that Gideon will die in his absence or wake entirely alone to the blurred and pale cloud world of the infirmary. That he will be frightened and confused, crying for his dead Ma, crying for Denny the way he did when they ran from what happened to the Indians and he split the skin of his knee open on a taut and rusted wire fence. It occurs to him in a blank sort of way that he is the only one who can speak to what happened – Minty was unconscious for the majority of it, Gideon feverish and dying. He force-fed them half-melted snow from his busted canteen, from the shaking cup of his palm. He ought to have tried harder, remembered more. But all the details are mixed up, the focus all wrong. Pa's hand is an anchor, and the only thing he really knows.

Outside the mess, there are rows of mourners – heads bowed, hands clasped – arranged neatly along the wall. Denny scans the crowd in search of Opal, but she is not there. He only sees women in dirty aprons, men who will have to work twice as hard now with their numbers cut by a quarter. And they know it was all him, because it was he they wished luck to before the final descent, he they congratulated on such a responsibility in his Pa's absence. Miss Gunn packed their sandwiches, their water, Jerry made sure their headlamps were in good working order, and Buster manned the truck, reversing it slowly and quietly well before dawn painted the cabins. All Denny had to do was make sure nobody got hurt.

'Listen here!' Pa speaks and every eye falls to him, cutting through Denny as if he is but a small tree in their line of sight. Pa tells them how it is, how it was; what happened. Who died. Who lost their leg and who lost their head and then he points to Denny, and all of a sudden he is more to them than a slant of the horizon. He is an obstacle, a face to condemn. Their only pity is spared for their leader, who has to punish his own son for these unforgivable blunders. Pa never mentions the silver or the escape; how Denny dragged his mangled friend through the space they had dug all those months before. How the stopes he drilled and Minty filled back in March held up long enough for the three of them to squeeze out of there and haul themselves back up the adit, Gid's body slung into a cart like a sorry clump of ore. Not once does he say why they were in such a rush to get down the shaft in the first place.

'You can understand,' Pa says. 'How this might be difficult for me. My own son. He was responsible for these men and it's under his watch that one of them died. A horrible, slow death at that. And our poor Gid! Only one leg and a baby new to this world. To take away a man's ability to provide for his kin . . .' Pa's nose curls, his grip tightens. 'My son, hacking the limb off on his own misguided whim.'

Denny flinches.

'But I know my boy, and y'all know him too! Wasn't it you that fed and clothed him, taught him our ways?' Not a single nod is given, but their silence says enough. The shame is clear, the pain in the dozens of pairs of eyes that spill water at his very feet. 'We raised him up together with our own hands. Became a family for him after he lost his dear mother.'

Denny's insides churn. The trees above spin of their own accord, curled ribs closing in. Pa is no tether, but a hook that's made its cut bone-deep; that's been bleeding sluggishly for decades with each little tug. There is no air here with these thousand eyes and their unbridled sorrow. He sees their faces and he can't remember even a single detail of what hers was like. *His dear mother.*

'I—'

'Quiet now, son,' Pa barks, pinching the bones of his hand. Denny holds fast. 'Don't you think you've done enough?'

For all his stealth and stamina, Denny has moved through life as if sleepwalking. He knows quite well that he is ill-equipped to deal with a world beyond his father's curation – brutal in his ways, savage in some others, but made easy. Denny could be good, could be all Pa ever wanted, only Pa likes to change the rules for no good reason and leave Denny in the lurch; knowing that no matter what he does, good will never be good enough. Denny let him. Truth is, Pa could ask anything of him and he would do it gladly.

'You do this for us, son,' Pa says, lingering long on the end, all the space left to fill with whatever terrible thought occurs. Fit to be skinned alive before all, scorched or sliced or hung in damnation. Denny can no longer feel his feet, his hands; nought but the fierce thrum of his heart like a warning. 'Spare us the pain.'

Where else is he supposed to be if not here? What is he meant to say to make it better? Pa never gave him the right words, not for this. Maybe he's gone for good, left below with James, who is nothing now other than dead. Dead like his own mother. Oh, his dear *mother*.

'I—' Denny breathes, slow and deep; a crackle and catch in his throat. 'I'm sorry. I'm – I'm really sorry.'

He breaks apart under the watch of those faceless masses – who have always stood and been voiceless too; not for it having been taken from them, but for the way they gave it willingly. Pa won't hold his hand anymore, but Denny still follows – herded by Sarge – because what is there to do but place one detached foot in front of the other? What is there to say but his sorrys, over and over and over until it is just the three of them on the short and winding path to the big house, where he will fall as easily as flesh from the bone and be swallowed, digested.

'Pa, please,' he says. Sarge's hand makes a fist in his shirt, nails catching his skin. 'Please, don't . . .'

He longs for Old Buster and the quiet of the shed, for him to make it go away somehow. To feel the walls close tight around him and press careful hands to his back, his arms and shoulders. For the light to cradle his face and not burn in such a hurry. He's had many chances, opportunities to put a stop to all of this before things went further than they could come back from. But Denny's a rotten coward, and he loves his father, far more than he's ever loved himself.

So, inside the house he kneels by his bed. Shirt off, head bowed. This is his lot, and it's been their way for as long as he can remember. Say your prayers, Dennis. His dear mother, did she know how rotten he was? Rotten down to the very middle of him. He braces himself.

But the rules are always changing; this time, the blow never comes.

'This here's all mine, Den, but I'll let you have it to keep you going at your new place.'

Pa's got one leg crossed over the other as he gestures broadly. He's always thought these objects so silly, childish, pathetic. Ornaments, buttons, brushes, empty photo frames and only one filled by anything worth looking at: Maude in her dungarees, with redcurrant jelly dribbling down her chin. That belongs to him. But none of it – not the books or the playing cards, carved woodland animals, or dried flowers – means a thing. His friend is dead. Denny sits on his bed while Sarge stands in the doorway, both shoulders brushing the frame. There are all of these things and at the end of the day, it's only dressing. What is there to take but the clothes on his back? And even they don't belong to him.

'What – what you said out there . . .' he starts, gravel in his throat. The lump on his head stings enough to blind him, but he carries on. 'That ain't what happened, Pa. I know it's still bad, but . . . it ain't.'

'Ain't it?'

Pa tilts his head to the side, all curious like. It's a funny story to tell at supper, the punchline of a well-spun joke. Denny burns, skin steaming.

'No. I did – well, I did everythin' I was s'posed to. Like we planned.'

With a put-upon sigh, Pa sits next to him on the bed. Their knees are touching, but Denny's won't stay still. His head is split apart, and Pa only makes it spin faster.

'Are you going to lie to them, son?' he asks.

'It's not. I'm not—' A whisper, then louder. Holds Pa's gaze for as long as he allows.

'So, you're saying it didn't happen?'

'No, he's . . . James, he – Gid lost his fuckin' *leg*.' James is dead. He wasn't even supposed to be there. James died and Denny spent days with that death; slow as molasses, a whimper in the pitch-black.

'And whose fault was that?'

'You said it was *safe*.'

'Did I? Seems to me that was your responsibility, boy. You're no fool – you know to survey the equipment before you go picking away at something that might crumble.'

'You said you already—'

'Oh, so *I'm* a liar now?'

'Pa, *c'mon*.'

Denny remembers the night in the big house, months prior. Maude was playing at his feet, tying the knots of his shoelaces, when his father told him of the plan as if it were brand new and never before discussed. Pa wanted more. They didn't have the gear to sink another shaft. They could chip away at the adit for a few months to see if there was a way into the deposit through the tunnels – only it was taking too long for Pa's patience. He never liked to wait around once he set his sights on something. Forget the repairs to the shaft and the lift mechanism – the one Buster warned them against ever using, for its age and terrible wear – Pa wanted to hoist the cage with a truck and some chains or a steel cable. Three men could do the job, but he stuck James in there anyway, like the extra weight was worth the risk. Their land, their product; they'd find a way into it. It was a way out that they never considered, how to get back up the shaft if it was obstructed; if the rubble got knocked loose and fell heavy like hail showers. Not to worry, so long as there was the potential for more product, more money. Every bit is a success, Pa always said, no matter the loss. A good yield trumped a lost leg, a lost life.

Denny could not find it in himself to agree – the silver that was mined on a daily basis, they saw none of it. Off it was sent to Pa's contacts, the ones he met with on a bi-monthly schedule – with Sarge driving the truck, rifle between his thighs. Eyes were never set on the lustre, only clumps of dry earth, chips of silver hidden within. It wasn't knowing where it went, but having it pass through your hands, if even for a single moment. Pa likes gold because it keeps. But silver is better, silver is softer.

Pa snaps Denny's face between his large hands, fit to mould it into a shape he likes best. Denny's skin still burns, strips peeled, hot and stinging. A song he's heard a thousand times over. Fingers in his mouth, stretched wide in a smile, Denny coughs and groans and tries to pull away, but the hold on his skull is ferocious and burrows so deep it ought to make fissures that split him all apart. There is love in here somewhere, time spent and devotion; did Pa hold him like this when he was little?

Sarge clears his throat. At Pa's glance, he taps his bare wrist.

'Myself and Mint are gonna map out a new route tomorrow,' says Pa. He drops his hands, but the pressure remains. 'See if we can't get back in where he did all that work down the adit.'

Denny gasps greedily at the air, wipes the spit from his chin. 'I can help.'

'Nah, I want you to fill the shaft.' Pa dusts himself off. 'No use in it now.'

Denny never wants to be there again, and yet: 'James is – is – he's still—'

'You deaf?' Smack. 'Is that what happened to you down there? Never listen to a damn thing I say, boy.' Nose to nose, he doesn't remember ever standing, or how Pa's hand got so tight on his collar. 'I piss in your ears and you tell me it's raining.'

But Pa said. He *said*. Denny knows because he always listens to Pa, even when he hates what he's hearing. Denny knows because that evening they talked about it, he washed Maude's hair over the tin basin and thought needlessly, foolishly, that this would be their lot forever. That he could always be this close – to wipe the suds from her eyes and kiss her rosy cheeks. He made sure to dry inside her ears and tie a tight braid down her back – just like Opal showed him – so as to not soak her pillow. But he will never again get to sequester himself inside those minuscule moments in which the world appeared perfect. The absence of it will exist as a drone, a pitchy whine, that tunnels inside his ears; reminding him of all he has lost in such quick succession.

'Pa,' he tries in a great heave. Every limb does its best to defend, protect; curl in and keep the heart safe. Because it knows how this is supposed to go. Knows that his voice will never matter again. 'We oughta tell people the truth. It's only right.'

'We oughta?' Pa bites, like he's fit to take a whole chunk out of him. 'This is on you, Dennis. You wanna tell them that you buried what little of our silver's left so far down that they'll never meet it in this lifetime? You did that. Buried young James down there too, didn't you? All because you couldn't wait to get your hands on his bitch.'

Denny rears back. It's a blow that cuts deeper, bruises darker. That's not what he wanted, it's *not*. For James, for Opal – he ought to be with her, should have gone to her first, told her the truth in his own words, because that's the least she deserves. But is Pa really wrong? This terrible solitude in him had nowhere to go. He willed it into being with such blindness and disregard, he might as well have killed James with his own two hands.

'Well,' Pa says, smiling wide and dangerous. 'Congratulations, son. He's dead and gone.'

It's Sarge who takes him – hauls him out of the only home he knows – down some old game trails to a shack with a hole in its roof, windows broken by him and Gid's childhood dares. Sarge, who never says a single thing when it actually matters, leans over Denny and tells him that this is his lot now, and he best learn to live with it. Denny is his father's son. He is his sister's brother. He had a mother once, but she's faded so far from memory now that maybe she doesn't matter at all. He is a lot of things, but he can't fathom how to be this.

When he thinks of Opal and how he would have told her if he'd only been let, Denny feels, for the first time since it all happened, like crying. It's not something he deserves to do when he so longed for a world that was smaller, when he couldn't figure out how to make James fit. How to fit *with* James. And now they are both without him and everyone is half as happy as they ever were. Pa is wrong about this – Denny wishes he was still down there, laying beside his friend.

He walks out his new front door to where they buried the dog last winter, scrambles through the brush and along the crick that tumbles over slick rocks and moss. He almost popped his ankle out from his socket on that trip – so wound up and wrung out like a wet rag – and near does so again.

Denny knows that, like the most ugly things inside, he will remember this moment in feeling only. Not the words Pa spat, the things he did. There is pain and hurt and many things that he will never let himself think of again. He can go somewhere else: to a pocket in his mind, a door that he can open. Beyond it, there is a room and there is Maude.

He never got to say goodbye.

From here, he has a direct line of vision to the trailer that was once the Asters', but now belongs only to Opal.

And to the east, his sister's window, where the golden light of the walls cuts a beacon through the dark trees. He can see the whole world, but from the outside. His hardly whole self, from above.

He will lose himself in these woods if he's not careful.

May 1970

Leslie's contractions begin just as a thunderstorm rolls in from the west. She clutches the carved edge of the pine dinner table with her cherry nails and flails blindly for Denny's hand. He places a chair beneath her, brings water and a damp cloth for her sweating forehead, because he knew this was coming. Pa said to keep an eye out for it while he and Sarge drove down as far as Owyhee with the bi-monthly deposit; late, by Denny's estimate, but Pa showed little concern. Said they might even stop off in Boise for supplies, despite summer rearing its head rather early and the land feeding them well; despite all the canning they did last fall and the large sacks of flour that will soon gather mites in the storehouse. The signs of a storm were obvious by then too, that even a man without eyes and ears could feel down to his bones – the humidity, for one, aching joints and ozone with the kick of something cooling in the air – and still, Pa left.

Pa likes to leave when it's important. Six years ago, he left right after beating Gideon's daddy on the floor of his office and locking him in there to die, slow and howling. Denny was just gone fourteen at the time, and Pa made him sit outside with a .38. Told him that if Mr Bass got out, he was to shoot him right between the eyes. But Denny never needed to do that, because Mr Bass died just fine all on his own; in a puddle of drool and piss, corpse too swollen to do anything but burn.

This isn't so bad. Leslie paces the floor of the den, then lies there, back flat to the rug. She smokes long cigarettes because she likes them, because she says they make breathing easy, and Denny comes to her with the matches every time she asks. Mostly, he sits, legs folded under himself because there's nobody around to get mad about it. Waits until another one of the pains comes upon her and holds her hair back while she chokes bile up into a basin. Wonders if the baby will look like him at all, whether he even looks anything like his Pa or if he's just been told time and time again that he's the very spit, cut from the same cloth, fell in the shadow of that broad and daunting tree.

Leslie says he's hard to look at right now, so that should tell him enough. He makes himself scarce for as long as it will take her to have a nap – leaves a glass of water and a damp cloth at her bedside – and sits out on the front porch with nothing but his pocket knife and a small, soft piece of wood he's been shaping into something. Even his shoes were forgotten in his hurry to get out of her hair, so he peels his socks off and stretches out his bare feet before him; watches as a soft smattering of showers begins, making dark circles on the dirt ground.

It's a long time before he sees a soul – everyone seemingly content to coop up, the clouds above growing heavier and darker. First, it's just some of the kids running from the schoolhouse, then a flock of women who wave in passing on their way to the mess to make dinner. Only Gideon and Minty approach him, loftily fanning themselves with filthy hands, they swing their elbows onto the porch railing and regard him with playful scorn.

'All that frettin', Bass, and look at him,' Minty says, smacking Gid on the shoulder.

'What you got there, DB?' Gid grins up at Denny, snaggletooth stuck to his bottom lip like always.

'Dunno,' says Denny. The face is too narrow for a doll, now; overeager and heavy-handed as he got. 'Some little thing for the baby, I s'pose.'

'Who's havin' a baby?' Minty asks.

Minty's new – rolled in fresh a couple weeks back from down near Mackay, face all busted up, only a knife to his name – but he knows enough about these parts and the mines beneath that it feels as if he's been around forever. This feeling of permanence is not one Denny can often trust in – nothing stays the same, not really; the rubble always shifts. But Minty seems accustomed to such things – slightly older, more worldly than the pair of them combined. He's steady as bedrock, coarse and cool. Smokes like a train, too. One after the other, rolled and ready to go. He spots them both a cigarette before lighting up his own.

'Leslie,' says Denny. 'Doc said I should stick close in case I'm needed.'

Minty hums, exhales, sizes him up with a quick glance. 'She your girl?'

Gideon's smoke goes down the wrong pipe.

'Nah, she's Pa's woman,' says Denny, kicking out at Gid with his bare toes. 'But he's beyond with Sarge 'til Sunday, so I've to hold the fort.'

'You're in charge, then,' says Minty.

Pa might have said as much, hand to the nape of Denny's neck to pull him in close enough their foreheads touched. At nineteen, he's been a man for far longer than a year, but he's so rarely been without his Pa. Were it a year or two prior, were Leslie not inside, stuck in pains from the impending baby, he might have sickened himself in despair; let himself sit in wait – any and all mining be damned – for Pa to return and make sense of the things that move around him. What people want, what they say. A currency he's unable to deal in for the intricacies it presents. Denny nods at Minty, timid all of a sudden, and carves curls into a tail that grows too thin and snaps into a stubby end.

He's in charge, he *is*, but it hardly seems to matter. Not when Leslie gets to screaming bloody murder and the boys hastily stub their cigarettes out to run and fetch Doc Froy right before he sets down to eat. There was a plan, made by Pa and the doctor, but it's all gone now. Set the fire, hold her to the mattress; boiling water and towels and his belt for her to bite down. Each layer of tissue cleaved like the earth: topsoil, eluviation, subsoil, parent rock, bedrock. Not a shovel, but a thin surgical blade in steady hands. Leslie cries for him, for Pa, but Denny can only hold her hand and hope that the hurt isn't so great that it's all she'll feel. Because there's joy in the sight of this little pink creature unfurling two perfect arms and two perfect legs;

a joy that burrows down to the bone and takes root there. The baby comes out. Not a peep, let her mama do all the howling. He thinks the baby dead, until Doc Froy delivers three swift thumps to her chest and the cry that follows rings sharper than the thunder rattling the windows.

The blood doesn't stop. Pack the wound, stitch Leslie up. At least *try*, it's what Pa would want. Doc Froy has painkillers, a small rubber mask to wrap around Leslie's sunken, sleeping face, with a tube that winds up and around a tank of air. He passes the baby to Denny, both men painted to their elbows in red. Froy wants to let her go, says it's no use, but Leslie made the nursery nice, had Denny do two coats of buttery yellow to cancel out the dark. She has a list of names – for both boys and girls – that she fusses over every night by the light of the fire, but she never said her favourite. How is he to know?

For days, he lives by the sounds of the baby's cries. He sleeps only when she does, barely eats a bite for how difficult it is to make the time. He is always holding her and being told not to by the women; which seems counter-intuitive when holding her is all that stops the terrible crying. It's quite possible that she knows about the state of her mother and that she hates him for it.

Leslie is in pain, Doc Froy tells him. She's holding on so tight to something, fighting for a life with her little girl that will never come true. Infected, resisting the medications; even the yarrow does nothing for her. But she deserves her goodbyes, at the very least, even if she's not all there inside her head to say them. Pa deserves them too, and should get to make the final call. He'd like that, Denny thinks, as if to soothe himself; to feel as though the decision he made is the right one and Pa will thank him for it when he returns; when things will be made better by the very weight of his presence.

On that last morning, Denny parts the curtains and opens the windows. Light breaks through the clouds and floods the whole valley, warms the sick room and the crisp sheets that have been tucked neatly down Leslie's sides. He brings fresh water for the flowers, sits with the baby at her bed and reads from the list of names until one comes about that gets any sort of reaction. Leslie's lips are dry and cracking, stained red by the lipstick they never got to wash off, but he swears that she smiles; two teeth peeking out, a hitch in her breath.

But when Pa finally comes back, his eyes pass right over Leslie's pale, bloodless body and land on Denny with a frown heavier than his hand. Denny holds the baby, waits for deliverance, for any kind of sign of grief that matches how he feels on the inside. Pa only runs his fingers across the top of Denny's head, caresses the soft part of the baby's skull with his pointer finger.

'What were you waitin' for?' Pa asks. 'Put her out of her misery.'

Doc Froy twists the top of the tank and removes the mask from Leslie's mouth. It wasn't making her breathe – she did all that on her own. She kept on, despite Pa having one foot out the door; receiving commiserations and congratulations in equal measure, his back to the sick room. Leslie is a porcelain doll, not dead, only sleeping, with the flush of fever still high on her cheeks. Denny should have fixed her lipstick.

'I'll keep her safe,' he whispers pointlessly. She's already gone.

As Doc Froy turns up the sheets, Denny stands and cradles the baby close. He hums to her, hopes she won't notice the absence of her mother's heartbeat; that his own is strong enough to make up for it. But he is so tired, left to carry her down the steps and back to the big house while Pa delegates, admires his new kit from afar when others compliment him on her dark hair, her button nose, like he has even come close enough to see for himself. Denny wishes he would, so he might understand that the sight of her, his baby sister, is enough to stop a heart or send storms chasing; that in making her, Leslie struck a vein of something far more precious than silver or gold, rich and glowing iridescent in the light. He folds Maude – her name chosen from the long, flowery list her mother left him – neatly into her crib, beneath crochet and embroidery, a spinning mobile of felted birds flying above her head. When her eyes crack open to regard him, her brother, they are inky-black pools, infinite wells that echo soundlessly far beyond his reach. She is different, and though it hurts, she is better for it.

Denny knows now what it means to make up someone's entire world. To be not the sun or the moon but an entire sky above their blank face. It is good and it is bright. He finds he does not like the feeling.

Baron 1935–1962

IN ITS PRIME, the Coeur d'Alene Mining District laid bare the treasures of ancient America for any person who wished to plunder it. For Baron Rowe, the Silver Valley was the sole constant of a tumultuous childhood. A promise for a future that went unfulfilled by parents who could never line their pockets with enough funds to make the move back to their home, their birthright. This left Baron, at the tender age of fourteen, with the distinct feeling of having been robbed of something.

He could recall, in his early years, making the long drive up to Shoshone County with his father. The feeling of purpose that sustained him throughout that journey of meandering conversations and poor attempts at placating his hopeful heart. His father was a weak man. Nothing was ever so clear to Baron as that. Men were not supposed to just let life happen to them, nor were they meant to cower at the words of their hollow wives, flinching from nothing but scorn and the wave of a wooden spoon. Baron's mother was strong, that much was evident, though there was little about her he thought admirable. He loved her, of course, but that was where the buck stopped. Love did not feed a family of seven, nor did it keep the lights on and the water running. Love was a frivolity, a nice addition to a bountiful life, but felt like more of a kick in the teeth when others expected it to sustain you. Besides, it was rare that Baron ever felt that love reciprocated. His mother thought nothing of sending her husband and eldest son to the mountains, be rid of them for a month as they perused the land that they could not afford to mine. *My father found a mighty rich deposit there, right beneath your feet. Made my mother's ring from it. Used to have a shack right up on that hill, could see the whole valley.* Bull, the lot of it. Talking in circles about the past, recounting fond memories of things they had all done and said, and Baron saw no sense in any of it. The future called to him. Prophetic. Dreams of a life without wanting, to take the knife in his own two hands and twist. To be *home* again and mine what his parents could not. He dreamt of digging as deep as the planet's core with only his fingers, just to see how far the jurisdiction of land deeds would go. *Rowe.* It was his to inherit, nobody else's. And what lay beneath? That was his too.

Then came Minnie Dufresne. Daintily perched on the slopes at Alta with skis she could not use. Skirts of rich silks and satins. An account at Bergdorf Goodman. Saks Fifth Avenue. Baron had never set eyes on New York City, but he could imagine himself as an infinitesimal dot on its golden horizons. There was money to be made, but certainly not a home. Still, the silver called above all; the mountains that were promised to him. Minnie rejected any and all attempts to follow this augury, arguing for

Manhattan. They would summer in the Berkshires, winter in Salt Lake City; New York for the seasons between. But he wore her down, coaxed her west with the vow of marriage. And in the year 1950, despite her best efforts, their son was born in Utah: Dennis, named for her youngest brother who died of tuberculosis in infancy. Baron cared little for the name, she could have that much. It was a son he had wanted most of all. Entirely his. Made in his image, the spit. Apples and trees. His boy, who followed him like a shadow, fastened by a stitch. Denny enjoyed living in his pockets, spouting innocent nonsense into the shell of his ear. Like the reincarnation of the living, his son would undoubtedly make it back to the valley, even if Baron could not.

Minnie tried, with as much effort as she granted anything, to keep them to herself. At first Baron's boy was stifled by starched shirts and table manners. He could not run or play the way Baron wanted him to. Mountains and the valley, there was freedom in all that, a place that was entirely one's own and could not be governed by state or in-laws. Denny was softening into some other creature that he could no longer recognise. Baron had hoped that Minnie's untimely death would harden him, but it did no such thing. Denny all but climbed into his mother's open grave, closed casket, clawing and tearing chunks out of his uncles and aunts.

Baron spared them the inconvenience. Bolstered by the life insurance claim, fate set into motion a perfect circle. On the long, meandering drive to the Coeur d'Alene, there was no placating, no music and conversations that ran around into nothing. Denny sat through all the stops and starts, the motel rooms and the roadside diners, and he listened to his father. He did every little thing he was told to and did not once object. He understood, Baron knew, in that intrinsic way that only a child of his could. Calm eyes, blue as frozen winters, met his across the booth of a diner in Boise. Yes, Denny understood.

But Denny was too young, still. He couldn't drive the truck on his own or shoulder the kickback of a gun without heading for a tumble. Sarge could do both and then some. Despite Sarge's dishonourable discharge (Baron himself had dodged the draft), they had all the tools and skills between them to cultivate a society worth keeping. Fate was at work now, urging him through Montana for the final leg of their journey. Missoula brought Baron a bar that brought him a fight that brought him to Sarge: who reefed Denny clean off the floor from hands that pried and pulled and doted, dropping him in Baron's lap before kicking the bum to the pavement and knocking his teeth into the gutter. A fierce man, he was, with morals so ambivalent and indeterminate that it was hard to gauge what he felt about anything. But Sarge wasn't afraid of getting his hands dirty, at least, and spent the night feeding them from his tab – mid-shelf stuff, a glass of milk and buttered bread for Denny – in exchange for a layout of the plans, the projections, the going rate for silver. See, Sarge had money burning a hole in his pocket: alimony, jobs done for the Boston Irish that paid well but required distance from the East Coast for a spell. He saw no wrong in sourcing from scrap, cutting corners where it might tighten things up. Said he may not know much about mining, but he knew money, he knew construction, and if Baron could deliver the people, he would build homes – cabins, single- and double-wides from a derelict trailer park over on Polson Bay – where they could rest their weary heads.

Because fate meant nothing if they didn't have people. So, in the truck stops that lined their journey, Baron spoke loftily of his plans and promised jobs to those without; easily swayed, every carriage slotting into place on the long and winding tracks. *Come to the Silver Valley! There's always a job for those who are willing to work, a home for those who wish to make one.* They came in small clusters at first – families who had been made redundant by steel mills, other mines in the area – but soon word spread to smaller towns in the Northwest, logging communities and unemployment offices. There were no requirements, no experience was needed. It was a free-for-all, with urgency smothering any sense that might have been had over contracts and housing. They were building from the ground up, after all, for independence and to sustain, through generations, something worth being proud of. His grandparents had only left so much behind – small, crumbling shacks, a useless mining shaft and a single, cavernous barn – but it was enough to work with once Sarge's people shipped the timber and trailers, with all the belongings still in them.

Their numbers had doubled by then to a humble thirty. With the smaller crowds from the cities came Leslie. Leslie with the black hair in pin curls, red lips and dark paint on her eyes. From down as far as Grand Junction, not looking for a husband, just a job, and getting both within the month.

*

Denny paid no mind to her, but Denny paid no mind to anybody in those days. His child mind drifted from one frivolity to another, and during the nights that Leslie began staying in their house as a full-time resident, Denny took up his own residence in a tree. A black gum tupelo by Buster's shed, filled to the gills in its knots and hollows with trinkets he had obsessively gathered. There was nothing from before. His daddy didn't believe in sentimentality. Didn't believe in his mama, either. Like she had been torn from existence and all memory. Now everything worth remembering was right in front of him, in the holes of a tree; tied to its branches, dangling between bright red leaves like grapes on the vine.

Denny was nine when his mama died. All black and carnations and his face pressed to the bosoms of strangers. The needle kicked across the vinyl, a smash of the piano keys, ice in his daddy's drink. He remembered her blood and how it never stopped, the taste of it stuck under his nails. Pa got mad at him for picking them, for biting the skin raw. Torn to strips, pink and white and red all mixed up and stinging dreadful. Crying is for babies and women. Crying is for Democrats. Something ate him from the inside out and there was nothing to be done about it without his mama. She always knew best, and now she would always be gone. He understood. His mama belonged to the worms.

At night he would lay, tied to his tree with the worn bungee cords he'd stolen from Old Buster Chaps, and think of the worms. Eating her. Maggots, too. Their writhing bodies pulsing with pounds of flesh, whittling her down to a skeleton woman wearing pearls around her skeleton neck. *Bag of bones*, that's what his daddy used to call her. *Not a pick of meat on her* – the worms' feast would be cut short. Denny could recall the feeling of his mother in the tight wrap of his embrace. His hands used to meet one another at the base of her spine, where lumps poked out like a pea shoot. But she would fling him around, regardless. Tossing versions of himself that were infinitely smaller into laundry hampers and washbasins. Laughter like a song on the wind. In his mind, she was forever spring, and he, trapped in winter. Even six feet below, hundreds of miles away, he imagined flowers sprouting from her eye sockets in full bloom.

June 1976

As soon as the evening bell tolls, Minty and Gid are in the wind. Seasoned as they are, it's nothing to leave their clean-up to someone as green as James. They'd never pull something so bold with the likes of Buck and his crew, but it's easy to take one look at James and figure he's too nice to say no. Easy to kick someone down when you stand a rung higher on the ladder.

'Thanks,' James says, smiling as Denny takes the other strap of Sarge's weighty toolkit. It's another thing crossed off the list he keeps in his mind: secure the ore, the equipment, check the lights, make sure everyone's clocked out and nothing's been left in the canteen's sink to go bad over the weekend. Sarge had asked Gid to bring his tools back to the big house, being that Gid was the one who wanted to borrow them in the first place, but there will be hell to pay if it's not done. And, since it's Denny's crew, Gid won't be the one paying it.

James shoulders his own load on the other arm; rusted rods and drill bits clinking together inside a cement-caked bucket. They're about halfway up the adit, Denny can tell, by the breeze that blows before any daylight meets their eyes; damp earth cut through by the lush scent of the forest.

With the longer days of summer here, it's something to look forward to. The end of a shift is not the end of the day – there's always more to be done and Maude's bedtime isn't for another three hours. Tomorrow's Saturday, and his shift at the patch doesn't start until noon. So, he can take this time to make sure things are done right; to make sure James isn't being taken for a ride by his new friends.

'Shouldn't let 'em tease you like that,' he says. In the densely packed earth, his voice is far from an echo and instead sounds closer, tighter, as if he's just whispered into his own ear.

'It's all right,' says James. 'I'm used to this part.'

'How d'you mean?'

'Until now, I hadn't found my thing, y'know?' Denny does not know. 'So, I've worked just about every job you can imagine. Meat-packing, steel yard, postal service for a while. Jack of all trades, master of none. Yet,' he adds, his smile like a secret between them.

'Take a lot of shit, then?' Denny asks. That, he knows.

'Nothing crazy. I can hold my own for the most part.' James is strapping and golden, but he's soft in a way that none of the men of the valley have ever been. 'What about you? I bet nobody would even *try* to mess with the boss's son.'

'Got all that over 'n' done with when I was a kid.'

Sarge and Buck and all the men would drag him below to work – hollering, clipping his ears, mussing his hair. He knows now that they were tasked with whipping him into shape, keeping him busy like Buster had; only Pa hated to see Denny cooped up in that shed and wanted him working like a man, acting like a man, to put some hair on his chest and some steel in his spine. Denny took the verbal lashings easily, so long as a smile followed. Once Gid came along, he could give it all right back. It was easier to mimic his ways of smirking and sneering and throwing rocks at animals. He could follow the steps once he knew what they were – but that didn't mean he had to like them.

James laughs; a flash of sound, warm down to the quick. 'Tell me about it. I'm the baby back home and they'd never let me forget it. You should've heard my siblings when I said me and Opal were coming up here to settle down. Though, they never did like her that much.' Then, quietly, he says: 'Never liked me much, either.'

This is something Denny cannot fathom. As they break into the light and the birds call them home, the fact of James's goodness shines brightly as the sun. He is kind, hard-working. There is lots of liking in James, despite his inability to see something through. That's the kind of thing Denny had beaten out of him before he ever set foot below. Pa hates aimlessness, but James wears his with the air of an explorer. The boy in Denny is jealous. The grown man in him aches for anything at all.

'Should head to the bar,' Denny says, wanting the dip in James's spirits to vanish; for his buoyancy to return and keep them both afloat.

Denny is gifted a grin. Straight teeth – no tobacco stains, no chips, none missing.

'I bet you we'll have to play catch-up,' says James, as they near the big house. Already, cheers weave through the trees' thin trunks; by the sheer volume, the bar must be full to the brim. These sunny evenings are a blessing to some. James's feet move faster beneath him – he loves it all and can't seem to help his eagerness. No matter how endearing, there is danger to such devotion. Denny winces as a glass breaks in the distance to waves of raucous laughter. James's grip on the toolkit loosens; Denny picks up his slack.

December 1981

THE FLEECE OF HIS SLEEVE soaks poorly, and still he wipes the wetness from his face and presses the heels of his hands so hard to his eyelids that colours burst through the endless black. Denny quietly inhales against his running nose, lest he wake the dog who snores loudly at his feet. It was the same dream again – earth crumbling, giving way to an infinite wall, rock-hard and impenetrable. The edges always close in and hum a song so deep that it spreads through his bones and drives down, down; past crust and mantle, to the core. Into his chest, where his father's fist sits as if its home has always been there: in a vice around his stuttering heart. It was the final blow that did it – caved in, the powdered bone that dusted Pa's skin. A feather bloodied for every life he took in rage and contempt; bloodied from a bullet to the brain. Because Pa did not have a heart of his own and wanted to rip Denny's right from his chest, toss it around, measure the weight of it. Vacantly, he is aware of a presence. James is always there, because James never left. Denny sits with him after each of these bad dreams and accepts his appearance as penance. It is easier to sit with James's judgement when the words cannot be spoken aloud, when there are no strikes to leave his skin rotten and soft. James, who is a far heavier weight to bear than Pa. James, who followed him down into the dark that day, who has kept the dark since.

Denny sits up, blankets pooling around his waist. The heat from the fire has vanished completely, turning the air a deep blue, and he is struck by a cold so sharp that his hair stands on end. His pyjamas are thick and cottony, with buttons missing near the collar. The skin there is dotted with gooseflesh. He rises despite all this, socked feet meeting the floor, curling against the unpleasant coolness. He won't sleep, not with what greets him there. Perhaps he'll never sleep again. It's the proximity that's killing him; walls instead of long and winding paths carved through trees far older than any of them could begin to imagine. He knows she is there, they all are, behind doors he is so afraid to open. An exile, but one that he's imposed upon himself this time, where to be alone is as much a punishment for others as it is for himself. The baby must be cold – small thing that she is. She is not strong like the other children, not big enough yet. She is defenceless and, perhaps, taking her was the one good thing he's ever done. But Opal has the baby, and though she has expressed many times now that she thinks he ought to sleep next to them, it feels like something that Denny is incapable of doing. The state of him now, so flushed with fear and shame, eyes tacky, is nothing worth inflicting on another; not with James still heavy in the air, his broken bones rolling with each minute movement he tries and fails to make in Denny's shadow.

There is a woman, too: playing the piano with fingers like the legs of a spider. He can close his eyes and follow the patterns, each note struck aloud in his mind. These memories possess a clear edge that refuses to bleed into his reality now, and try as he might, that life feels like a prior one in which he was a different person, born to a different father, with a different name. A different heart, that didn't bleed so fruitfully with every little touch. He thinks it might have been better, back then; but were he given the opportunity to wish it away and renounce this life to spare that one, he would choose this one every time. Because he wanted Maude. Surely he could hold her with blood-slick hands, so long as he was holding her at all. But he and Maude, they are not the same. They are not equal in their devotions, and that's OK. He has the children now, all three of them. Bound to him and he to them by some brittle, splintered twist of fate. It's funny, really. So funny that he and Opal were the ones to take them away from that place. That the five of them survived, when they had spent all of that time before, dying.

Denny smacks the flat of his palm against his forehead. It hurts. Rings in his ears. His hair is longer now and he can make a fist full of it. He does so, but only for as long as a single, deep breath, before he rights himself and steps quietly over the dog. Before he changes his mind.

In the bedroom, Opal has one eye cracked open, a shock of white in the dark. He sees the outline of her, the space she has left for him beyond – clothes folded neatly at the bed's foot from the day's laundry and a pillow, plush and untouched, for him to rest his head. The door creaks when he closes it to keep the heat in. He sits on the edge of the bed, moves the pillow blocking Baby in, and glimpses her slow and soft breathing, whistling through her nose. When he lies down entirely flat for the first time in months, Denny again feels a terrible weight land on the very centre of his chest. The urge to cry, to curl himself away from Opal is strong and persistent. He thinks of the press of a steel-toed boot, and the pressure on his ribs is hard enough to snap. She can see him, he knows, with her eyes blowing wide under the shadow of night. She who carries scars from the worst of his mistakes. Who stands on the precipice of each little hurt with a defiance others can rarely muster. Who accepted her lot and took them with her, out into the world, where she rightfully belongs. Opal should never have come to the valley, should have stayed far away from them all; from James too. But here she lies, the shape he mirrors, coaxing the cold away with a heavy hand. She never asked for anything but this, so Denny tries to sleep. He can do that for her.

Opal says nothing, eases the child closer and closer to Denny so as to not disturb her slumber. Baby's fuzzy hair sticks to the stubble on his chin. And with her small head resting right above his heart, with Opal's eyes on him in long, slow blinks, it is easier to breathe, if only for a moment.

*

Four months prior, the Liptons had Bobby Cannavino working the early morning shift at the Silver Bullet gas station just off the I-90. It was building up to a muggy day, blistering heat beating down on the blacktop, fellas lingering with Wranglers hanging loose around flat asses, spitting and pissing into the same glass bottles.

A woman came through the door at the crack of dawn. Young and pretty with her hair twisted on the top of her head in some kind of intricate knot, fixed in place with two stubby bingo pencils. She had blood on her hands but didn't look much like a hunter. Maybe she was on the rag. He learned not to question such things after that one time Patti Umansky gave him a boxed nose for his efforts and stuffed a tampon up there to quell the bleeding. Besides, this woman had a dark look to her.

The woman was quick, efficient like. When things got too many for her to carry, she began dumping some on the counter, thinking he'd start adding it all up without even asking. Diapers, two loaves of Wonder Bread, formula, cigarettes, iodine, Band-Aids, beef jerky and a tube of toothpaste. Bobby tried to look at her – really get a good look as he punched in the figures, rang up her total – but when his eyes found her own, cloudy and muddy as they were, he felt terribly cold in the heavy heat; almost as if he was sitting in an empty grave.

She paid in cash – fresh, crisp notes that slid easily into the register – and before he could utter a word that might make her feel as discomfited as him, she was out the door and sending bells and whistles in her wake.

It's winter now, and he is shuffling a dead rat out from behind the freezers when he sees it on the TV. Way on down in the Silver Valley: mass murder-suicide, the rotten corpses of men, women and children encased in a frozen winter scene, with a wake of vultures circling, blood-soaked earth crusted black.

'Good Lord.' Jimmy Burns takes his hat off and holds it over his chest. 'The things some people will do.'

And Bobby, too occupied with the dried-up rat carcass, does not make a connection between the two.

May 1981

TODAY IS MAUDE'S ELEVENTH BIRTHDAY. Denny marks it with a sugar sandwich warmed slightly on the hotplate and a view of the setting sun. It's the fifth one she's spent without him; almost half her life where he is not there just as he always promised to be. By now, she ought to be out with Sarge, a few spoils slung over her shoulder – rabbit, squirrel, maybe some fish if they figure the weather is good for it. He hopes she's with Sarge, but it might not be one of those days: where things are easy. Pa takes fits about it all, decides when the rules are going to change in the blink of an eye. Maude may be good at it, cute as she is, but playing the game never matters when somebody is mad enough. Rage paints the world in sweeps of charcoal; the truth gets crossed out. Why not do as you please if the consequences happen regardless? Play and eat cake and run around in the spring sunshine before the rain rolls in heavy and floods the valley. Denny did so as a child, knowing well that he would never be right, not in the way that Pa wanted him to be. There was something missing inside, an innate fracture that could not be cured by all the bolstering in the world. He was soft, and softened further when Maude was born; into some pathetic, simpering thing that would gladly sit and watch her all day. He should never have relished in her birth, knowing what he knew; what he knows now. But it was hard not to, when it meant he was no longer alone.

It's a trap he walks into willingly each time companionship is dangled before him on a golden thread. Stuck in a snare, a bear trap closing its teeth around his leg. He could cut it off, just as he did to his dear friend – not a clean slice, but something that required hacking in the dark, crushed bone splintering under each blow. Denny is well practised in laying waste to any living thing that inches too close.

The wasps are dead.

Hard shells that curl around one another, not black but dark brown in the dwindling summer sun. He is so caught up in them that it takes more than a moment to recognise her face through the window.

Opal's honeyed eyes meet his, with a jar in her hand half-empty, refracting the light and breaking the beam with each sway of her arm. He opens the door. With her, she brings the smell of rain. Denny never wears shoes inside, but he'd let her footprints mark his floors. Gentle as she treads, scuffing her soles on the ledge.

'Sorry, wasn't expecting company,' he says pointlessly. She looks more sorry than he, with her shoulders high and hunched under the thin drape of her coat.

'The rain let up.' Her coat stays on. 'Thought I'd bring you this while I had the chance.'

The jar floats between them, topped by a slice of gingham wax cloth. The sugar inside is glitter in the setting sun;

though he can't recall ever seeing such a thing, he knows well the sparkle on bows, ornaments, painted around blue eyes that gather water with each urgent blink.

'Why?' he asks.

'I spilled it when Yvette came in for her week's lot. Figured if you're using it for your wasps, they won't mind the dirt so much. Felt wrong to just . . . scoop it back in.'

The sandwich is laid plainly on the table and though its contents are not obvious, the lack of buzzing tells the truth that his manners reject.

'Wasps are gone,' he admits. 'Some died – near sixty by my count – but the rest flew off somewhere new.' Much like the people of the valley who, in months past, have fled in the night without breathing a word of their plans – shift posts abandoned, taking only what can be carried – because of the watered-down soup and milk, the ignored repairs, the questions gone unanswered and thoroughly discouraged by Pa's fickle temper.

'To protect their queen?'

'Nah.' He found her first – bigger than the rest, a halo of mourning in ripples around her empty shell. 'They'll make a new one.'

'It's good to move on,' she says, despite herself. 'You should be glad for the quiet.'

He should. 'Soon, we'll all have to.'

Opal places the jar on the table with a delicate clunk. 'What do you mean?'

He's been thinking about it: the after. Pa never said, but there's nothing to keep them here once everything dries up; when what they need to get at is deeper and further than a handful of men would be able to dig. And had they more people, more equipment, had Buster succeeded in his endeavours to make it a solo mining and processing operation, things might have been different. Had Buster succeeded, he might not have ended it all and left Denny alone.

'Got a year or two left at most.'

The lightness of trying to be something resembling friends has vanished from their midst. 'Of silver?'

'Of anything.' He feels shy, ashamed. 'Lead, zinc, silver. Can't get down that far without . . .'

Without the mine's shaft.

'There's no way down there besides how we came back up, and that were a tight fit,' he says. Miles of earth above and beneath, an infinite dark with no light to crawl toward. Minty, barely lucid, climbed through the gap between flat rockbed toward the adit, and took Gid by his arms, dragged him where Denny struggled to push with his injured shoulder – didn't know where to grip when the hastily cauterised stump was still giving heat to the air, when the risk of infection was already so high.

'Can't you go back that way? Open it up? The – the four of you used to work down that end all the time.'

'Ain't an option anymore, not with everyone leavin'. Don't have the equipment or the manpower.' And there's the concrete now, filling the entire shaft, the tunnel too. But he doesn't want to talk to Opal about that; about the concrete filling the space around James's body like an embrace; a tight and hardening vice to keep him there, fossilised forever. Lungs that were so briefly empty, packed with sludge and hardened to rock with veins of silver running rivers back into the earth. Denny buried him twice over, yet the body was never laid to rest.

She holds him still in her gaze with no amount of pity. There's a hardness to Opal that can only be seen from this close; she hides it well under pleasantries and what he imagines is normalcy. Gone is the easy smile, the charming gap in her teeth, trapped between the hard line of her lips.

'Who else knows it's running out?'

'Pa, Sarge. Now you.'

Buster did too, but there's nothing he can do about it anymore.

Her hands curl like talons around the back of his lone chair, voice measured carefully. 'They're going to be mad, Denny.'

'Not at Pa.'

'*Yes* at Pa.'

Not for the first time, he thinks she must have mistaken the rules. She should know by now how these things go: the facts were presented and the people made their choice. It's simple to blame the man unscathed. Denny came out of a crack in the adit looking strong, because that's how his Pa raised him to be. Get right back up, brush your brothers off, put one foot in front of the other. That was his job. They were his team.

'Look . . . if I hadn't—'

'If you hadn't what?' she asks. The answer floats in the black water of memory above all other sunken things. 'What *really* happened down there?'

He shakes his head, slowly. 'It all went bad.' A glacial descent to the centre of the earth that all at once became hell. It was their realm for over a decade, and naively they had let their blind hopes swing on a single chain made up of links in their hundreds. It only took one of them breaking to get buried in the underworld. 'I can't—' He takes a single, trembling breath. 'I can't. It was my fault.'

'*He's* the one who told James to go.'

How does she say his name without flinching? Opal should be long gone, far away from this place and the curse that has salted its soil. To see her before him is to feel something, anything, when all but sorrow has been lost to the caverns in his head. And yet, there is a part of him that wishes to never see her again.

'Why'd you stay?' he asks.

'You didn't answer my—'

'Could go anywhere in the world.' When Denny imagines city streets and deserts, lush fields and stormy beaches, it is her shadow beneath him. He could see the entire world through her eyes alone and feel no loss; because in her eyes there exists a place so vast and unexplored, a place that he was never meant for. 'You could go on home.'

'So could you.'

'Opal.' He has no right to plead or bargain, not with her. 'I ain't got a home.'

'And I do? Why in the hell d'you think I came here in the first place?' Her voice is rough, from disuse or exhaustion, he can't tell. 'James wanted sleepaway camp – I'm the one who needed out. It wasn't supposed to be forever, but he was—' A shaking hand covers her mouth, drops heavy like a ragdoll. 'There's no place for me back in Chicago. Everybody was gone before I could find my own two feet. I can't go back, can't move on. I mean, look at us: don't know how to do a single thing without somebody showing us the right way.'

There is no right way, he ought to tell her, but the words get stuck.

'Doesn't it eat at you?' she asks, eyes full of sorrow. 'That it was all for nothing.'

Except it was his whole life, not a fragment – a third or a quarter, even a half. Denny spent every second of his life, beyond even what memory can reach, following the path his father carved out of dirt and bone. He always had a place at Pa's side, and when he didn't, Pa made one elsewhere for him to fit inside neatly, safely; made this special pocket of the valley for him to sit stagnant and do little else but breathe. That's all he does: one more breath, one more bite, one more step. Push that boulder up the hill again and again and hope that there's someone waiting for him at the top. Been doing that for nearly five years now, living each day like the next will offer a change; like tomorrow's going to be better when never in his life has that proven true.

'Why'd you ask me that?'

She gives him a long hard look. 'Because, if what you're saying is true, then it's over. We can't stay here. People need to start making plans about where to go.'

'Pa said not to tell.'

'*Denny*,' she says, laden with disappointment. 'You can't be serious.'

'What? You were good 'n' happy to stay here all these years, but now that things are gettin' hard you want out?'

'Gettin' hard?' she parrots bitterly. 'They've *been* hard. Jesus, Denny, you're a damn idiot. You think it's all going to magically work out because your Pa said so? He's not *God*. He can't fool everyone. Soon enough, the money will stop coming in and there'll be no booze, no medicine, no damn cigarettes. Hell, half the food we get ain't even from the patch. People are talking, you know. They'll leave, because that's what people do, and you'd be wise to get out while you still can, or else he's going to get his teeth in and swallow you whole.'

Denny's heart is a clump of ore, chipped down to nothing. If he were to take it into his own hands, the skin of his palms would split a canyon that can never heal, no matter how far he stretches the reach of his bones for her. Going well beyond his own limits for one single chance at closeness.

But he can't grab for a life in two different directions. Might not make a lick of sense to anybody else, but Denny loves his Pa. Loving Pa is the easiest thing about him, and when time runs far between one meeting and the next, he feels it fierce like a knock to the teeth. Misses the long nights with stories spun from thin air, sleeping on a pile of coats in the bed of a truck. Perched high on a stool with a tall glass of soda pop, leaning up against his Pa's arm, eyes drooping with every blink. They used to find their way by the stars, name trees by the shapes they made, catch frogs in the crick to cook them up for supper. Pa smelled of woodsmoke and leather, pithy like the dirt from below. One time, when a rattler sank its teeth into the flesh of Denny's ankle, Pa latched on and sucked all the poison into his own mouth; held Denny while he cried from the pain, never spit the poison back out between them. Pa loved him as much as he could love anyone. Denny misses all the good things so much that the bad things can't even touch him.

Opal looks at him like she knows this; like she hates him for it. She doesn't want to stay, but she wants to leave about as much as he does.

'We'll go together, when the time is right,' he says, but it sounds false even to his ears. It's all empty – his words, his cabin, the earth beneath their feet. The wasp's nest is but a grey husk feathered in thistledown and there's nothing of a home in this place beyond the touches left behind by those they can no longer reach.

Opal's sigh takes every bit of breath from her. She leaves the jar, leaves him for the door; braves the shower that's blown in with the hood slung over her dark head.

'Do what you want, Denny.' She does not twist the knife – she holds it tenderly, as if it were a precious thing; as if the wielding of it is not power, but a terrible burden. 'But stop making promises you can't keep.'

He hopes that wherever she goes, she thinks of him just as he thinks of her. But then, maybe not. Maybe that's worse, and all the goodness is in forgetting.

December 1976

IT RAINED THE DAY James died, fat drops smacking the window of their trailer like a shower of bullets. Opal was hunched over the kitchen counter, peeling potatoes, beets and parsnips. She boiled water on the stove, drank it slowly from a cup to keep her hands warm. She waited. She ate an almost thawed hunk of bread, gnawing at the tough bits with her molars. She slipped into her boots and trudged through slush to kick at the generator and tighten the lugs when it started acting up. She waited. Too cold to snow again, the rain froze the ground solid, slippery under her heels. Her hands were red raw, humming to the point of pain in the trailer's sudden heat. More boiled water to drink, nothing to taste. Dinner was getting cold. She reheated it twice. She waited.

Baron had boasted of this expedition being easy, a quick one. Told James he'd be home to warm his wife in no time – all the while, he and Sarge drove off to peddle their spoils to the world she had so readily left behind. Opal was fine without the warming, and could keep herself busy when the weather demanded it. She wrapped up in bundles when bedtime came, scented with sachets sewn with lavender by Miss Gunn. Fingertips achy and stiff, she had to dog-ear the pages of her book and close it for the night. Nothing intricate could be done – if it wasn't the cold, it was the worry that shook her hands; the hollow feeling in her chest that begged for an answer of any kind to fill it.

She told herself, over and over, that she would be fine if he did not return. It was simply that she wanted him to. Her stubbornness soon dissolved into a simmering rage that readily crescendoed at even the slightest provocation. It had been two days now, and yet the world kept turning. Despite the news that there had been a problem with the descent, that the remaining miners were working on fixing it, every meal carried on as usual – smiles passed alongside bowls of piping-hot soup, chatter about nothing of any consequence – and Opal felt herself slowly maddening at the ignorance of them all. Were these men not sons, brothers, fathers? Was it not the very depths of winter, when even a trip to the storehouse was a precarious journey? In Chicago, anyone missing in conditions so severe was considered dead after one day. Human beings could not withstand the worst of winter simply by virtue of hailing from Baron Rowe's land. And yet, she couldn't avoid this line of thinking, not when the turn in weather meant credits were rationed and meals could typically only be eaten together. Eventually, she retreated to the trailer and when she and James's rations ran out, she stopped eating altogether.

She let grief in the door. It burrowed like a tick, taking root in her spine, and the pain was so tremendous that she succumbed to her bed, feeble and pitiful. Made up of her doll parts, doing her Coppélia dance as if she was once more nineteen and scanning the crowd naively for signs of a father whose heart stopped beating en route to Northwestern Memorial before the show even started. Opal always came to things a little later than everybody else – slower to walk and talk, to see people for who they were and not who she so desperately wanted them to be. Cheek pressed to James's pillow, she watched the rain pool at the curved corner of the window, arranging her limbs as they became rigid and impossibly cold. She waited. Left to linger in a moment; the moment right before every one of her thoughts decided to become a reality.

That evening, Marcia knocked repeatedly on the door, claiming in an urgent whisper that the boys had returned. And when Opal discovered that James was not among their number, well, she had all her grieving done by then.

*

Opal did not attend the funeral. She had seen many, and had no need for another in her lifetime. What terrible things they were, made worse by the fact that nothing of James lingered in these mountains; not in the rivers and lakes, nor the trees that sprouted from its back. The very air felt different without him there to breathe it. She did her best to feel another way about things, but couldn't shake the shroud of indifference that sat comfortably across her shoulders. Like a winter quilt, patchwork, each square lovingly sewn with sorrow at its seams. She wrapped herself in its embrace, allowed the knowledge of having been loved so tenderly for such a short time settle her spirit. But the loneliness never left her; it grew like weeds when she wasn't looking.

One week later, Baron came to her door.

She spotted him on his journey toward the trailer, carving through dogwood and boxwood; a hunter's path, never straight. Opal watched from the window and within her rose a sensation so specific that she stood still as prey and hoped desperately to remain unseen. Then came three loud knocks, like the hammer of her heart. She greeted him at the door, opened it wide. Coat off, he hung it over James's on the hook. Trailed slush across the welcome mat. He looked at her as she settled her gaze on the approximate area of his brow, and a smirk grew wide and leering on his old face. Where Denny's eyes were the beautiful blue of scorpion grass, the sky on a new morning, Baron's were a shard of shattered ice, floating menacingly across Lake Michigan. Opal remembered standing on Navy Pier with her own father over a decade ago and worrying that they had reached the very edge of the world. That bottomless despair that made its home in her as she held his gloved hand and took three breaths for every one of his. How safe she had felt, in hindsight, with such a man towering over her, shielding her scrawny frame from the cutting wind. This moment – a lifetime and almost 2,000 miles away – was nothing like that.

'Can I help you?' she asked, surprising herself.

'There she is,' said Baron, so playful and familiar. His fingers grazed her back in passing. 'You doin' OK, honey?'

Opal busied herself with the door's latch, the water's boil. She adjusted the pot on the ring, the hair behind her ear.

'Better, thank you,' she said. *Fine* was not acceptable, even though it's precisely what she was. Fine conveyed a flippancy, made her appear uncaring, when the truth of it was that her care ran so impossibly deep. She was not *sad*, nor was she bereft – for Opal knew this lack, had lived with the blank spaces for so long that she'd learned to cultivate within them fanciful habitats of longing, dreaming, desires to be kept locked out of sight – but she was lost. Set adrift within these worlds she'd let herself forget for the sake of drowning in a love that was taken from her in the end, the way all things inevitably were. It was fine because it was familiar, that's all.

'Why are you here?' she asked, curt and to the point, though she felt anything but.

'Won't be long,' he said, idly admiring James's mother's teacups, hanging daintily on their hooks. James had never said what kind of gift they were, whether they were supposed to be kept. In fact, he never said much about anything to do with his family, not since they scoffed at his decision to move states and made clear their disdain. How could she ever go back to Chicago when she had no idea what she was stepping into?

'Just checkin' in,' said Baron. 'We didn't see you at the funeral.'

She nodded. What else was there to say?

'Didn't you wanna say goodbye?' he asked.

'To a hole full of dirt?' she countered, regretted it immediately for the precipice she now dangled over. The edge of the world, indeed.

The slip came sooner than she thought it would: a gap in the mask he wore so well. His smile grew sharper and, for a moment, with the length of the galley kitchen stretched between them, he looked at her as if she were something worth picking apart.

'Oh,' he laughed. Something pointed that had lanced her enough times, it felt unremarkable. 'I sure am glad you folks came here.'

Her hands shook. From within her rose a disgust so acidic, she feared it might burn through the walls of her throat. He would be glad. As would anyone. Glad that the loss was not one of their own. Because it had been less than a year – that's how far they got. Opal tried making a home here, and she hadn't made it past Christmas. A pathetic attempt, truly.

She could not play this game with him. 'Where's Denny?' she asked before she relinquished what remained of her composure.

'You expectin' him?' Lecherous, conniving, he leaned his elbows on the counter, low enough to catch her eye as she tried to avoid his. Baron made traps for every kind of creature.

'No.' But, of course, she felt that longing in her; for Denny to pay her a visit, to assuage her worries and tell her how James's end came to be. This want felt abstract, yet she could pick from it a single, fine thread to hold between forefinger and thumb. She had one tether to this world and it was as thin as an eyelash.

Baron stood to his full height. 'Don't you wanna know about the others?' Her home halved in size, the world shrunken down to the width of his arm span. He took it all up, every last bit.

'I know how they are.' One bruised, the other severed. Marcia wouldn't talk about Denny. Neither would the other women, who delivered nothing but kind smiles and condolences with every supper.

'Well.' Baron weighed situations just as she did, took the temperature of each room he entered. But where she adapted, softened her edges and melted back down so she could fit a new mould, Baron shaped each place to his liking; made holes in the walls when the doors wouldn't open. 'Denny's been dealt with.'

Her mind conjured images of Denny prone, bleeding, with that little girl cleaning him up just as he had taught her. But some wounds ran deeper. He, like Opal, had plenty of lines scoring his bones. It should have been something to bind them inextricably, a commonality that made him easy to be around, but James died and Denny did not come. Even when he was likely the last person to see him alive, to hear his voice. The only person who might have understood what she felt and what she had lost, who held the other end of that fine thread which was forever unwinding to infinite lengths.

So, Opal kept the terror close. Put it away. She was not herself, but a puppet version – the girl who saw what Baron wanted, and kept still and calm. So he would look at her and see a likeness, not an other that he ought to be rid of. Not his own son.

'Enough about him,' said Baron. 'I came here to talk about you.'

'About me?' She sounded so dull to her own ears.

He smiled again, wider and wider. Though his arms remained at his sides, she felt his touch all over.

'What will you do now?' he asked.

'I . . .'

Baron regarded her much the way she regarded the children she had cared for, the ones who threatened to run away with nothing but a knapsack full of their favourite toys and a single candy bar smuggled from the pantry. Caught red-handed, trapped in a lie. Opal had no plan. She could hardly conceive of setting foot outside the door, let alone past the threshold of the valley and out into the whole world. She had aced geography, once, and knew every state and their capitals in alphabetical order. And yet, where could she go?

In her hand, she held that fine thread as if it were a treasure. If she tugged on her end, would Denny feel it in his chest? Would he unravel like her, or would he remain twisted in knots, choking on Baron's leash?

'I'll be back at work tomorrow,' she said. 'I just . . . I needed some time.'

Coiled tighter, limbs wrapped around herself in a brutal contortion. She grew smaller until the space she occupied was slighter than a child. His was no shadow to stand tall in, to feel brave by. She wilted, shuttered, loathed herself for it. But, oh, how tired she was; cheek flush to her shoulder, she longed to sleep forever, but her hibernation was over.

Baron reached between them, held her face in his rough hands. She felt the urge to recoil, but her body did not answer. Maybe the leash was hers to wear too.

'You take all the time you want,' he said, sweet and gentle. 'I've got it covered.'

It was as though Baron had taken that thread, woven it into a shroud that expanded, a blanket for the whole sky. It was muffled under there, warm; a place she need not worry over the million minuscule agonies that besieged every heart she had come to touch. A quiet place where the passage of time needed no accomplishments, no progression to be seen, for it was all there in the turning of the leaves, the blooming of the flowers; in the dying.

There was a calm that came with knowing you were already dead. She faced the predator, she took him as he was; gave in to his hold, his comfort, anything that meant he would not eat her.

When he kissed her cheek, let go, Opal walked him to the door and offered his coat. He slipped his arms into the sleeves, turned his back to her. She knew then that she had succeeded; that surviving in this way was better than being alone in any other.

The porch creaked under him as he stepped into the cooling evening. Baron turned to her, tipped his imaginary hat.

'Why . . .' she started, stopped. 'Why did you send him down there? You knew he wasn't ready.'

Baron sighed, but she had not lost him. The smile he gave her was kind, or the best imitation of a kindness he could achieve. 'Don't matter what he was – it's what he wanted. That's all any of us are, at the end of the day. What we want.'

Like this, she could see how Denny might care for him. How James had revered, fawned, been eager to drop down to the very depths of hell for even a glimpse of his alleged warmth. It was not some grand game in which they were all willing and aware participants – these people *loved* him. And there they had been: over a dozen hands outstretched, tossing dirt onto the empty grave of her great loss. Baron trapped them hook, line and sinker – trapped James in the deepest of graves – but he held them too. He made the cut, let blood stain the earth, then pried the wound apart to massage the heart.

She thought of Denny, of Maude. James was enough to make her come to this place, and they – despite their father and his ways, despite the distance that grew and the danger felt from closeness – would be enough to make her stay.

'Thank you,' said Opal, giving all but a curtsy, her final *révérence*. She had played this role many times before, and she would do it again. For a fraction of a second, Baron's relentless gaze faltered, his arctic eyes flitting down to her lips, before bouncing back up with double the vigour. His hand cut through the air as he waved, his bejewelled fingers shining gold in the grey light. You catch more bees with honey, her father used to say. But bees were never what Baron was looking for.

December 1981

THERE IS A CRACK that spans diagonally across the bottom-left corner of the kitchen window. It is in the afternoons that Opal sees it most clearly. After wiping away dust and fingerprints with newspapers and vinegar, she pushes a large milk jug in front of it, as if that will scrub the fissure from her mind. That morning, she sent Maude off for a day in town with Mrs Schweers, to help run some errands – dressed in her new trousers and shirt that she got for Christmas; a pretty floral thing, rolled at the waist so as to not appear too long. She tucked Maude's hair in at the collar, for some warmth to her nape. Denny's thick socks would have clashed terribly with the bright red of her shoes, so they decided against them; even if her poor feet would suffer the consequences. Over it all, she wore Opal's coat: felted grey and double-breasted with big buttons all the way down to her knees. It swaddled her completely, which was equal parts comforting and endearing. If Opal had a camera, she would have taken a photograph.

'Ma,' Billy says from the kitchen table. He has a box of beheaded crayons and a sheet of newspaper next to him; colours the faces, paints grins on the otherwise dour frowns. He's written his name on the top, the way she taught him.

'Yes, honey?'

Billy nods at the window. 'Bet my daddy could prolly fix that for ya.' He means Denny. It's easy to distinguish, because Gideon never was Billy's daddy – more like a creature that lurked miserably in the corner, both hoarding and ignoring the boy in equal measure.

'That so?' she asks.

Billy nods viciously. Defensive. 'Seen him do it prior.'

The children's bedroom has a window that used to whistle in the night, until Denny sealed it with duct tape that made a perfect line where dappled glass met rotting wood. Billy drew a series of figures along the silver strip in black marker pen that he no doubt stole from Mrs Schweers' kitchen. Five people, a dog and a cat. Each of them has a smile.

'What's he a' yours?' Billy asks.

'Well, he's my husband,' she says plainly.

'I a husband?'

'No, you're a boy.'

'A boy?!'

'Myself and your daddy are married. Like husband and wife. You're our boy.'

She knows how it was for him: utter silence punctuated only by the sound of bottles clinking, the stifling smell of snuff and stale smoke that draped across the air like a winter quilt. Billy sometimes babbles to himself like a newborn, talks to his own reflection in the bedroom window like a person is staring back at him. There are things he does not understand. His mother killed herself in the winter. That first one following the accident. On account of Gideon's condition, she was left there for days, frozen in the wood-shed he had built off their trailer. Poor thing, curled up like a cat to stave off the cold. Best guess on Dr Froy's part was that she had drunk some ethanol, thinking it was moon-shine, yet his eyes told a different story.

But Opal comes from a long legacy of dead mothers. She has shoes to fill, regardless of whether or not the children can recall what those shoes even looked like. Maude rejects and embraces being mothered with varying efforts; Baby thinks nothing of it. It confuses Billy: he figures Ma is another of her many names, just like his own.

'We still friends?'

She does her best not to react. That's how she coaxed him out, took his small palm and dragged him off Gideon's porch. What's a friend? Who is you? A friend is someone who holds your hand. So she became Ope, then Ma, and sometimes Mama; but she hopes that, above all, she is still the first thing.

'Do you want to be?'

Billy looks at her with those serious eyes of powder blue. She thinks of home – before James and the valley, before this – and how the cold of the lakes never left her. But Billy's made of spun gold in the weak winter sunlight, and though he tears his crayons ferociously across the thin paper, makes the world into a single, sharp void, he smiles at her and she smiles back.

'Well, *yeah*,' he says.

'Lucky me, huh?'

She knew motherless children, bound to a life of governesses and nannies. Dressage and fencing and lullabies of jazz music, glasses clinking and breaking, like glitter on herringbone floors. Workers: imported. Nutcracker soldiers the size of giants; polar bears and Santa Claus. Jewels left carelessly on antique sideboards; wallets and check books. Billy was not so different to them, in the end: uncultivated and coarse for entirely different reasons, a small treasure aching for any show of love.

'C'mon,' she says, fingers skimming the length of his hair. 'The others will be home soon. How about you and I get a start on dinner?'

'A'right, Ma.'

*

Mrs Schweers says a lawyer is a man who knows what's what about the rules, how everything is supposed to go. Mr Brinkley looks like half of Pa, with his long arms hanging well below his waist and swinging uselessly as he greets Mrs Schweers. Suit and shoes too big, his tie knotted crooked around his collar. He holds a hand out to Maude – which greets her at eye level – and she forgets to shake until Mrs Schweers does it for her.

'Nice to meet you, young lady,' he says.

Maude nods. At her back, Mrs Schweers stands close enough to ward off the breeze blowing in through the door to the office. There's a fireplace in the room, which is silly, because the only person sitting out here is the lady at the desk. In her sky-blue suit, with her big hair, her clacking nails, it's hard to imagine that she would stoke the flame or add coal to the pile. It's dwindling, and Maude would like very much to fix it herself for the chill she feels, but she'd only get a scolding. Instead, she sits as Mrs Schweers directs her, next to a table with magazines and newspapers.

'Quiet, isn't she?' says Mr Brinkley.

'She's a good girl,' Mrs Schweers says, voice sharp like it gets when she's not all too happy. 'Lives with her mother and father out by my Leroy's place.'

'And do you like it?' he asks. Maude looks away, eyes fixed on the glossy pictures.

'Bunny? Answer Mr Brinkley.'

'Well, yes,' Maude says, off to the side of her, pulling the cuffs of her brand-new shirt down over her palms. 'I s'pose I do.'

Mr Brinkley laughs, like any of what she said was funny. It's maybe only Bear that ever thinks she's funny, and that's because Ma and Da are decidedly not. Baby is funny, when she tries new foods and cries over the taste, or when she poorly mimics new words. She's pulling herself to a stand now against the kitchen chairs and sofa – she did it for the first time on Christmas morning, two days ago, and has had plenty of practice since – but she falls flat on her diaper with an almighty *poof* every time.

'Well,' Mrs Schweers says with a pat to her shiny brown handbag. 'Let's get this over with.'

It doesn't take long, and while Maude doesn't touch the magazine or the bundle of newspapers on the table, the covers are plenty to look at. Mrs Schweers seems eager to leave, but they are still nice to Mr Brinkley. Maude tries shaking his hand herself this time, and it's not so bad, if a bit clammy. The doctor's office is next, and while she knows what a doctor is, of course, she only ever set foot in Doc Froy's office when she twisted her ankle out by the patch and his cabin was closer than the big house. Everything here is much brighter, with pale blues and stark whites. It smells sharp and unpleasant, and the people who wait look incredibly unhappy. But Mrs Schweers doesn't have to wait – they call her name before she can even sit down.

'You stay here,' she says. 'Play with the toys.'

On this table there are wooden blocks in red, green, blue and yellow – the kind Baby likes to put in her mouth. Lincoln Logs too, like what Bear got for his Christmas present. Ma wouldn't let Maude bring her Christmas presents – not the blue bicycle Mrs Schweers got her, not the Speak and Spell neither – but that's not so bad. Because a girl around her age sits in a squeaky seat in the waiting room and Maude doesn't want to play in front of her, not when she has a magazine in her lap, turning pages with nails painted a garish fuchsia. The girl catches her looking and her mouth widens to a smile – but her teeth are wired and black, screwed in place as if they might fall out otherwise. Are they rotten? Doesn't that hurt? A scowl replaces the smile as she stares and Maude tries to look apologetic, but her gut twists, her chest tightens. She sits on the floor and plays with the blocks, winding them around metal bars of corresponding colours and being careful to fold her legs in a way that won't scuff her shoes on the ugly tile.

Mrs Schweers is gone longer this time. Maude wonders why she was asked to come at all, when nothing has happened but sitting and standing. Waiting. People cough into their hands and take tissues from the box next to her. They blow their noses and hack, scratch at the skin of their elbows. Maude imagines all of it flaking and falling, imagines it in her mouth. When she stands to create some distance, the doctor's door opens.

'Take it easy,' he says, guiding Mrs Schweers out. 'Call me if there are any problems.' She nudges his hand away, shuffling across to Maude, who follows her to the door. On the street, Mrs Schweers takes her arm. A man tips his hat as they pass and a woman smiles, but it's not a real one. Mrs Schweers hardly acknowledges any of them. Instead, they dip through the door of a tiny storefront with linen frills in the window. A wall of heat and the overpowering smell of something syrupy sweet hits them upon entry. Maude's cheeks are bright and rosy red in the mirror that hangs at an angle from the ceiling; she burrows deeper into Ma's coat.

'What will you have?' asks Mrs Schweers.

'What can I have?'

'Whatever you want.'

The glass case at the counter holds all the colours in the world: mint green, buttery yellow, a pink the exact shade of the foxgloves outside the storehouse. There is lilac and magenta, white, silver and gold. Chocolate smooth as glass is topped by dark cherries and cream. There are biscuits shaped like men, with white beards and white hair under red hats.

'Can I have that?' she asks.

'Two gingerbread men,' Mrs Schweers tells the lady at the counter, who takes some silver tongs and grabs the little men by their middles, placing them on a plate. Maude slides it across the counter as Mrs Schweers places some change there, and there are lots of seats to sit in, but they silently choose the window. Plate between them, Maude leans over to nibble on the arm of her gingerbread man. It's very sweet and nothing like the gingerbread Miss Gunn used to make. It has a face, too, and some pants painted on in red-and-white striped icing. She kicks her feet as, outside, people pass by in hats and coats, scarves billowing behind them like capes. Parked across the road, three young men in denim jackets warm themselves over the cooling bonnet of their car and hop from foot to foot. The black-and-white sign above their heads reads "Frank's Fine Food".

'Ain't that where Ma works?' she says to Mrs Schweers.

'Indeed it is.'

It's OK. Bright colours and rusted chrome, cigarette butts on the pavement. The windows are wet with condensation, hearts and stars drawn in a corner where some teenagers are sitting. They look like they're having fun, faces pressed to the glass and leaving kisses behind. She bites the inside of her cheek, breaks the arm off her gingerbread man and stuffs the sweetness between her teeth. It's far too much, sickening even, but she eats it all. Mrs Schweers picks at her biscuit, nibbles away in increments. She pauses, gingerbread clenched mid-chew, and shoves the remainder of the headless creature into her purse.

'We'll go home now,' she says, clipping it shut. 'Have a pudding on the stove.'

'But we haven't finished that other one yet.' Bear has tried his very best, but Ma says it's too rich for eating all at once and they will have some more on New Year's Eve. It's also ten pounds, which Da says is heavier than Maude was when she burst into the world.

'No, not for you, Miss Maude,' Mrs Schweers says with a smile more playful than usual. 'I'm making it for my husband and the boys. Forgot to have it ready for the holidays. They'll never let me live it down if they have to wait another year.' Maude looks at her. Ma and Da said that Mrs Schweers' husband is dead. She could have another. Ma had one before Da, and Pa had plenty of wives, she's sure.

Mrs Schweers waves goodbye to the lady at the counter and lets all the cold in when she opens the door. The snow here is slush beneath their feet, the only crunch coming from salt. They hold hands again, but this time she feels Mrs Schweers squeeze harder, leaning a little more to the left. They make it back to the car in one piece, albeit slower than they left it.

*

Leroy. Maude knows him well. Brown hair, brown clothes, brown eyes. Skin a greyish white, the colour of the sky that stretches behind him. The mountains, the trees, no sun in sight. There is a cow and a horse, some chickens pecking at his ankles. He smiles, despite all this, at the person who is holding the camera.

'He looks nice,' is all she can manage to say.

'He is nice,' says Mrs Schweers. 'Too nice for his own good, I'd say.'

Such a thing is hard to imagine – Maude's never met anyone *too nice* in all her life. No use in being too nice. What does it get you? Soft. Silly. Being too nice never did a thing for nobody, not like being nice in just the right amounts. Ma's good at that, enough that sometimes it scares Maude. She smiles at the strangers who wave to them on the street, at the people in the stores, and even those who look at them funny. Ma smiles at *all* of them, then calls them *sick bastards* under the loud chug of the engine turning over. Nothing but a car door between them and the whole world. But Ma's got thick skin and a way about her that makes Maude both frightened and jealous. She never holds tight to much for too long, knows what to let go of. Maude tries to let go too, but the bad things follow her around, as if stitched to the hem of her trousers. In the night, when Bear sleeps soundly, curled around her arm, she hears the past echo in her ear like it's living in the next room over. If she were to press her ear to the wall, she might hear the hurried footsteps, the flutter of hearts and bullets; her own desperate, smothered cries. She might hear the monster and find that it is closer than before; that it has squeezed itself under the door like a great, dark shadow and found its way inside of her, nestled and humming against her heart.

'What're you thinking about?' asks Mrs Schweers. She pats the seat next to her. 'Come sit for a spell.'

The sunroom is warm despite the white expanse of winter beyond. Maude can't understand it – nothing but thin sheets of glass separating them from the elements. It's not safe, being so exposed, but Mrs Schweers looks quite comfortable, her sore and swollen ankles propped up on the magazine table between them.

'You worry too much,' she says as Maude settles onto the sofa and its fluffy, tasselled cushions. 'Just like your daddy.' Da worries about the sun and the stars as if they are hung from above on thin strings that are liable to snap. Maude is made of granite.

'What's there to worry about?' she asks. 'I can handle myself.'

Mrs Schweers nudges her, urges Maude to put her feet on the table too. It's a stretch.

'That's what I worry about,' she says. 'You, out there, handling things.'

'I handle things just fine.'

'Used to keep a penknife in your shoe,' says Mrs Schweers. 'Those pretty red things.'

Maude's eyes flit sideways; she dares not look at the woman head-on. There is nothing to defend – she never used it – and still the shame creeps across her wavering resolve. 'My daddy told me I could.'

Mrs Schweers sighs. She is tired, Maude knows, and has been for a while now – long before they came to live in her husband's cabin on the ridge. 'You mean your other daddy, huh?' she says. 'The one from before.'

A gnawing in her gut, the familiar burn. In fact, Pa never let her carry knives – not unless they were days out hunting – and neither did Sarge. Da was the one, she remembers, Denny then; when she was small and he would do her hair. Just in case, he said. In case I'm not here. Well, he never was after that. In case of what, she soon learned the answer. Maude never got to use her knife, but sometimes she longs to. A longing so fierce that it sits heavy in her gut like a peach pit, still sweet at the edges.

'Stop it,' says Mrs Schweers, and Maude does stop her fretting, because she has to. It hurts to go on like this. 'Lay back.' Mrs Schweers' joints click as she rearranges her limbs, one arm coming to drape across Maude's shoulders. Her neck cranes at an uncomfortable angle, but she shoots Maude a sideways smile; impossibly wide this time, gums and all. 'Listen. You're out of the woods, now. Time to look up. Promise me you'll try, hm?'

Out of the window the trees are naked of their leaves, fine black lines curling upward, dustings of snow clinging hopefully to the branches. Mourning doves leap from one bird feeder to the next, picking at the balls of fat and seeds Bear rolled last week. A voice in her ear.

'No need to be a wolf, my girl.' Mrs Schweers' eyes find the sky, pale and unflinching. Her bony fingers curl around Maude's; she holds tight. 'The birds do just fine.'

*

'Ma!' Billy wears a smirk so bold, pleased with his own cleverness. Thumb in the pie, cheeks flush with delight. 'Your husband's home.'

Denny jerks as if burned. Boots off, door shut. The world tilts at an awkward angle. It's not right of the boy to say such a thing. Denny thought so desperately of it in those early days when the Asters first arrived – the family they could be: he, Opal and Maude. He was brutal in his exclusions; the world was fit only for the three of them. He dared not think of how his father might cram into the picture, how he would colour all the shadows an infinite black, swallow the whole frame. There were so many times when he had wished that the others were gone. Simply no longer there. Now they are dead.

He can recount every detail of James's appearance almost as if the man still exists before him as a painting or a distorted photograph. How he thought of James felt unreal, unlikely, and nothing like what he had ever truly experienced of him. James was sainted in death, put upon a pedestal that called to mind an innocence, an altruism that did not always fit the make of the man. No illusions were had about Gideon or Minty – he and they came from the same places, and yet it always felt that they were moving further apart, in vastly different directions. But could he claim to be any better? Denny did nothing of note in thirty years of life, when he had been given plenty of opportunity to do so. There were the ways of his father that he inherently disagreed with in some kind of bone-deep sense, which went entirely against his upbringing; something that cringed away from the callousness and cruelty that made up this giant of a man that everyone feared. But what did he ever do about it? He never went against Pa's plans and their vicious reasonings. Denny did not have a gun to his head. Pa never beat him that bad. He never.

'What?' asks Opal, tying an old work apron around her hips. The hairs on his arms stand on end. Things are getting away from him, sand through his fingers. 'That's who you are.'

Denny swallows. 'Ain't.'

Her eyes roll as she turns on her heel. The boy scuttles up next to him with one of those old newspapers from Mr Schweers' pile.

'Drawed this for you, Da.'

''S good.' Four people holding hands, a washy pink circle in the arms of the largest figure that must be Baby.

'Is you not a husband?' asks Billy. Opal doesn't even spare him a side glance; keeps fussing with the hunk of deer she left in the sink last night.

'Nah.'

Billy frowns. 'But Mama said—'

'Go to your room, honey,' Opal says. The boy glances at the canyon between them, his bare toes curling over its edge with no fear of what lies at the bottom. He takes his drawing from Denny and crosses the room in purposeful strides, despite the trousers that have unrolled at the ankles and threaten to trip him.

'I'm no Baby,' he says.

'I know you're not,' says Opal. 'Go to your room.'

'Go on, now,' says Denny, though he knows it won't help. 'Listen to your Ma.'

A scowl, a huff, the sound of paper shredded down the middle. He'd like to tell the boy that he's done nothing wrong, but it feels like a betrayal. *James* was her husband. Everything after is make-believe.

'Don't take it out on him,' Opal finally says, facing him, arms folded over her chest.

'I'm not the one who sent him to his room.' Each button of his coat is released, gloves torn off and dumped on the mantel to dry off. Some of their logs got damp last night, snow blowing near horizontal when the wind picked up. There will hardly be enough for burning in the days that follow.

'He doesn't need to see you wallowing, Denny.' Her long fingers fold over the back of the kitchen chair, nails digging into the grooves in the grain; carved with the kind of delicacy that few would spare in a hunting cabin. Her hair is shorter now, which makes little sense for winter, and hangs in line with the severe cut of her jaw. There is a feeling that Denny gets when he looks at Opal, one he can't quite resolve. It leaves him raw and exposed, as if the top few layers of his skin have been peeled off. He knows the true feeling of that, the sting and the shame, because he couldn't hold onto the chain long enough to keep James alive. Things were easier before, with James between them. He was a buffer, overeager but gentle and loping in the way of a foal; he could soften their abrupt and abrasive tendencies into something that looked, from above, like the beginnings of a friendship.

'Your husband's dead,' he says.

She stares, withering before him, brow pinched between forefinger and thumb. He's grown accustomed to disappointing her, to seeing the inevitable dismay; the weariness of hoping upon hope when he has given her no reason to.

She sighs, a drawn-out thing that comes from deep in her chest. 'When James died, you wouldn't even look at me. It was like I died too.'

A clean cut: the switch of a birch tree, a near surgical incision that cuts so close to the bone. It was cruel of him. Whether or not Denny was welcome in the valley anymore – by its people and their tight circles – he should have known better when it came to her. Their shared history being what it was; defined only by its tragedies. Did it all need to happen so that they could be this to each other? How wicked they are. What an awful little life they spun from those threads of sheer terror. There are some things that a soul ought not to come back from, and yet they carry on, they do more than just surviving up here on the ridge, in their new home that they have nestled away. It's like inhabiting someone else's body, climbing inside a corpse, trying their skeleton on for size. There are days when Denny feels like every bit of it has been pretend – a game that he invented inside his child mind to cope somehow with the things he saw, the pain he felt; that he dragged Opal along with him and made her believe it too; that she sees through him now, right into his ugly centre.

She says, 'You just had to try. That was all.'

But there are things which she can never understand. His fists perch on the tabletop, whitened at the knuckles.

He is a mirror of his little sister, now his daughter, so petulant and splintered.

'I couldn't *just* do anything,' he says, in a bitter mockery.

'You're not a child, Denny.'

'But I was.' And no matter what, Denny will always and forever be his father's son. Escaping that is not something he can expect of himself – not the motherless little beast that he was, the frightened and cowardly man that he is. Denny never stopped being that boy; so long as his father breathed air before him, there was no way out. And perhaps he could have left the valley, were this world another and the people in it different, but he had Maude to think of. He was not so untethered to that place as Opal had been, with her dead husband and all the people she could barely tolerate. Maude was his responsibility, whether their father allowed him to see her or not. How could Denny abandon her to Pa's swinging whims, his rage? Maude is only a little girl, it's not her fault that she was born into such a place. But Opal chose. Denny did too, in his own way.

Opal looks at the floor and takes little gasping breaths. He'd like to place his palm carefully on her chest, slow the frantic rise and fall, but he's never been sure of how to go about comforting her. He couldn't do it before, and to do it now – when she is so angry with him, so tired and hurt from the years that tumbled into one another and grew insurmountable – feels like an act that will only serve himself.

There is no longer the numbness that shrouded him in a cave, that kept him from crawling toward the light and the truth and all the things he had been so afraid to touch. Denny can't look at Opal without imagining what her face might have been on the day James died: wide eyes and gapped teeth biting into her bottom lip, only to drop her body into the snow like a ragdoll. The blankness. He thinks of the blood on his hands, his clothes, his face. The blood in his mouth. It's crisp and cloying on his tongue like a copper coin every time he sees her. The ghost of James's rotting, bloated corpse between them. Nothing to mark his grave but a stick in the frozen ground. A dented helmet that was not even his. None of them were wearing helmets, which is another secret. All the prayers knocked loose from their heads before they could ever speak them aloud.

Her heart thumps in his ears, a vicious and relentless beat. He can taste her in his throat. And she, him. She wonders what would it have been like if they'd met else-where. On the L train, the back of a Greyhound, heading far away. At work – he, a gardener, a driver for Mr Goodwin. Spring break, a picnic at the Great Lakes. The pianist in her dance rehearsals. Perhaps simply in passing on the street; a collision of bodies that swapped one soul with the other like telephone numbers. Playing pool with the blow-ins, he'd let her break, grin when she sinks each ball. Rain-soaked and wanting for nothing. An altercation in the grocery line. A dent in her car, a note pinned to the windshield, penned in his immaculate scrawl.

Opal had not wept once for her dead love. She had the distinct feeling that if she were to start, she wouldn't ever

stop. There are many things to cry about in this world –
some that don't bear thinking about, others that confront
her daily in the form of her hungry, grieving children – and
she need not waste time on tears when she has a perfectly
good husband before her. A husband who cannot cope
with the weight of the title, who flinches away as if flayed
by the lick of it. He muddies the waters with his instinctive
repression; the need to withhold all like a child who has
gone without for most of his life. But she cannot pity him,
nor could she see a single thing but the man in front of
her – as a man is the only way she has ever known him
– and his inability to forgive a single thing about himself.
She resents him for it – not for James, but for the way he
carried it all after; as if it were his alone to cradle, to press
against the jackrabbit of his heart. He robbed her of the
one thing that was hers in the entire world, hid the grief
away at the edge of the valley and refused to share. Opal
never wept for James, but for this, she weeps gladly. They
never stood a chance.

'You need to let go,' she says.

'But I did,' says Denny in a painful whisper. 'Opal, I
let him go.'

She looks at him, he at her. In his eyes, she sees the
terror of that moment – the final drop, a plummet toward
hell itself – reflected plainly. Tears salt her cheeks. Denny's
thick thumb smudges the wet away. The sadness wells up
with such speed and ferocity that her sobs double her up;
his own cries emerging as he stands there, still holding
her face.

After a few moments, Opal is able to speak again. 'Denny . . . I was never mad at you, not for that. There was nothing you could've done.'

'You don't know that.'

'I do,' she insists. 'You can't save everyone.'

'I could have tried harder.' His voice cracks.

'And what? Leave the others behind?' she asks. 'James is dead. That's all there is to it.'

'I should'a done something.'

She laughs, despite the hurt. 'You'd live and die for everyone but yourself.'

'*He* was your husband.'

'James and I were never married.'

There it is: that indecent thing between them. Denny is not a replacement, nor is he taking anything that she's not perfectly willing to give. It should assuage his worry, remove the need for forgiveness in that regard. Apologies will do nothing for the rest, heal little of what occurred between them, but he ought to let her have this for making her live so long without.

His thin lips bite down on a cry, maybe, a consolation. Pinched and pained, he looks as ugly as she feels inside; with his flushed face and sweating brow, deep-set eyes alive with pinkish veins that only darken with each quick blink.

''Kay,' he says. A small nod. The light begins to fail around them, but there is nothing to obscure the fact that they did what they had to do; the understanding that it is what they have always done. His palm fits to her cheek, grazes the corner of her mouth. It's as close to a promise as they can give one another. Nothing resolved, nothing decided. They hear a whine nearby: their baby is awake; their son is waiting. Soon, their daughter will be home for the dinner they will share. Their cheeks touch in the first embrace. He holds her for a time and she, him. When she lets go, the warmth remains.

While he goes for Baby – crawling around, no doubt, at the foot of their twin bed – she opens the door to the children's room. It's sticky on the turn, hinges creaking. It's cold. Tiny shreds of paper blow like autumn leaves. The bed is unmade and beneath it, the stuffed bear with its long, errant limbs is missing. Opal scrambles across the room, knees burning, palms stabbed by a thousand splinters, and pulls her body up against the sill. There is a break in the seal where the wind flies through. A slice through silver. The window is ajar.

*

The room smells of citrus.

Behind her sounds a quiet exhale that drifts like a breeze up to the glass sky. Dust dances in motes that move apart and come together again, light passing through like stars. Maude takes Mrs Schweers' hand, made of bones and veins, skin but a thin film – mottled and translucent like a sheet of white tissue paper – and she presses a kiss to the jut of her knuckle. She tucks the hand under her chin. Oh, how fond she feels for such an old thing. Maybe Mrs Schweers could have married Maude's Pa and made him into a man like Leroy; who was broken into a million different pieces by the severity of his own tenderness. Maybe things wouldn't have ended the way they did – she could walk around the world unwounded, no scabs to pick at, no more blood to spill. Like the photographs in Mrs Schweers' basement – visits to Hawaii and New York City, Niagara Falls and Mercer Island. All the places Maude's never been and will likely never go. Everything untouched and perfect, kept inside a miniature world in which there's no space for the bad things. Maude has no photographs of herself, but if she did, she'd cut herself out of them and paste her little paper body into the Schweers' life.

She eases the lavender blanket over Mrs Schweers' slight chest. On the stovetop, the pot whistles at the boil. Numb to the heat, Maude slides it off the ring and turns the knob until it pops out again and the gas stops hissing. Her socked feet pad across the sticky linoleum. She finds her shoes, the droplets of melted snow still sitting on them, and buckles them at a crouch. Her head spins upon standing, but it's OK – she'll be home soon.

She walks down the drive, past the bushes misted in powder, the rusted buckets filled to their brims with water, frozen solid right through to the base. Once at the road, Maude scuffs her feet across compacted snow; slips in the smooth tracks left by cars and bicycles. She fits so perfectly inside these lines, almost as if she never trod them to begin with. Invisible, like always, melting seamlessly into shadows, smaller feet landing in the larger footsteps of her father, of Da. But she is a black mark against the vast white snow. The trees make way for paths and roads, severed and carved apart. She imagines a bird swooping down, bursting through the black branches and picking her apart. The beaks nipping at her stomach, tearing at her beautiful new clothes. Not much meat to feed on. Her mind takes her back. Did something feast on Pa? Lick his bones clean? Was his flesh rotted by then? Was there anything left of him? Did they want to eat him at all?

Maude vomits into the ditch.

Her knees are wet. If not for the shock of the cold, she'd believe herself back there: shattered windows, her brother's soft whimpers dissolving into the silence, the desperate howl of her own breathing. There is snow in her hair, her shoes, fisted beneath her palms. She releases a single breath that makes a thick cloud in the air; a cluster of things she remembers, things she wishes so desperately not to. Some of it so make-believe in her mind's eye that she ought to be proud of herself. A life in the mountains, gilded in silver, and the gold that shone from the sunbeams on morning dew. Children playing. Abundant growth. Houses with stairs, animals for company, family holding hands around a table laden with all kinds of things: corned beef and buttered green beans, Ma's purple *borscht* and tinned pine-apple with heaps of whipped cream from the can; peanut butter and jelly with the crusts cut off the Wonder Bread; nougat, Skittles, potato chips and ketchup. If you get full up, you can save some for later. Plenty of water to go around – for baths and teeth and drinking. Plenty of blankets and toys, clothes and heat. A kiss to the forehead at night and tiny, cold feet pressed against your shins. Washing your hair over the bath, the sink, careful combing and drying with soft cotton, head in the sky.

Imagine a life punctuated not by silence, but by a soft song of laughter – your own, maybe, or the sound of someone you love.

But imagine: Da, with blood in his mouth, rivers running from his eyes. A head in his hands; imagine it's detached from the body. Imagine that a child is crying. A wound shared between two people. Rot in the hollow of a tree, the floorboards warping. Anger climbing the walls, swallowing the whole world in a single gulp. Imagine that you are a monster.

Imagine.

Maude is walking. One foot, two feet. Good toe, bad toe – a dancer, just like Ma. A navy ribbon carves through the snow, the richest velvet with creases and ripples and frozen edges. The stream is doing its best to move along and she matches its progress; hops across to the line of the property. Back to the drive and the muddy tire tracks – somebody left the gate open, somebody left in a hurry. She slips on the slope, heaves herself across a mighty drift, spindly branches poking out like gnarled fingers.

Smoke rises from the cabin's chimney in skinny lines that fade into the terrible grey of the sky above. It's going to snow again; a final shudder from the clouds, shaking off the cobwebs of the day. They will be buried, all of them, in husks of dens and burrows built for creatures far smaller. Maude could fit in there, live under the porch like Bear did all those years, without a mama or a daddy to care for him. She doesn't need any of them – not Ma or Da, Bear or Baby, not even Mrs Schweers.

She traipses across the yard and up the steps, shoes avoiding puddles of slush from the salting. She skids on the porch, catches herself on the splintered railing. The screen door is wide open, the door unlocked. Ma is there, pacing the kitchen with Baby on her hip.

'You've been cryin',' says Maude. They both have. Baby's hammy fists rub at her eyes, swing toward Ma's face, pull at her hair. 'Did I cry like that?'

'What?'

'When I was a baby. Did you and Da get any sleep?' Maude remembers the calloused fingers in her hair, gentle songs in the night that lilted long into the dawn chorus. Tears smudged from her cheeks and soaked onto hankies, embroidered with carnations, lilies and purple hyacinths.

Ma holds Baby tighter. 'Maude, that's not—'

'You and Da put me to bed.' Warm water to sip on, a cloth scrubbing the dirt from her face. 'Every night.'

'Oh, honey.'

Baby's cries have quietened to sniffles, vague mumbles of upset sent in Maude's direction. Maude was never such trouble, she knows that much; she never made Ma cry. Even the thought of doing so cleaves her heart in two.

'I remember,' she says, and it's getting harder. 'Ma, I do.'

'That's good,' Ma says, taking a single, shaking breath. Baby is gone now, on the floor, crawling around and pulling herself up to stand against the couch. She holds Maude's hand. 'Do you want to sit down?'

Maude cannot imagine moving past this moment in time. She can only look back to the very start of herself; to a whole host of feelings and situations that she was too young to navigate. There was no mother, no father in the sense of the word she has come to know. There was a lump of a man who cowered at the hands of another and there was Da. There was Ma, and the three of them liked to swim down at the crick. And Ma had a bathing suit with blue stripes on it, her toes painted a bright colour like Mrs Schweers' pink fingernails. Maude held Ma's hand then too, when she was still small; held both their hands, down the dirt paths and through the pines.

Growing is painful, Maude has learned. A keening, a rattle of the bones. A complete reshaping of the self into some other creature entirely. Not a wolf or bear or a rabbit at all, but something immeasurably small; a bug crawling around in the maw of her father, between festered molars that crush and grind, cartilage worn down to grit. She never had the wings to beat against his gums. Maude did not simply fall and cut herself on Pa: he chomped her up, gristle and fat ground between teeth. Da was the first and their father loved him, Maude knows he did. She has to know this, or every bit of her tiny world will fall to pieces.

'Mama?'

Opal's hands press fervently to her cheeks, her forehead. Maude's scalp is wet to the touch, hot and clammy despite the cold of the snow. She heaves in great breaths, punctuated by whistles of air that do nothing to cool her scarlet skin. Neck flush and swollen, hard under her fingertips. Opal wedges her hands beneath Maude's arms to feel there too and is met with the same thing. There is something so terribly wrong about all of this that her time caring for children hasn't remotely prepared her for. Were they the Goodwins, she would only need to call the family's paediatrician, any doctor would suffice. In an emergency, there was the hospital, paperwork she could fill out easily – with social security numbers, insurance. Maude doesn't have any of that. Not even a birth certificate.

'Sit, Bun,' she says, finally coaxing the girl into a chair. She sways, keels forward. A small thing, still, but dead weight. Opal makes a gentle bundle of her on the kitchen table, Maude's head cradled in her own slack arms while Opal fills a bucket with clumps of snow off the porch. The pipes to the pump are frozen, the barrel itself coated in inches of ice, like a miniature rink. She takes a clean rag from the shelf, and hopes the heat of the fire will melt the snow quickly.

'Bunny.' Maude hisses at her touch. Opal sits her up, supports what little she weighs, and holds the cloth to her neck. 'Your daddy will be home soon. He will. It's all going to be just fine.'

Maude whimpers, bloodshot eyes so wide and fearful. 'Billy?'

'He's fine,' Opal insists.

'Pa's going to – he's going to—'

'Pa's *gone*.'

They have no medicine, no thermometer. Baby is crawling toward them, tufts of hair bouncing on her head with each jerky movement. It's hard not to panic, when she has no idea what they're dealing with. Baby's never really been sick like this, none of them have ever been to a real doctor. She can't fill the bath alone; she can hardly carry Maude by herself. There is no one to watch her. No one to watch Baby. Denny is gone searching, and Billy may be gone forever if he forgot to take his shoes. It doesn't bear thinking about.

They did not account for many things, but this is the worst of them.

*

His bear was in the lake. Stitched back together by the red wool from Baby's old sweater that she outgrew before winter truly reached them. Denny held it, worried the soaked fabric between his fingers and under his chin for a moment, let the worst come to him in preparation of what he might find. It's hard to breathe. The cold saved Gideon that night; slowed the flow of blood, froze the mangled stump.

But it will kill his son.

Boots full of water, Denny wades along the lake's edge in lengthy strides, hoping the indents on the shore are from small feet and not hooves, paws – but it's hard to tell, because it's snowing again in soft flurries. He rushes to cover more ground, eyes flitting back and forth to track any change in the landscape. The prints lead away from the water, but that matters less and less with every second that passes. It's freezing, Billy has no shoes. Opal may have forgiven him for James, but she would never forgive him this. Maude too would add to her tally; a slew of strikes for every wrong he's done her. Denny's heart clenches painfully at the thought of losing their boy. He curses, smacks a palm against his forehead, scans the water once more through smudged vision for a ripple or a splash. He is no Buster; he's his Pa through and through. He's Gid – neglectful, angry at such a precious creature for daring to exist in the same vicinity as his misfortune. Every tree looks the same, every gnarled root and severed branch. A shadow slithers into the corner of his eye and had he a weapon, he might have used it; but it is only a memory, the switch swinging down to lash at his skin; snipe and spite in some twisted punishment for doing no better than his father before him. Pa's voice rattling in his head to a chorus of bullets. Denny clutches the bear in one hand, a clump of his own hair in the other. He pulls, listens for a sound that might tell him what he's supposed to do, how he's meant to be a father to a wild thing when nobody ever showed him how. But he never really needed showing, not when loving was so easy. He recalls a winter just like this one, Buster's smoky coat a shield from the wind's worst whips. Denny fell from the sky and was caught in arms that, for the first time in memory, held him without the promise of hurt.

He looks up.

Up in the tree, Bear likes how the snow feels on his tongue. But Da's eyes are red and wet, so maybe he doesn't like it so much. Bear's got no hankies to offer up, nothing but his sleeves that are all muddy from when he fell on his ass in the water. He can't reach, anyway, because he's so high up in the tree and Da can't see him. He's not sure he wants him to yet. It's good to be quiet and hide away when people get sad. Don't know what they're going to say; or maybe they won't say anything at all, and Bear can be invisible for a while – a day or two, a week, or however long it takes for the hunger to make problems.

'Look who I found.'

Da does see him, because Bear stomped around lots at the bottom of the tree, trying to get enough grip to climb. But Da's not talking about Bear: he's got Billy in his hand, the toy's legs dangling like they might fall off. Da stays put – he won't touch Bear sometimes, like he's afraid it will hurt – but Bear folds himself tight just in case. The bad feeling crawls around inside him like maggots.

'So loud,' he says. Ma had shouted and sent him to his room. She was crying.

'I'm sorry 'bout that, bo',' Da says.

'Is you?' Nobody ever says sorry. Not when they shout or they throw brown bottles and it gets all sticky in your hair. 'Did you know my Gid?'

Da looks right up at Bear. 'Gave him that nickname myself.'

What? Da is a nice man and all – shows him how to work snares and fix his laces so they don't get loose. Few weeks past, he showed Bear how to use the toilet without calling for help. But he never saw Da before the night they ran. Never saw most people.

Bear asks, 'He your Gid too, Da?'

Denny may not have liked Gideon, but he loved him enough to make up for it. 'Sure was,' he says. They were not one another's keeper, and Denny owed him no loyalty – but this boy, *his* boy, deserved it, given to him freely and gladly. Not for Gideon or poor little Julie Hirsch, simply for the fact that Billy was *theirs*. Opal chose him that day, so Denny did too, with his frozen feet pressed against rough bark, swinging lower now for Denny to reach out and take him.

'C'mon now, bo',' he says, tucking the toy under his belt, arms raised and waiting. 'We miss you awful. Your mama needs a hug.'

'You too, Daddy?'

Billy slips from between the branches and into his arms; only small, nothing so heavy as who he has carried before. His trousers are crisp with the cold, perished feet latch at the base of Denny's spine. Tiny hands wind under coat and collar, warming against his neck. Denny holds his boy close for a handful of heartbeats and carries him home.

August 1981

THERE IS A GIRL who sleeps inside a trunk. Skin pinched, splinters rooting themselves into the leathery soles of her feet. She likes it there: the dark dankness of it. The smell of mothballs and what must have been her mother.

It is summer. Her face is flush with the heat of it. A day spent by the crick, soaking sore hands and their hot welts, wiping from her cheeks all the dirt and tears. It's been hours, but she feels them still. Light between the wicker smatters her shirt like stars. There is shouting from the mess hall; which has been happening more and more since people started leaving. It's because there's no silver left – she heard Sarge say so. He and Pa have been at each other's throats all week, and this morning Pa lost it when Sarge started meeting people in private, all secret like; that's why her hands hurt, that's why she's hiding. Pa got worse when people started packing up their things and dug their tires from the caked soil – giving up on the valley, not a lick of loyalty to share between them – and the anger has kept on since.

As people entered the mess, Maude took count from her perch at the front window and found that of all who remained, only two were missing. This was not unusual, though if not for Pa's rantings on the matter, she'd have thought Denny and the lady from the storehouse had fled months ago. She stayed, waited to see if they would come, until Sarge caught her watching and shooed her back into the house; told her to stay put and keep her nose out of it. But everybody is there – even Gideon on his crutches, no boy in sight; which is also not unusual, as Gideon seems to forget he has a son on the best of days.

She's supposed to stay in her room and wait for Pa to come get her, but the shouting only grows louder with every passing minute. In the trunk, it is quiet, and she will hide in it until she hears the thunder of her Pa's boots on the floor. But there are no footsteps, only a sudden, single, loud bang followed by five more in quick succession. Maude swallows her breath. She knows the sound of bullets from her days out hunting. Pa and Sarge are the only ones allowed to touch the guns – locked away with a key she can never quite get her hands on – but they've shown her how, given her proper training now she's hit double digits. Maybe she can help.

Lifting the lid on the trunk, she climbs out and lands softly on the floor. Like a mouse, she rushes from her room and down the hall with heels up. She can walk clear under the high windows, down the porch steps and across the yard; where casings and shattered glass litter like leaves in the dirt. There's little need for quiet or stealth now, what with all the noise: more shots through the air, screams and gasps and guttural cries. She soon wishes she had stayed in her trunk.

In the doorway to the mess, Sarge lies with a single, round hole in his head. The back is mushy, and for a moment she wonders if maybe she can put it all back inside, fit the fleshy pink pieces together, but then the noise stops. She looks away from Sarge – from Mr Kepner, Gideon, Miss Gunn, some ladies from the kitchens, Jerry or maybe Minty or *oh*, Prue and Letty are holding hands, how will she fit it all back inside? How will she find her brother among all the red? Hold him careful as he held her, tangle their fingers like he did when they'd go off hunting to get away from Pa and Sarge and all the things they did. She knows the hot feel of blood on your hands, field-dressing a deer and burying the innards far from home so the predators won't come looking. She knows the smell of death.

There is Pa, a lunging coywolf – gun thrown to the side, ammo spilling from his pockets – straddling legs that kick like an animal caught in a trap. She has seen this before. Pa is killing Denny over and over and over and she will never escape the cycle; moving like the seasons, the migration of birds across the solid sky. Pa will never stop killing him.

'It's your fault,' Pa growls; sharp teeth, pointed ears, claws instead of nails. She flinches. 'Look at me, Dennis! You look at me right now.'

A swing, another pound of flesh. It's always been Denny. He sees her, but his eyes say nothing. She doesn't know him anymore, not since Gideon lost his leg below; four men went down and only three came back up. But he will die and then she will only have Pa, forever and ever in this forsaken place. No more silver, no more people. No use in begging: Pa would never end it – he loves her too much. But he will end it for Denny: the only person she has ever loved back.

'This place is *dead*,' says Pa, pressing hard against her brother's throat. 'I built this for you, I kept you so *close*. Look how you thanked me, huh? They weren't askin' any damn questions. Would'a kept diggin' circles with my say-so if you hadn't put ideas in their heads – you and that two-faced bitch. Don't worry, Den, she's next. What y'all made me do— You think you could'a led these people? You're pathetic. They're all *dead*. Might'a been my gun, my hands, but you people made me do it!' Pa's temper, so quick and terrible, has once and for all breached the walls of the big house; through the busted window, not so precise as the kills of a hunt, but more an explosion that caught every living creature in its sweep. Pa's gone and done something this time that won't heal up nicely; that will leave far more than a nasty scar.

'You forced it, Den. You went and put notions in their heads about shit that they don't understand and *no* – don't try an' tell me you didn't, 'cause I know *you*. That weepy little heart, you're just like *her*. You were never mine, never – I'm made of *stone* and *God*, Den, I'm just sick of lookin' at you.'

Maude shakes as she moves, crouches low, grips the discarded gun by its barrel. She rights her hold and comes to a stand. Pa paints the walls with the blood of his son, beating him over and over. Denny kicks. They're all dead. Everyone is dead. Pa promised forever and lied. She stopped believing him a long time ago, when he hid her away from the world and her brother.

'You did this,' Pa lies. Again and again. He spits. 'Should've left you to rot in the ground with your mama—'

Denny kicks. Denny chokes.

'With Maude's mama—'

She chambers the gun, the noise its own bullet. Pa turns his head, makes to yell, throw, fire all this hate back and forth between them like he's always done, the sole constant of her short life.

But Maude shoots.

Pa is a roman candle. Her legs give way with the force of it. The world is ruddy with carmine, ruby, cherry red. Her tongue darts out to taste it. The corpse of their father collapses, headless, spurting still. Denny is there, then he is not. It's too warm and she cannot stand. He appears above her, her brother, hand outstretched. How does she take it without touching him?

'Oh, sweetheart,' he says. Maude begins to cry.

Denny knows the sight of him must frighten her – eye swollen shut, mouth bleeding, the ring around his throat – but this is their time and they must use it wisely. He hauls her to her feet, keeps her there, moulded to his bloody torso. What a horror, to be reunited in this way.

'Don't worry.' It hurts to say. He manoeuvres the weapon from her shaking hands. 'You run along now, go to Miss Opal at the storehouse. You know Miss Opal?'

Maude shrugs.

'She's good. She'll help.' Opal wasn't at the meeting, but she will have heard the shots and known she was right all along. She won't flee empty-handed and she will take Maude, even if she won't take him. 'G'on now. I'll be right behind you.'

Maude slams the door open. She throws her slight body out into the night in chase of the salvation he promised her. The only traces left of her are the footprints of blackened blood, the fresh drops that fell from the torn ends of her pitch-dark hair. She wasn't supposed to be here, but she came regardless; followed the noises that tore a wound into the trees and echoed long and lasting toward the mountains. What she did for him, he will never forget. If he draws into himself enough, he can feel the delicate press of her feet in the foliage as she vaults across fallen logs and swings left around the black gum that was splintered by lightning in the year of his nineteenth birthday. The year she was born. If he does this, he will not have to feel the soaked insides of his boots, the way that something he can't and won't identify is rolling around beneath the sole of his foot. He won't have to smell it – the thick fog of fear in its most absolute form, knowing the way it all spilled out of them and seeped into the gaps between the floorboards. If he thinks of her and how they are never going to be here again, he can focus on the hope and fear that reality holds, and not on how the people he has known for the entirety of his life lay around him, fragmented, for finally finding a collective voice.

Through the murky swell of buzzing in his ears, a cry sounds, pitchy and young. Minty is on the floor, his lined face blank and still next to Marcia. Denny rolls her, watches her neck swing. And there she is: little Frances. Bathed in blood and born again. His hands shake as he reaches out to touch her. She howls, screeches, the small cage of her chest grabbing quick breaths. His body remembers: how to coax and ease, quiet the cries. Gentle little thing that she is, rubbing at her eyes. He uses the cleanest part of his shirt to clear her skin of the blood that's drying there; spit on the fabric to loosen the flakes. She'll be all right, safe and sound. Pretty as a picture, his girl.

December 1981

'Denny.' a voice, a whisper. 'Hey.' Fingers in his hair, palm flat against his back. A hum and chest to chest. Breaths taken in tandem. He struggles to keep up.

'You need to calm down,' says Opal. 'I need you to do that for me. Please.'

His body won't let him. As if there exists at the very centre of him a hole, a cavern so wide and deep, but there is no space left; stuffed and overflowing, hot in his throat; tar, coal, ashes, the blood of his father just sitting there in the well of his tongue. A silence that echoes long into the night, lacking the words he was never taught to say.

He is not there. Not anymore. Pa has been dead six months now. Maude killed him. Shot him through the head like Pa did Sarge. Like he did everyone. And now she is dying. Poor little thing, hot to the touch, boiling in a bathtub of melting snow. Shaking, a bird stripped of her feathers. It's not fair.

'She's going to be fine,' says Opal, making a promise she can't keep.

'You don't know that.'

This is what you do know: you will always be her first sight. The boy who named her, kissed her downy head.

You will comb her hair, pinch her toes between calloused fingers, hum a song into the shell of her ear. Feed her, bathe her, hold her. You will know her as your child; the boy and the baby too, wrapped safe and warm in the bed you share with their mother. There is comfort in this truth.

Maude wheezes. A buck dies quicker from a lung shot, suffocates long before it can bleed out. The world owes her that at least. He owes her far more. Maude's heart thumps inside him in a cluster of five. Denny climbs into the bath, folds her limbs between his own.

He remembers being caught in the maw of a beast greater than this harsh winter. Sliding down on crimson knees, head in crimson hands. Surely, that is hell. He cradles Maude to his chest like she is once more a baby. There are always worse things.

August 1976

THE AFTERNOON SHIFTS into sharp shades of amber that cut across his vision and dapple the world with concentric circles of white and yellow. Denny tastes fall on the air, but there's still a stretch of summer left before harvest. It's another day where James wants to drag them all down to the crick like he's never seen one with his own two eyes before; like he's not from Chicago, of all places, with its lakes like the ocean. Gid's packed nothing but brown bottles of Buster's home-brew, rolling paper and a box of matches that are soaked the moment Minty pushes him into the water. There are sandwiches, wrapped in wax paper, that surely cost Opal a hefty sum of credits at the storehouse; lemonade clinking merrily in her basket; boysenberries, green-tinged plums, a jar of golden honey made by Jeanie Specker's bees. It's all laid out on a blanket, stitched together with threads of different colours, soon to be muddied by footprints and splashes and cigarette ash.

Denny stands a few feet away, ducked under the brush of a black cottonwood. Heart-shaped leaves graze the bare skin of his back, fluffy seeds bobbing happily atop the water's mirrored surface; which has finally settled after Gid's intrusion. Denny shoves his own matches, papers and envelope of tobacco into the vee of the tree, far from prying hands, tossing his shirt over the top. It's all he brought with him. There was an idea that struck him in the early hours of the morning, scraping eggs over the stove, that he ought to make some food for the excursion: bring a tin of peaches, maybe, or berries from around the big house. But the berries hadn't ripened yet, and Denny had to clear out soon after: Pa was in a mood, woke up stewing in it, spitting a chronic vitriol that Denny failed to remedy with the most placating of words. Sarge says Denny tends to press against his Pa's hair trigger, set him off without thought for the exit wounds. Like it is a conscious thing, a choice each evening before bed, chewed on alongside his whispered prayers. Denny left the house because there was no other choice. He agreed to James's overeager invitation if only to get the ruckus of three idle men off his father's front step.

Opal wears a striped number with frills along the collar. James runs his fingers under the seam, and she swats his hands away like a swarm of flies. Denny's cheeks burn under the harsh bursts of sunlight. To cool off, he jumps into the lake with a grand splash that echoes in green ripples and rolls onto the shore; touching the tip of painted toes. James joins them, Minty has long since submerged. Opal seems content to watch, squinting against the sun, eyes lined by the intensity of her smile.

'C'mon, baby,' James calls, before Gid drags him under. Denny wades toward the trio at a leisurely pace, treading water that shimmers under the afternoon sky.

'I'm good right here, thanks,' says Opal. Denny's never seen the likes of it – sunning herself like a cat, stretched out on the blanket so the sand won't dirty her togs. If not for her presence, they'd all be swimming with their asses bare, buck naked and not a care in the world. But none of the other women have ever come along with them in the way that Opal does – not to say that she's one of the boys, as she distinctly, most obviously, is not; but that it's a wonder she hasn't yet made some more friends. The storehouse is a social place, a perfect fit for her, where everyone is liable to pass through at some point or another – Denny can't go there himself without stumbling gracelessly into a minefield of questions that he is well-equipped to answer, yet knows not to. He hates for her to be lonely. James passes his days below; near every day, now, what with the deposit Pa reckons is hidden right under their noses. Does she miss him? Though they are his friends – James spends an awful lot of time in Minty's shadow, in Gid's back pocket – Denny can't imagine that Opal would feel a sense of peace with them. This is her day off. Were it Denny's day off, and were he welcome in the big house – to stay as long as he so pleased, without the noise and the simmer of something on the air, fit to light with a single spark – he would not be here, at the crick. He would not be with these people. There is Maude, and there are the things and people that pale in comparison. But Minty is laughing, it's bold and vibrant and vibrates in his ears, and Gideon is spitting water from his mouth like a spout. This is preferable to whatever lies behind him: to his little sister in her sleep clothes, gumming at a fresh loaf and asking to come along, and their Pa, always telling them no when he's like this; always calling her back and keeping her out of the sun as if she is a foxglove or a begonia, too fragile for such harsh light. If Denny brought Maude, it would have been the perfect day. Pa knows this, knows that Maude takes to water like a fish, and still he kept her home. Denny perhaps should have stayed too, been better, quieter, but no such thing seems to matter on days like this; the rules are always changing, a slip in the story. Denny is a liar and a leech, he's a good boy and a fine man, but he's also pathetic. All he wants is to survive the afternoon.

From across the water sounds a yelp and a splash. James has Opal slung over his back like a sack of grain and when she kicks, she does not miss. While James howls and the boys laugh, she dunks her head beneath the water. Denny counts Mississippis in his mind, makes it to twelve before he feels his heart start again. Opal's hair floats up around her shoulders like snake grass. The boys are familiar with her in a way that she seems to find strange – large hands patting her head, sliding around her waist to pick her up and toss her into the sky – but Denny keeps his distance. He watches her swim far past where her feet can touch, pull carefully at moss-covered stone, smile at the feeling beneath her fingers. In the sun, her hair is the precise colour of her eyes, both having shifted from molasses to honey; brighter and brighter, to lemon curd, buttercups under her chin. He stands in the water, dirt between his toes, and watches with such intent that, at first, he hardly notices his sister.

Maude is on the shore, water high as her protruding and petulant stomach. It hitches with the effort of withholding frantic breaths. Her mouth is full of blood: thick globs of it drip down her chin, half congealed and wetted by spit. Denny stumbles toward her on all fours, like some terrible mare, hooves digging deeper into the silt the closer he gets. She is still crying, a wail that echoes through the valley like a murder of crows, and he is the only one running. The boys know not to interfere. That's about all they know.

'Where is it?' Denny drops to his knees in front of her, thumb and forefinger coaxing her mouth open. Maude says nothing, points a bloodied finger at the centre of her belly. Stringy hair falls around her moon face, which is swollen and reddened at the jaw. The tooth will rattle around inside her like a penny in a jar; a single milky incisor embedded deep. He kisses her cheek, takes her small hands into the palms of his own. He ought to ask her, make her talk about it, but he knows: a string and a doorknob, a slam or a smack, a quick jimmy with a pair of pliers. Maude ran for a reason, and the reasons that have always existed between them remain unspoken.

'Oh, dear.' Opal is behind him, bent over his shoulder. The pendant on her neck swings at the corner of his eye like a pendulum on a clock. 'Let's get you cleaned up.'

She does not ask or wait. Maude watches her warily, large black eyes tracking each minute movement back up the shore and into the trees. James calls something that blurs into a single word in Denny's mind – he can't parse a thing right now. He lifts Maude onto his hip, where her cotton shirt sticks to his wet skin. She paws at his chest, his ears, slides her chin onto his shoulder. He follows Opal step for step, though he knows the way well. Dried dirt is caked at her calves from when James dragged her into the crick, frizzing strands of hair stuck to the middle of her back, dripping water onto the forest floor. Opal walks ahead, down a path of firs and red cedars, by the patch, the glass house, and it's plain to see the home she has made here; the ease with which she moves through the valley, despite her unease. Maude breathes deeply, her crying slowed by confusion – never has Denny taken her to the home of another person. He's not supposed to take Maude places without Pa's say-so, but she's hurt, and the source of that hurt cannot be explored for fear of what kind of reaction it might cause. Nobody will know, the boys won't tell: James will surely think nothing of his wife helping a little girl – he speaks regularly of her job from before – and Gid's been giving Pa a wide berth since he got into that trouble with Julie Hirsch. Minty's fair, and he likes Maude well enough. Denny needn't worry about the repercussions. Opal turns as she climbs her trailer's steps, shoots him a smile.

He pats Maude's back. 'Be good, y'hear?'

She answers with a huff, wrists wiping at her sticky eyes. Inside, the air is a cool reprieve – James likes to boast the benefits of a trailer in the shade – and smells of lilacs.

Opal shakes salt into the bottom of a tin cup and twists the faucet, fills it halfway.

'Give it a rinse,' she says.

Denny deposits Maude onto the counter, conscious of the filth on her feet. 'Thanks,' he says, lifting the cup to her lips. She gags a little at the taste and he rubs circles against her back. 'Spit.' He holds the cup under her chin; red clumps in pink-tinted liquid. It's poured into the sink and Opal repeats the process. Still, Maude regards her with the level of caution she might spare a venomous snake. 'This is my friend,' Denny says, plain as anything. No room for doubt. 'Her name's Opal.'

Maude nods stiffly. Her bare heels kick discordantly at Opal's kitchen cabinets, dirt dusting the floor like snow. Her foot is the size of his whole palm, but he holds one in place while the other swings, unaware of its partner's capture.

'It's real hot in here,' she tells Opal. It's not.

Opal smiles with her gapped teeth. 'I should crack a window, huh?' Hip tilted into the countertop, she reaches across draining dishes and a glass container filled with baking soda to flip the latch. Outside, the birds sing.

'I'll go fetch us some towels.'

He's grateful for the otherworldly tact she possesses, the innate ability to read a room. Denny wishes so desperately not to alienate Opal by the facts of it all. She brushes past on her way to the bathroom – no longer a scullery now that everything is in working order – and Denny does his best to make Maude look at him.

'Was Sarge there?' he asks. Sarge is a bluster of a man, built to withstand storms and heavy-artillery fire. He is made of pure granite. Pa spits bullets that could hardly make a dent; but every time he swings, Sarge goes down like a bag of rocks.

'He said "run on now". So tha's what I did.' Maude nods, entirely satisfied by her position and the choice to stand by it. The watery sheen to her eyes remains, but the resolve holds fast in the whitened clench of her fists against the peeling counter.

'Good.' His hand covers the top of her head like a helmet. 'Good girl.'

Opal returns, the trailer so small that their conversation must have carried. He pays no mind. She hands them a towel each, rough and worn from washing, and Denny wraps Maude's around her shoulders, leaving his own by the sink.

'I hear the tooth fairy pays extra when you swallow it,' Opal says sagely, leaning against the table.

'What's that?'

Denny remembers this in some absent way that bleeds slowly into the forefront of his mind. There was a time before the valley, he knows, and maybe that is when these things existed to him as something much more than stories – a childhood treasure, lavender and vetiver, cold fingers curling around the shell of his ear. His Pa would never bother wasting time on things like that – couldn't get a dollar in the valley anyway, despite all the damn silver. The thought of him gently lifting Denny's dream-heavy head to place a shiny coin under his pillow, kissing his crown and bidding him a good night – such concepts are novel and stupid. He and Pa have never been that way, which isn't to say that there's anything at all wrong with their way; he's happy to survive on the only kind of love his Pa can manage to give. He can grow in it, warping his branches in the quest for sunlight. And Maude, she is too small to know any better. She has Denny. Now, she might have Opal, and he will no longer feel worry press heavily against his heart in the darkest hours of the night.

'It's a city thing,' Denny says. 'I'll get you some peaches tomorrow if you're good.'

Opal's jaw ticks, lines deepening at her temples. 'Sometimes it's a mouse, not a fairy.'

'Don't want no mice in our beds, do we?' he says.

'And they leave candy.'

'A mouse leavin' candy – I've heard it all, now.' He nudges his nose against Maude's temple, delivers a kiss to her cheek. 'We best be off. She's gonna bloody your towels.'

Opal makes like she'll try to stop him, offer a drink or a dry change of clothes from James that will hardly fit his broad shoulders. She'll endear herself to Maude in ways that Denny can't manage, and the world will be made far too big for him to protect her. He passes her the towel, spots a patch of browning blood on stark white as his hand touches Opal's; if he's lucky, that's all the red she'll see. Maude was born to this place, to this family, just as he was. What kind of person would he be to invite another into the fold?

But Opal, for all her smiles and her easy way, offers up a hard edge too. Something sharp – no flies, feet firmly rooted to the ground. She needs no invitation, seeks no permission. This is not something worth praise; it scares him. Maude looks to this woman with her forever smile and sees a gift; her wide black eyes absorbing every minute detail, committing it to memory. Come bedtime, she will have questions that Denny won't answer because he has no idea how; how to find this closeness with terror only a room away. The knife that twists inside him. Rot that has taken the foundations. Maude need not learn these feelings, not if he can help it; but to let her feel the joy of this gift is to let her see what she must go without.

'At least let me braid your hair,' says Opal. 'Don't want you catching a cold.'

It's a battle easily won. She knew that it would be. Denny is not soft by any means, but there is still blood on Maude's tongue, and the wet ends of her hair fall like teardrops onto the counter. They will go home after this. Denny will bathe Maude, slip her arms and legs into fresh clothes. He will make her supper and do his best to settle her for the night ahead. Pa will be there though. Pa will see Maude's hair and Denny's sun-pink face and he will know. So, Denny lets them have this – a single moment in time to fall back on when things must return to how they were only this morning.

He lifts Maude down, reminds her of her manners. He watches as Opal threads three strands into a single rope and fastens the hair with an elastic from her own wrist. Then the delighted twirl, teeth with matching gaps – does Maude smile this much when it's just him? She likes Opal's toes, the pretty colour painted onto the nail. She asks if she can have some too, and Denny should say no, but he wants this. A want so terrible and small that he could swallow it, let it rattle around his insides and act as a reminder. But Maude laughs, skips the length of the galley, tooth forgotten. She waves her foot around for him to catch, presses the sole against Opal's as they lie on their backs, toes to the sky. Denny sits and he watches, pockets it for the times when he will need it most. The sun gets lower, the light turns from amber to a deep, burnt orange. Crimson soaks in the sink. The dark feels darker. He ought not have wanted so much.

January 1982

THE BROWN-PAPER PARCEL he'd wrapped up so neatly two days prior has turned translucent from blood and fat. It has frozen again in the night, no longer safe to eat having been left on the porch this long. It crinkles in the soft breeze, sending a sharp scent across the yard. Death, he knows, in all kinds. The front door is unlocked. It's OK, he tells himself, over and over. She said he could. Denny is not a dog or a cat or any other creature. And they are friends, in some capacity. She takes care of his children and he takes care of her food. He twists the handle and crosses the threshold, follows the unease, the smell, to the sunroom, and steps back into a version of himself that was not dead, but simply buried.

Buster was like that. Even with the rope tied around his neck, his face ballooned and shiny, he looked peaceful. Denny held him by his legs before he could think to cut the noose. Yelled for help when the weight was too heavy to bear. Nobody came, and maybe he was too late anyway, but nobody came. Even when he begged. He won't touch Mrs Schweers, not when she looks so comfortable; when her pretty face is pale and made-up. He knows that feeling: the waxy smell of the lipstick, a shimmering powder that made his chin itch. Her nails aren't dark enough, lacking the clean lines and pointed ends. Fingers missing rings of gold and heavy jewels. She was younger, his mother. But she was dead too.

He stumbles backward out the door, catching himself on the parcel, eyes watering in the high sun. Peg felt sorry for him. The game made her smile, how he gutted it so politely and tidily and used that cabin for what it was created. Maybe he did what she couldn't and made a home there; she had to love him for that.

She fell asleep in that pocket of sun, Maude laying on the other end of the couch, feet tangled together. *Pink Cognac* nail polish, chipped at the ends and stained by tobacco. The soft linen of her dress, tartan for winter; lipstick in the lines of her mouth; earrings weighing her lobes; white hair piled in pin curls, clipped to one side as was the fashion in her youth.

Peg died there.

The little girl could not fathom what such a thing looked like – to go peacefully, a quiet exit. She was sick, too, until Opal rid her of the fever. But, in the end, it did not matter a single pick what Peg knew, what she did not know. There was a little girl, with her eyes so wide and open, like looking through a telescope into the inky-black night to search for a star, anything, to take hold of. Peg did not need to hold anything in the end, but she was glad to be held for the length of a season. In her lifetime, she had three boys, each three years apart. Every bit of Leroy and absolutely nothing of her. Only one comes to sort things – Murphy, the youngest, a financier in Wichita – and reads her last will and testament with Mr Brinkley in town.

As for the Hirsch family . . . It starts with this and ends with three words only: *Leave them be.*

Murphy sells the house and its contents for less than it is worth, and the money is split evenly, to the very decimal, between he and his brothers. He clips his briefcase shut and catches the next red-eye out of Toronto. Soon Peg is easily forgotten by all but five. A perfect number, really, and quite enough for her.

*

The sun is a blown lightbulb in the sky, white flash against crisp snow. Bear stuffs his big boots into the ends of a drift, clumps crumbling down the slope as if he's on the edge of a mighty cliff. He tumbles, crash-landing on his ass in soft powder that puffs up around his covered head. Something to smile at, he thinks; to catch on his tongue. Bear wants to catch everything, but Ma says he is not allowed. It is dirty. But the snow is white and bright and hurts his eyes to look at for too long, so he figures it's pretty clean. It makes his teeth hurt. His tooth fell out yesterday. Da lost a tooth before, and let Bear feel the gummy gap in his mouth; says he's got to put it under his pillow and he'll get something nice. But only if he's good. He's been very good, until now.

There it is, floating like a teardrop on a long green stem: a flower.

Though he knows he is not supposed to, Bear picks it. He's careful, rolling the root between his frozen fingers. The flower spins, melted snow smattering his chin and cheeks. It's beautiful, catching the light. He can take it someplace it won't be so cold; fill a cup with water and put it on the kitchen window where it will get plenty of light through the clean glass.

Memphis strolls around the yard like a big, grey lump. His fur is long and scratchy and catches between Bear's fingers. Later, they will lie by the fire, two roly-polies on the carpet, and they will eat what scraps Da yanks from the flames in silver foil balls – onions, or maybe some potatoes if he's lucky. Memphis has a nose so cold it feels wet when he kisses it. Memphis licks Bear's nose, so he must like it very much. He'll like the flower too. Bear moves fast.

He walks then runs as soon as his feet hit the threshold of the house. Across the carpet and hard floors, to Bunny's sickbed. It's their bed that they share, but Ma and Da have been taking turns sleeping there. He doesn't mind, because it means he gets to share with Baby and hear stories from the library books. It's only for a while, until Bunny gets better enough that she won't make him sick. There was a long time where Bear thought it would happen to him too; that Bunny was a body in Da's arms and there was no coming back for any of them. They lay in the bath like a boat on the ocean, rocking back and forth with Ma leaning over the edge, drowning. Baby was asleep – maybe she had gone too – and Bear suddenly felt so strange inside his tummy that he thought he must be dying.

Oh, how he had cried. Cried and cried and cried. His breaths wouldn't come and got stuck in his chest, tangled in a knot that was far too tight to loosen. Ma said it would be OK, said lots of things, but Da was crying too. His face wet and smudgy, holding Bunny like a doll he broke by accident.

'Here,' he says now, hands outstretched to the bundle his big sister makes beneath the blankets. His elbows poke Da's arm as they both lean on the bed.

Bunny takes the flower carefully, her skin warm when it touches his own. 'That's a snowdrop,' she tells him.

'Oh,' he says. 'Thought so.'

'You did, huh?'

He chews on his thumb, she smacks it away from his mouth. 'Picked it for ya,' he says with a smile. 'Can share, if ya want.'

Bunny has a real good think about it. She looks at Da, who's smiling. Bear nudges him with the top of his head, Bunny kicks him with her bare foot, which is clean and not black with dust like his own.

'Fine.' She's careful when she gives it back to him. Bear is too, bolting for the door. 'Put it in some water or it'll die.'

'I *know*, Bun.'

Ma has been in the bath all morning so as to warm herself from the cold outside. A while ago, Da brought more hot water and dropped Baby in there to splash around. Ma said that Bear could too, only Bear doesn't mind the cold outside so much when he can make shapes in it. He traipses in and finds Baby standing, hands on Ma's knees so she doesn't fall over.

'Good job!' he says, leaning against the rim. Baby reaches out for him, feet slipping in the water. Ma steadies her.

'You coming in?' Ma asks. 'The water's getting a bit cold.'

'Not done playing yet,' he says. 'Will ya put this in some water? Bun says so it grows.'

Ma runs her fingers through Baby's hair, then his, making it wet. 'Go get some logs from the shed and I'll sort it for you. Deal?'

Deal set in stone, he thunders back through the bathroom, the kitchen, out to the porch and down into the yard; where the dog waits, hopping on hind legs and licking flakes of snow from the air. Maude fingers her knotted hair and listens to the yapping, the constant stream of chatter from Bear, the excited barks of the dog. She understands better now – the worth of a person, a creature.

Maude killed her father, their father. Put him down, just as she had seen him do to her dog when she was five. And perhaps she could have done otherwise – attempted to reason, bargain, beg. But there was no talking to Pa. Truthfully, Maude rarely spoke a single word to him for the fear that thumped right through her. She did not love him, she couldn't. Because love had filled her eyes before even the sun, the sky. It had been shown to her, given in generous helpings. She knew the shape of it, the words. She knew, even when Denny was gone, that he loved her how birds love the trees, how fish love the crick. What Pa gave her – that was not love. He learned her well how to hurt, and hurt others in return. How to gut a fish, pluck each feather from a bird. How to field-dress a dead thing and make it so nobody would notice the cuts that were made. What Pa gave her, she gave right back.

She will have her own bath later, when dinner's been eaten and the fire has long since heated the house. She will wash her hair and comb it out properly, no matter how it hurts her arms. In the bed, her world is soft and rounded at the edges, safe from even the slightest splinter; with Da sitting vigil, his bright eyes steady and unmoving.

'Give it here,' Da says, unwinding an elastic from his wrist.

No move is made until Maude turns her back to him, shakes the few snaking strands from her shoulders. Some stick behind her ear, down beneath her collar, but lift readily when soft fingers draw them away; a tug to her crown by only the calloused pads of her father's fingers, for his nails have long since been bitten away with worry. He is careful, as he always was, not to pull too hard, not to get the elastic stuck on the twist. Her hair is longer now than it has ever been and he handles it well. Three times around and a snap, draw it tight. The beginnings of a braid, maybe, sways in the cool breeze like a fishtail and whips in a wide arch when she turns. There are thanks to offer, then a companionable silence as she returns to her reading, and he to his. So much to get through now that they have the world on their doorstep, every little thing she could ever wish to know at the tips of her fingers. No more asking and getting half-answers, half-truths. No more hearing the words from the mouth of another and wondering if any of it is real. He taught her to read, she thinks. She knows. He gave her that and everything else, before and after, that was good and whole.

In the kitchen, Opal stands in her pyjamas over the rusted sink, a towel twisted atop her head as she dries the dishes. Still, the windows are wide open, airing out each dusty corner where the light hits like copper flecks of glitter floating, breathed in. On her feet, she wears thick socks that slip down her ankles and are far too big at her toes. Bear's snowdrop sits in the jar on the windowsill, next to a row of carved animals and the crack in the glass. It fractures the sun, makes glowing shapes on the wall. Outside he sprawls in the snow, arms and legs waving, face to the bright blue sky. Footprints all over the yard and winding through the house; he calls to his Ma, asks if she can see him.

The birds sing above and beg to be chased further off into other worlds that have more distance, more space, from what they left behind. But here there is a cat and a dog, a job at a diner and another at a garage. There are meals made from the things they grow and hunt and buy and soon, very soon, Baby will be walking all on her own. Maybe they can fall and the bruising won't bloom so dark; and it won't mean falling at all, but something closer to the way a seed can drift on the wind and grow elsewhere.

The floorboards creak under Denny, when he stoops to lift the baby, when he swings her in an arc across the sky; naked and pink. Maude laughs along and he catches himself watching, a joy that no longer needs hiding. She fusses as Ma's fingers dig into her scalp, making small circles, coaxing away any impending migraine that might linger at the ends of her sickness. She is glad to have made it, glad that she gets to try this again. Because there were times when Maude thought she'd never see the whole sky through her little window. That she only knew fragments of a life which got broken. She couldn't see past her own two feet, her next birthday, the long barrel of a gun.

But in the kitchen that once belonged to Leroy, that he draped lovingly with lace curtains, carved intricately for the sake of his wife, there is a window so wide it fits a full picture. Her own photograph to frame, not to bury in the basement: her little brother with logs falling in his wake, chasing the dog that tries to catch its own tail; Ma over the sink, Da at her shoulder, rubbing Baby's gums with whiskey to ease the agony of teething. Their shapes are stark against the sky, but she'd know them in any light.

You're out of the woods now, Mrs Schweers says, a forever echo in the chambers of her heart. *Time to look up.*

And in the setting sunlight that drapes down across the sugar tyme, fruit like dollops of crimson in the snow, Maude makes good on her promise; she surrenders to it. Like all worthwhile things, it keeps.

Acknowledgements

Like this story, let's start somewhere in the middle. Thank you to Oona Frawley, Fíona Scarlett, and Catherine Talbot, who I met through the Creative Writing Masters at Maynooth University. Thank you to Jen for getting me there every week. To Belinda McKeon, for her guidance then and ever since, and for making this all so very real.

Thank you to Máistir Ó Fearaigh for his encouragement. To Paula McGrath, who taught my first Creative Writing class in UCD and whose advice has stayed with me to this day. To Maria Stuart, who propelled my love of American Literature to impossible reaches in a single semester.

To Sharmilla Beezmohun, who was the catalyst for this journey; who chose my book as one of the twelve winners of the Irish Writers Centre Novel Fair. To everyone who facilitates the event. To Ger Holland for the care she takes with her craft.

To Sophie Orme at Manilla Press and her immediate faith in this story. Her passion for these characters has inspired my own, and I am forever grateful for her kindness and consideration; for the work that she, Helen Reith, and everybody at Manilla Press and Bonnier Books UK have put into this book. To the team at Gill Hess, for their wonderful vision.

Most of all, to my agent Brian Langan, who was my first successful attempt at manifestation. From the very first read, he understood what I was trying to say, and helped make this story into a novel. I could never have done this without you.

As always, to Jules and Luke, for taking it around the world. To Paula Stokes and everyone at *Folio: The Seattle Athenaeum*. To the Library of Anthony Foster, which I imagine is of similar size. To Baby Cara and the library she will make.

A special thanks to Granny, Nanny, and Breege. To my great-grandmother, May Nelson. To Granny Nan and Granny Margaret. To Margaret Hayes and Kay. To Mam and Dad for their unwavering belief in me and for seeing this path so clearly, even when I could not. To Joe and Susie forever and ever. And finally, to Matthew, who made worlds upon worlds with me, down in the streams and up in the trees.

Reading group questions

1. We read *Dirtpickers* through the points of view of Denny, Opal, Maude and Billy. How do they all see the world differently? How do they experience the novel's events differently?

2. The novel's timeline is not linear, with time shifts which allow us to piece information together gradually. What effect did this have on you as a reader? Can you think of any scenes from the past which particularly built your view of a character, or their relationships? At what points did you begin to piece together what had happened in Silver Valley?

3. Denny, Opal, Maude and Billy have no choice but to become a family. How are the relationships between them different at the end of the novel compared to the beginning?

4. How does the complicated relationship between Denny and Opal change? What do you think the future might hold for them?

5. What role does Mrs Schweers play for the family? What do they learn from her? What does she learn from them?

6. What are some of the different ways in which Baron manages to wield power over people throughout the novel? How does he control Denny, James, Sarge, Opal, Maude and the community at large?

7. How do gender roles operate in Silver Valley? How are the women viewed and treated compared to the men? How far are these gender roles different in the society Denny and Opal encounter when they leave the community?

8. We meet many different kinds of parent in *Dirtpickers* – from Baron, to Gideon, to Opal and Denny who eventually come into their own kind of parenting. How are these parents different – or similar? How do characters' life experiences or personalities impact their approach to parenting?

9. We follow Denny, Opal, Maude and Billy from rural Idaho to the mountains of Canada, with the natural world as a constant presence. What roles do nature and setting play in the novel? How do they impact the characters?

10. How is the theme of trauma explored in *Dirtpickers*? How does trauma continue to affect the adults, compared to the children? Were there any particular portrayals of the impacts of trauma that you found memorable? What do you think the novel ultimately says about trauma?

11. What did you think about the ending? What do you imagine the future might have in store for the characters?